orchids are deadly

Vincent Ray Butler

To Clint

"Make The Play"

Best Wishes

V.R. Butler

ISBN
978-1-4602-2810-4 (Hardcover)
978-1-4602-2811-1 (Paperback)
978-1-4602-2812-8 (eBook)

Produced by:

FriesenPress

Suite 300 – 852 Fort Street
Victoria, BC, Canada V8W 1H8

www.friesenpress.com

Distributed to the trade by The Ingram Book Company

Acknowledgements

I would like to thank and recognize my mother, Elsie L. Butler who encouraged me to start and finish this book. In addition, I want to thank my girlfriend Christine Allen for having patience and being tolerant. I appreciate Nicole Morgan who is a dynamic writer and working on her third book. She recommended Tweedy Poole who was copy editor for me and gave me lots of guidance throughout this final process. Shots go out to all of you.

Chapter 1

Blood gushed down McAlister Johnson's arm and the knife that he held in his right hand. Thick red droplets fell from the tip of a blade that had just seconds before been shiny. Blood struck the carpeted floor leaving remnants of a struggle for life. McAlister's right hand was clenched tightly around the ivory handle of the knife. Without much thought, he used his left hand to feel for the warm spot on his rugged face. He winced when he saw that his left hand was now covered with blood from his face.

Tremors of fear rendered his body motionless as he cursed loudly at the events that led to his latest misfortune. Once again, he had proven to himself that he was not a man who possessed the talent of making the greatest decisions in the world. It was evident when he looked down at the still body of the transgender that was lying in a small pool of blood on the carpeted floor.

As the reality of what had just happened to McAlister began to set in, the bedroom started to take on an eerie presence. He had little fear that the neighbors had heard the struggle for life that had taken place in the duplex. It was a lavish bedroom that he and the victim were in. Even though he had been highly intoxicated when he and Natalie entered the driveway, he remembered noticing that there were no other cars around. The cross-dresser who had called herself Natalie assured McAlister that the neighbors weren't home. She knew he was married and put his mind at ease. It was unsettling to know that other people were speculating about his lewd activity, especially when that activity was adulterous. He wanted to ensure that his reputation as the best criminal defense attorney in Greenville, South Carolina remained intact.

McAlister began to regain some of his composure. He felt perspiration on his forehead but decided to ignore it. He took deep breaths and let them out slowly. His heart began to take on a slower rhythm as he walked towards the king size canopy bed. Before he could reach it, he caught a glimpse of himself in the mirror that rested heavily on top of the mahogany dresser. It was an ominous mirror, quite large for use in a bedroom. He momentarily allowed himself the opportunity to check out the remainder of the bedroom's furnishings and felt disgusted at himself for admiring Natalie's taste in interior decorating. Returning the focus on himself, he looked back to the mirror. There was a hideous gash that marred the side of his face. He wondered if it mattered now that his wife had often remarked that she was attracted to his rugged, but extremely handsome face.

Sick from the sight of his hideous new face, McAlister walked over to the bed and sat on the lower corner of it. Noticing the knife still in his hand, he let it fall to the floor. It landed a foot away from Natalie's body. He noticed that the blood had stopped flowing from her chest and her eyes weren't moving. They looked as if they were trying to locate the top of her forehead. McAlister knew that checking her pulse would be sense-less. He lowered his elbows onto his knees while looking downward at Natalie's body. For reasons he couldn't explain, he wondered what her name had been before her phony dressing habits had turned into an alternative lifestyle. Nathan maybe? Perhaps Ned? "Who the hell cares?!" he shouted out loud.

McAlister's eyes drifted away from Natalie, and then scanned slowly about the dimly lit bedroom. They stopped in the corner where there was an oak wood end table that held a vase containing orchids. Staring at them reeled him into a haze of memories. Now he remembered that the orchids had been instrumental in resuscitating his relationship with his wife Kelly after the night when a long argument nearly ended in a boxing match. The argument had come when his wife discovered a slip of paper in his pants pocket with the name Carolyn written on it and a telephone number beneath.

****

As Kelly stood in the laundry room looking at the piece of paper she held in her hand, McAlister walked in and gently hugged her around her waist. He leaned his head to the right side of her face and planted a kiss on her cheek. He looked down at the piece of paper Kelly held and his heart skipped a beat. "I can explain that," he proposed.

At that time, a visual picture formed in his mind of Carolyn's lusty looks. "Let's see if you can!" Kelly shouted as she shook free from his embrace and rushed away from him.

She stopped in the den of their Spanish style house, looking through the patio door where she watched their seven year old son Dane dive into the swimming pool they had constructed two summers ago. "Look, don't you think you are jumping the gun a little?" McAlister protested.

"Hell no! This isn't the first time you haven't been faithful. As a matter of fact, I'm tired of all your crap! You waltz around here as if we have the most perfect marriage and you expect me to pretend with you. I made you what you are! You were nothing once, remember?! Now you're a lawyer!"

"You seem to have learned very little from serving five years in prison for credit card theft. I put you on your feet again. When you had nowhere to go after your release from prison, I took you into my house, fed you, clothed you, and shared my body with you. Then, if I wasn't already a fool, I became a bigger fool by sending you to school!"

McAlister turned his head slightly sideways and sighed. "You weren't a fool by doing that," he said.

Kelly continued on as if she had not heard him. "I helped you day and night studying different methods to help you prevent your slime ball clients from going to the slammer. So now you are a lawyer who thinks you're Mr. Hot stuff and have forgotten who helped you get here. Your only debt of gratitude is by crapping all over me and screwing every young creature that comes into your office wearing a short skirt."

****

McAlister's mind became a cornucopia of the now and then. He paid little attention to the body of Natalie, which was growing colder each passing moment. His stare at the orchids became more intent. There were no sounds in the bedroom of death. He knew that the now would somehow play an important role in the total destruction of his soul. Knowing that, at some future date, he would pay a huge price for the body that lay on the blood soiled carpet. He did not care to think about what was happening to him now. Somehow it seemed strange to him that if he had not thought of the orchids that things may have turned out differently.

Reflecting on the orchids, he went back to their argument. "So what is it that you want from me? Devotion – I tried giving you that! I was the perfect husband to you for nine years. I listened to all of your ludicrous nagging and ridiculous accusations." McAlister rubbed the top of his head while pacing the floor, "Did you ever stop to consider whether or not your accusations had any validity? Did you ever stop to think that maybe you were driving me crazy with all your insecurities? You didn't, did you? You kept on and on."

Kelly's eyes widened. "That's one thing you're right about, you're crazy," she said abruptly.

McAlister let the remark roll off his back. "You see Kelly, everyone has a breaking point. You ask yourself, when does it stop?" He paused briefly before continuing. "Well, it finally stopped for me, Kelly! During those nine years, I did everything in my power to show you that I loved you, but you kept on denying my love. The accusations kept coming. So I asked myself, '*when does it stop?*' I had to answer my own question. It was obvious that you would never give me an answer."

"Do you know what conclusion I came to Kelly? Never! Never, Kelly! That's the answer. You've really been answering for nine years and I was

3

too stupid to realize it. You kept saying never, never, never, never will I stop accusing you of adultery. It's only one word, Kelly. It's never!" he shouted. "Say it! Can you say it, or do you find joy in torturing me? Torture yourself now, Kelly! I stopped being tortured two years ago. We've been married nine years and for the last two years, I've felt no pain. Do you know why, Kelly? It's because I became the man you assumed me to be all along. It doesn't hurt anymore."

"You've never been incarcerated, have you, Kelly? Well I have. Do you know why? Sure you do. You've already told me my life story. Sure, I did wrong, and I paid a price. It was a big price – it was a price I can't place a value on."

McAllister ignored Kelly's ranting while his mind drifted back to that dreadful day in prison. "McAllister, are you listening to me?" Kelly said snapping her finger into his face.

"Oh yeah, yeah. Forget it Kelly, you don't understand."

"Try me," she said waiting for his usual excuse to get out hot water.

"Kelly, something happened in that state institution that I will never forget. Do you remember the Joan Lee rape case that took place in Columbia?"

"Yeah, but what does that have to do with anything?"

"Somehow they figured an eighteen year old black kid for the perpetrator. The kid's name was Willie James or something like that. Anyhow, this kid had won an academic scholarship to Georgia Tech. Everyone that knew him at the time said that he was brilliant. Circumstances weren't in his favor, because he was asked to stand in a police lineup. Some old, half blind bag identified him out of the lineup. The judge decided to give this James kid a thirty year sentence to the shithouse.

"I remember, because I knew judge that sentenced him. I didn't necessarily agree, but who was I to challenge a colleague. Besides, the case had already been tried. So, what's your point?"

"Kelly, that place was full of hardened types who were doing long term sentences. New guys were game for them. The James kid made fresh meat for them. Three thugs raped him repeatedly in the showers. One of them would stand watch while the other two took their turns. They would then designate a new watchman and the previous watchman would join what they called fun. When the officers did their body searches the next day for weapons, they discovered the kid was damaged. He was rushed to the infirmary. He stayed there for three days until he was able to go back into population. He was placed in a cell thirty feet from mine."

"Oh my gosh," Kelly said with her hand over her mouth.

"I remembered seeing this kid when he first got there. There was nothing unusual about him, except that he was ridiculously young for that hard man's joint. I watched the kid each day, Kelly. I've never seen anyone change that rapidly. The kid was losing his mind and the only thing I could do was watch. He would stay up all night talking to himself.

He would not listen to anyone, or if he did listen, he did not answer. He kept right on talking to himself. Those eyes! There was a fixed gaze to his eyes. I knew the kid had lost it."

Kelly eyes got teary as she listened to McAllister tell the story of the young boy. "My God, I watched the kid go nuts! It got worse, Kelly. One night, I heard him say repeatedly to himself, 'I'm innocent, I'm innocent!' He said it over and over throughout the night. The next day was strange. He didn't talk to himself. The gaze was gone. I knew that something drastic was going to happen. I didn't know what, but I knew it would be bad. I could not sleep that night, Kelly. I had a bad feeling in my gut about this kid. We were all locked down at 9:00 PM. It was a long day for me because I was worried about that kid. I cared, Kelly, I really did. Somehow I knew the kid had no reason being there. The kid knew I cared, but there was nothing I could do for him."

"That night, the lights were turned out ten minutes later than normal. I thought there must have been some bad activity going on, but immediately after my thought relinquished, the lights went out. I looked across that thirty foot space separating the kid and me, but there were no words spoken between us. We stared at each other for quite a while. Thirty minutes passed and the whole place became quiet. This bad feeling of mine worsened. The place became creepy. The kid never moved. At least, it seemed like he didn't. The next thing that happened startled me. Suddenly and from out of nowhere, the kid produced a candle. He lit it and produced a piece of paper and a pen. He wrote something very brief on the paper. He didn't take long at all, but I wished to God I knew what he was writing. I thought that he may have written a mathematical equation for a prison break out, but that was not what he wrote, Kelly."

"After writing, the kid blew out the candle. He looked over at me again, Kelly, and the gaze was back. My heart pounded loudly in my ears. I watched him pull his belt away from his pants. At this point, I knew what was about to happen. I wanted to scream for a guard, but my voice would not come. The kid stared again. I think there was a message there. He grabbed a folding chair from the corner of his cell."

Kelly continued to listen as if she were watching a movie. McAllister had told her a lot of stories, but never one like this. "Where the hell did he get that chair?" I asked myself. "The kid placed it directly under a barred vent attached to the ceiling. I looked at my own ceiling and there was no vent. The kid stepped up onto the chair with the belt in his hand. He had to extend himself to tie one end of the belt to the vent bars. I watched helplessly as he struggled to reach far enough in order to tie the knot. Why couldn't I make my voice work? He slipped the through the end of the belt to serve as the noose, then yanked on the belt to test the knot that he had tied. After testing the knot, he slipped the noose over his head. It fit perfectly around his neck. It seemed that if the belt had been any shorter, the whole plan would have been ruined. I found myself wishing that this kid had bought a shorter belt. He stood on his tip toes from the edge of the chair. He looked at me for what was probably only a minute, but felt like an eternity."

"From the thirty foot distance, I could see tears roll out of the corner of his eyes and down his cheeks. A lot of things went through my head during this short time. The biggest thought in my mind was how could you call someone who has enough guts to take his own life a coward? At the conclusion of my thought, and precisely at the conclusion, the kid jumped. He did not kick or make gurgling noises. He was ready for death."

"I finally went to sleep after fighting the nightmares away. I woke the next morning frightened by what I might see if I looked in that cell thirty feet away from me. While rising from my bunk, I hoped very much that what I had witnessed the night before was just one of the bad nightmares that I had gotten used to having. When I looked at his cell, his body was gone. I thought maybe it was a dream. I began to feel better. There was a guard standing outside of the kid's cell and there was a piece of paper in his hand. The door to the kid's cell was open. I summoned the guard over to my cell. His steps were slow and there was a blank expression on his face. When he got to my cell, I asked him what the piece of paper had written on it. He didn't speak. He just held the paper so I could read it. It read, 'I'M INNOCENT'

"I later learned that the guard who showed me the message inscribed on the paper was the father of the James kid. Two weeks later, a young black kid confessed to the rape of Joan Lee. The picture in the newspaper showed a remarkable resemblance to the James kid. They could probably have passed as brothers."

"You see, Kelly, for nine years, you were the old lady identifying me at a line up. I served a nine year sentence with you as the judge, jury, and worst of all, Kelly, the warden."

Chapter 2

Reality returned to McAlister like a flash of light when he heard voices coming from the other side of the wall that separated the duplex. He turned his head quickly away from the orchids, for now he had to accept his surroundings. Voices from the other side of the wall made McAlister feel weak hearing a woman's laughter. Then, he heard the bass laugh of a man. There was life on the other side of that wall. McAlister did not look down at Natalie's body, for he knew it was there, just as it had been before. He started daydreaming about his spat with Kelly.

McAlister stood up from the corner of the bed on which he had been sitting and walked over to the opposite side of the bed to retrieve his pants which Natalie had ripped away from him during the struggle. He reached into the right front pocket of the pants, hoping there were enough cigarettes to get him through the morning. He had always had trouble breaking habits. Smoking an entire pack of Style cigarettes each day was one habit he wished he could break, but they did help him relax. He also found his lighter in the same pocket and when he retrieved it he inspected it for a brief period of time.

This particular lighter had been given to him as a Christmas gift by his son, Dane. He thought of how Dane would grow up to be a fine young man one day. As he looked at the lighter he couldn't imagine how a seven year old kid could save his allowance money to buy his father a gold gas lighter. The thought of that Christmas, and how happy he and his family were, brought a brief smile to his face.

McAlister retrieved a cigarette from his half gone pack and threw the rest of them on the bed. After lighting the cigarette he threw the lighter onto the bed next to the pack of cigarettes. He took a long drag and blew the smoke out of his mouth in a straight cloud. Slowly, he walked back to his favorite corner of the bed, pausing to take a look in the distant mirror. The blood on his face appeared to be a darker red than before. It had quit flowing and dried up by then. He took another drag from his cigarette and watched the smoke come out in the mirror. After the smoke faded, he sat back down on the bed with his eyes roaming slowly about the room again. Nothing in the room held any significance for him, at least not until his eyes fixed on the orchids again taking him back to the familiar place.

****

Kelly was still standing facing the patio door. Her throat was extremely dry now and she felt as though there was a lump caught in it. McAlister's words had stricken her with a harsh reality. She knew that he had been right all along, but her pride stood in the way of her admitting it.

McAlister stood in front of the glass patio door with his back to Kelly staring at the acreage beyond their swimming pool. "Mac, this is very difficult for me to do, so please don't make the issue any bigger than it already is. I know you see me as a very insecure person."

Kelly walked toward him with her arms folded across her chest. When she finally reached the point where he was standing, she unfolded her arms, casually grabbed his shoulders, and spun him around so that she could see his face, wanting him to know her sincerity. "I love you, Mac." She continued. "I've always wanted you to be mine and only mine. I couldn't stand the way other women looked at you. It hurt me even more when you would return their stares. It always infuriated me. Ever since I've been old enough to be interested in the opposite sex, I've always held the thought in my mind that if I ever did marry, it would be perfect. I guess it's because my parents spoiled me with their attention."

McAlister spun around and flung his hands in the air showing frustration. "You need to get out of your little girl fairytale world. That's part of the problem. I'm not perfect and neither are you," he told her!

Kelly knew that he was partly right. As a young girl she had often fantasized what she wanted her life as a married mother to be like. She knew that no one was perfect so she would find the man she wanted and mold him to fit the image that she held in her mind. Now looking back she could see that the years she spent as an only child had led her to fantasize a lot. She told McAlister; "I would bet that other people have been ruined by being an only child as well. You're a very social person who doesn't need a lot of attention in order to feed your ego. I wish I could be that much at ease with myself."

Kelly's eyes became watery. She turned her back in an attempt to hide her self-pity. Her voice cracked with emotion. "I never meant to give you the feeling that I didn't trust you. I didn't realize how much you felt caged by my accusations." The tears finally began to stream down her face. She made no effort to wipe them away. "I'm sorry I haven't been perfect," she said.

Not giving McAlister a chance to reply, she grabbed her keys that lay on the coffee table and fled out of the den, through the living room, and out the front door. McAlister heard the slam of the little BMW's door but made no effort to stop her. The next sound he heard was the engine starting up. He walked away from the patio door, past the fireplace, and seated himself on the love seat that was pressed against one of the walls. He heard the splash of water from Dane jumping into the pool and then the loud squeal of tires spinning against the pavement. He wondered to himself how long she would be gone.

McAlister looked at the clock on the opposite wall that read 5:30 pm and wondered if he had enough time to make it to McKinnie's Flower Shop. Their closing time was 6 pm, but he decided to chance it anyway. Just at that moment Dane slid the glass patio door open and walked inside the den. "Hi Dad, where's Mom?"

"She decided she needed some air, son. She went for a drive. How was the water?"

"It was cold at first, but after a while you get used to it."

Remembering the time once again, McAlister quickly rose to his feet. "Hey Dane, how would you like to go buy your mom some flowers?"

"That's a great idea, Dad," he replied. "After the conversation you had with mom, flowers sound like a great way to keep me from becoming a kid from a single parent family.

"So you heard us, huh?"

"Dad, it sounded like Friday night at the fights, even with the patio door closed," Dane paused and thought for a moment. "I bet Mom would like some orchids. It's a change from the customary roses everyone gets."

"I'm glad you're a bright kid, a chip off the old block," McAlister told him. "Let's go son, time is money and the meters are running," he grabbed the keys to his Mercedes Sports Coupe from the coffee table.

Dane walked over to the love seat and scooped a plaid shirt from the arm. He pulled it on and the two of them walked out into the hot, humid air. The drive to McKinnies's was scenic. Dane was fond of the vast array of buildings that comprised the city. Greenville was full of strange people, and when Dane saw two women making out in front of a clothing store on Maple Street, he wasn't fazed by it at all.

On the way back from McKinnies's, Dane complimented his father on the "more is better" theory. McAlister had bought enough orchids to start his own nursery. Pulling into the driveway to their house, McAlister made note of the absence of Kelly's car. It was alright, because it gave him ample opportunity to carry out his plans.

'Those damn plans were fruitless,' McAlister thought to himself. 'The fun only lasted for a short period of time. Now here I am in the bedroom of some fruit cake who called himself Natalie and 'she' had a penis longer than mine! Life sucks! You get married, have an argument, make up, break up, undress a woman who turns out to be a man, and then you kill her. What's next?!'

Suddenly, there was a knock at the front door of Natalie's duplex. McAlister had never let the thought cross his mind that Natalie, the now late Natalie, knew people. He afforded himself a chance to peep at the clock radio that rested on a night stand beside the bed. Red digital numbers printed out the time: 2:34 am. He had been sitting in the bedroom that contained the body of a person whose life he had put to an end for five hours. He wondered how he had fixed his eyes on the orchids in the room and let them hold his attention for such a long period of time. Surely, he could not stay in the room forever.

The knock came again. It was louder this time. The sound of it made his heart thud. He was motionless, wondering if the knock came from a woman. He was tempted to stroll through the kitchen and living room, open the front door, and say, "Come on in, honey, and experience a real man!"

McAlister knew that would be a foolish thing to do and passed on the idea. He waited for what seemed like an eternity for the knock to come again, but it didn't. For a brief moment he found himself holding his breath. Finally, he let the air exit his lungs and thought he could hear his heart thumping.

A bathroom was conveniently located near the bedroom. McAlister felt that a splash of water on his face would help him calm his nerves. He walked over to that bathroom, opened the door, and felt around for a light switch. After briefly fumbling, he found the switch halfway up the wall and flicked it on. He had to make a turn to his right to find the sink.

On a small table beside the toilet were a number of Playgirl magazines. One of them was opened to the center and displayed its choice of the month lying on his back. McAlister didn't have to speculate much on why the magazine stand rested on the toilet. "So much for perverted thoughts," he said to himself, and commenced the washing of his face with water from the sink.

He felt small blotches of dry blood crumble from his face. After splashing more water on his face, the dried blood began to loosen and flow again. He turned the hot water off and the cold water on knowing that cold water served to close the pores of his skin better. Shortly after he turned the faucet off and dried his hands.

When he opened the medicine cabinet, he was fortunate enough to find bandage tape and gauze pads. He thought for a moment how lucky he was to have such supplies on hand. Then his mind turned to the luck he had earlier that morning and began to laugh out loud, slowly at first, then hysterically until his eyes watered and he began to cough. Finally, his laughter subsided as he bandaged himself and inspected the work he had done in the mirror above the sink. It would do for the present time.

His tank was crusted with blood, so he decided that appearing in public in that attire would be a dead giveaway to his foul play. He walked back into the bedroom paying no attention to Natalie's dead body. He reasoned that he could find a clean T-shirt in one of the dresser drawers. He opened each one of them, rifling through the contents. In one, he found a dildo, an electric vibrator, a pair of handcuffs, a leather whip, and some chains. He disregarded them. In the last drawer, he hit the jackpot. A clean white T-shirt was lying on a pile of underclothes. He quickly grabbed the T-shirt and closed the drawer. He pulled his soiled tank off and replaced it with the T-shirt. It fit his muscular torso as though he might have purchased it for himself.

After picking the tank top up from the floor, McAlister walked into the kitchen, put it down on the table, and searched the contents of the cabinets. He found what he was looking for when he saw a book of matches in a small brass dish along with a pack of cigarette rolling papers. He lit one of them, picked the tank top up, and held the match under it until it started to burn then threw the used match into the kitchen sink and held the tank top over it until he could begin to feel the heat on his skin. He let it fall to the sink, watching it burn until it would no longer served as evidence. He took the remains of the charred tank top and tossed them into a nearby trashcan.

Using the faucet from the sink, he washed the black soot from his hands, then walked back into the bedroom and took his seat on the bed. He let his eyes roam once again, taking in the rest of the contents of the bedroom. He noticed that there was nothing unusual about the room. Only the orchids appeared to have their own disproportionate space in the room.

Chapter 3

Lit candles gave the Johnsons' dining room an air of romanticism. A bottle of wine sat in an ice bucket on the center of the dinette table. The table was set for two, and a wine glass accompanied each setting. Musical tunes played softly in the background. The aroma of freshly grilled steak floated through the house. McAlister prepared a salad to compliment the steaks.

The clock on the oven displayed a time of 9:07 pm. With each passing minute, McAlister wondered more if his efforts had been in vain. He had sent Dane to his bedroom to watch television and found that to be the hardest of his tasks. Dane usually enjoyed hanging around the kitchen when there was cooking going on.

McAlister's plans were almost complete. He needed one more item for the plan to come together completely: his wife. He turned the temperature on the steaks down. The steak he had chosen for Kelly had reached its medium temperature, just how she liked hers, so he placed it in a container and covered it with a lid to maintain its warmth. He let his steak continue cooking until it was well done. He turned the range off and placed it in the same container with Kelly's.

McAlister went to the living room to get into better earshot of the music. He turned the light out and let the stereo system serve as the only means of illumination in the room, locating his favorite recliner and let his body sink into it. He released the leg on the chair and allowed himself to lean back and extended his body. He intended only to close his eyes briefly, but the music began to fade until there was none at all.

Warm lips pressed against McAlister's own. Without looking, he embraced Kelly and held her kiss. "What a nice way to rise and shine," he said.

"There's more where that came from," Kelly responded. "As a matter of fact, there may be some extra goodies."

McAlister laughed. "You have a way of jump starting my speculations," he said.

Taking in the lustful smile on her face, "And you make speculating orgasmic." Kelly grabbed McAlister by his arm and walked him into the kitchen. "Planning a little something for me?" she asked.

"Where would you get an idea like that?"

McAlister glanced at the clock and asked, "What nut would cook such a delicious looking meal at three o'clock in the morning?"

"My nut," Kelly answered. "Shall we dine?"

"We shall," he replied.

Plates were filled, wine was poured, and silence was sacred between bites of food. Looks flowing with chemistry were exchanged. "So, what are we celebrating?" Kelly asked.

"Reality," replied McAlister.

"Am I supposed to read between the lines?" she asked.

"That, you can do in the bedroom," he responded.

With that notion, they ended their meal. McAlister lifted Kelly into his arms and carried her into the bedroom. She was taken aback with the bevy of orchids that lined the dresser. Still, no words were spoken. McAlister released Kelly from his arms allowing her to stand and they exchanged a deep kiss. McAlister broke the kiss. He reached behind her back and unzipped her dress, letting it fall to the floor. He admired her neck as he kissed it.

Kelly's moans served as an aphrodisiac. His tongue flicked circles on the backside of her neck. It was convenient that she wore no bra. His member began to stir and strain against the fabric of his pants and Kelly sensed its need to be free. She unbuckled his pants and let them fall freely from his waist. His underwear was the next to go, causing his slave to spring free. McAlister's tongue found its way to her breast. It caressed her nipples with careful attention. His hands were clever and pulled the barrier away from her body. By Kelly's hands, the shirt was shed from his body. McAlister left her breast and replanted his tongue in her mouth. He lifted her onto the bed letting her body and head fall on satin sheets and pillows.

Still, there were no words. McAlister's tongue spoke for him. Kelly's moans did the answering. There was an entrance finally made. Simultaneously, Kelly's nails left their mark on McAlister's back. Sheets became twisted, pillows fell. The moans became louder and their pace quickened. The nails drew blood, but neither noticed and then came the explosion. The sounds of music silenced once again.

CHAPTER 4

McAlister wished there were enough orchids in the room to cover Natalie's body. His curiosity longed to know how long it would take for a corpse to begin to smell. He began to feel foolish for allowing himself to mirror his past. The bedroom of death had become a prison cell to him. He felt as though he was losing touch with the activity going on in the rest of the world. The room started to feel smaller to him. The air became thicker and more difficult to inhale. He became frightened, quickly directing his attention to the orchids again.

****

The sun rose with a bright orange flair hovering over the Johnsons' home. McAlister and Kelly were still clinging to each other after their passionate interlude. The house was quiet. A buzzing alarm clock violated the silence. McAlister moaned a fatigued groan that served to induce Kelly to start a new day. He freed himself from underneath the covers that provided the nest they had shared and as he stood and spread himself into a stretch that gave him the brief appearance of a scarecrow. He walked over to the bedroom closet that contained all of his office apparel. Opening it, he was presented with an abundance of like attire for the day. Suits of various colors were hanging within, but all very conservative. He preferred to display darker colors for office and courtroom appearances.

For nights out on the town, he made it normal behavior to wear clothes that reflected his outgoing personality. McAlister wished to himself that he could have already reached the part of the day that allowed him to select the outgoing clothing. He decided on a light gray, double breasted suit and selected a shirt and tie that complimented his pick for the day. He laid them out on his side of the bed and went into the bathroom and showered. After he returned from the shower, he found that Kelly was up and nearly dressed. "Aren't you going to shower?"

"No time for it," she responded. "I'm already behind schedule. The show can't run without your honor."

"Should I bow?" he asked as he proceeded to dress himself.

Kelly put on her final touches of make-up as McAlister fiddled with his necktie. "Well, I'm off to decide the fate of some hopeless people."

Kelly grabbed her bag, planted a warm kiss on his lips and departed. McAlister inspected himself in the mirror. Dane watched his father admire himself. "You look good enough to be seen with me, Dad," he said. "Do you plan on getting me to school on time today, or do you have intentions of making a stop at Madeline Ramone's Modeling Agency before we get there?"

"Ready now," McAlister said, feeling sure he looked appropriate to start his day.

CHAPTER 5

McAlister's law office was located on the seventh floor of the Greater Bank and Trust building on Main Street. After gaining wealth and popularity from Greenville's misfortunes, he decided to move out of a near dilapidated office on August Road. When making entrance to his office, McAlister greeted his secretary with a flashy smile. She was Pretty Girl Magazine cover material.

At one time, she had been a professional model, but had gotten out of the field because her age had been apparent. It was obvious she took good care of her curvy body. She had coal black shoulder length hair and light brown eyes that sat beneath long eyelashes. It was easy to see the Indian in her. Her name was Jeanette Littlejohn. She worked diligently and professionally and kept her desires for McAlister to herself.

They exchanged hellos, and inquired about one another's weekends. All the while, Jeanette radiated lust through her eyes toward McAlister. It had been going on for so long that McAlister had adapted to it, but made no advances toward her. He feared the obvious, and the obvious for McAlister was that his wife was smart enough to start checking her allegations out with his secretary.

It had become a ritual for McAlister to have a cup of coffee and read the newspaper of the day before starting any paperwork. He found a hot cup of coffee on his desk and an edition of The Courier Post. The front page headlines did not warrant reading, but the article entitled, "Police pick up lady pretenders," did make an interesting read. McAlister read that the would-be "Johns" had started to become irritated that their purchases were not legitimate women. One of the "Johns" had been arrested as well, and said that it had infuriated him when he learned that what he had given his money for was not actually a "Lady of The Night." He felt betrayed that he had been fooled into thinking he was getting a real woman.

McAlister put the paper down and laughed profusely. Jeanette began to join him, but wondered to herself what had brought on McAlister's instant hysteria. McAlister finally settled himself enough to relate to

Jeanette what he had read. He commented that never in his life did he realize how naïve people could be. He boasted that he could find a fiber of hair in a bale of hay, and there were people running around who could not tell the difference between a man and a woman. McAlister tossed the newspaper in the trash can beside his desk and started to work.

The phone on his desk rang, but he ignored it. There were enough legal papers lying on his desk that reading them would take up the remainder of his business hours. Jeanette relayed to him that Marvin Blackman; an old law school friend was on the line and sounded anxious to speak with him. McAlister picked up the telephone and spoke hello into it. "What's new on your side of the law and order business?" he asked.

"Nothing new, same system of blind justice," replied Marvin. "Did you read the article about the men who were thought to be women in this morning's paper?"

"Can't quit laughing about it," said McAlister.

"Boy, old Teddy Davis sure knows how to pick 'em don't he?" Marvin chuckled.

"Teddy Davis? You mean the same Teddy Davis that gave a two hour lecture on judging character of clients?" McAlister replied in shock.

"Yep, that's our Teddy," said Marvin.

"Well, doesn't that knock the hat off your head," McAlister said, then replaced the receiver on its hook. "Wow!" McAlister verbalized to himself.

The legal papers still remained unread. He considered it to be a relatively uneventful business day. McAlister's drive from his office took the usual fifteen minutes. During that time, he thought of the 3:00 am rendezvous he had in the bedroom of his house earlier that day. He thought of how amazing it was, how much he could accomplish in a twenty-four hour period of time. Then he hoped to himself that he may be able to encounter another session with Kelly and started to become aroused by the idea.

Upon entrance of his driveway, McAlister eyed a strange site. The orchids he had given Kelly were lying lifelessly on the front lawn. Sensing that he was in for another long night, he got out of his car and walked past the lifeless orchids, looking at them all the way until reaching the front door. After pulling his house key from his pocket and inserting it into the lock, he felt it give way once he turned it. Pushing the door halfway open, he paused and turned his head to look back at the orchids. Why were they not in the bedroom?

Chapter 6

The bedroom McAlister sat in felt as though there was a furnace operating at full capacity. Beads of sweat had exhibited themselves from the pores of McAlister's forehead. He rose from the corner of the bed and walked over to a window opening the blinds and peered through them. For some strange reason, he felt as though he were looking through bars from a cell inside of the South Carolina State Prison.

Outside, he could see a neatly manicured lawn that contained no furnishings. A distance away, he could see another duplex like the one he was in, but didn't see any signs of life anywhere. McAlister thought how strange it felt to be so isolated. He knew that too much isolation was unhealthy for a man. Suddenly he felt a surge of panic when he glanced at the clock that revealed to him that it was 3:34 am. He remembered that he had heard voices on the other side of the wall, but that was some time ago, he wished he could hear them again.

Now he'd welcome the sound of human voices. He heard nothing. The silence became irritating and his panicky state took on more intensity. A thought came to his mind: he had not eaten since he had prepared the steaks for Kelly that they enjoyed so much. Thinking about food made his stomach growl.

McAlister closed the blinds and walked over to the mirror which revealed the shadow of a beard outlining his face. He detested beards. He thought of how most men he'd seen wearing them looked like criminals. His eyes were bloodshot and black bags had begun to form underneath them. He felt his entire body tremble. Holding his hands in front of himself both shook at a consistent tremor. He began to feel disoriented and knew that he had to find a way to calm himself, so he took his seat on the bed and focused on the orchids. His mind went back to the past.

At first glance of the orchids that lay on his front lawn. McAlister thought to himself that he had better prepare himself for anything unexpected. Carefully opening the front door of the house, he heard voices. He felt at ease, thinking that Kelly's friend Torie Jones had come to pay a visit. He walked casually into the den where the voices were. Kelly greeted him with a toothy smile. "Hi, honey, you know Carolyn, don't you?" Kelly asked. She seems to know you quite well."

McAlister's throat felt dry and parched. Instantly he felt dizzy and at a loss for words. It had been two weeks since he had seen Carolyn. The last time he saw her was when they went out to dinner. They had enjoyed shrimp, lobster, and wine. They had enjoyed being together. "Well, aren't you going to say hello to our guest?" Kelly asked, with a cunning smile stamped on her face.

"Perhaps after you say hello, you can take her to bed! You were working your way into that stage set, weren't you, Mac? Maybe the two of you can put on a little show for me – I'll cheer you on!" McAlister cleared his throat but was at a loss for words.

Dane walked into the den through the patio door wet with perspiration. He had been playing basketball on a cement court McAlister had constructed for him in the back yard, "Hi Dad, hi Mom, who is our new friend?"

"Your father would be better qualified to answer that question," Kelly responded.

McAlister was still speechless and stood motionless and petrified. No one else spoke for a while. Then, Kelly broke the silence. "Dane, there's a basketball game on television, why don't you go to your room and watch it?"

Dane looked at his speechless father who appeared to him to be a different person than he had known. "Looks like you really have done it this time, Dad," he said walking towards his room.

McAlister watched without a stir as Dane walked away from the group. After he was out of sight, McAlister turned away from Kelly and Carolyn. His mind was blank. He knew he could no longer stay there. As he exited the house, he questioned himself as to what his next move would be. He didn't care to make any decisions as to where he would go, deciding that he would just drive his car until he could see a place that looked interesting enough to stop. He decided on one thing: he needed a drink. He knew that one drink would turn into many. Drinking was an activity he felt would numb his mind in a different way than how Kelly had numbed it before he walked away.

McAlister paid no attention to the evening's activity that surrounded him within the city as he drove. It didn't bother him that he had been driving in the same area in a circular pattern. A mental picture formed in his mind as he drove. It began to make sense to him why Kelly had returned at 3:00 am on the morning they had made love. He visualized her stopping at the telephone booth to dial Carolyn's number. He imagined that their conversation had been very honest and open.

Then, he imagined Kelly driving to Carolyn's apartment. He pictured her knocking on the door, Carolyn opening it with a courteous expression on her face. Kelly would have introduced herself resulting in being invited inside the apartment. He knew that behind Carolyn's door, there was a plot designed to destroy him. McAlister smiled at the imagery knowing that Kelly should have been an actress. Her performance surely would have guaranteed her an academy award.

At the conclusion of his daydream, he noticed a building with neon lights flashing the words, "The Phoenix." Abruptly, McAlister maneuvered his Mercedes out of the busy traffic and found an empty space in the mostly filled parking lot. He sat still a moment, looking blankly ahead. He felt a temptation to start the engine of his car, place the gear selector in drive, punch the accelerator, and aim the car toward the wall of the building. He thought of what headlines might read on the front page of the next day's edition of The Greenville Courier and Post. "Greenville Attorney Takes Mad Plunge into Wall of Popular Nightclub."

If there was life after death, he did not desire to look down from heaven and see how pleased Kelly would be without him. McAlister was bombarded with the sound of loud music as he made his entrance into The Phoenix. He paid little attention to the alluring comments directed at him from various glamorous women as he picked his way through the active crowd of people. The conservative suit he wore set him apart from the crowd, who wore an assortment of loud colors.

McAlister viewed the haircuts of those around him as extremely radical. They had arrows and lightning bolts cut as designs of many of the heads of the group of energetic people who seemed to be enjoying themselves. McAlister wondered if they used stencils to cut the designs he saw on their heads. He let the thought slip from his mind and seated himself at a circular bar.

On his left sat a distinguished looking older gentleman. He could tell from the way the man's head hung downwards that he had been there for a while. The guy was talking drunken gibberish to himself as he nursed the beer he held in his right hand. McAlister watched with an expressionless stare as the guy raised the glass to his mouth, but missed his face, spilling beer on the floor as a result.

Disgusted by the act, McAlister turned his body slowly to the right. The person on his right was certainly more pleasant to look at. She had shoulder length hair, light brown eyes, which appeared as though they could penetrate steel, and a medium brown complexion. "What do you care to drink?" asked the bartender.

"A double shot of rum to get started," McAlister replied. Turning to the figure on his right, he caught her attention and their eyes locked for a second. "And a single margarita for my friend over here," he shouted as the bartender walked away.

"Good choice," said the figure beside him. "You must have noticed the salt around the rim of my glass. I admire a perceptive man," she added. "Allow me to introduce myself. I'm Natalie."

"McAlister Johnson," he said as he offered his hand for a gentle shake.

"So, are you a frequent attendant of this place?" McAlister asked as he gripped his glass of rum.

"I am not a regular here if that's what you mean," Natalie responded.

"I make it more of a habit to check out the bodies that frequent the new spot called Character's. That's an interesting name," McAlister replied.

Natalie observed McAlister as he gulped his rum. As he finishes the contents of the glass, he summoned the bartender for another. "Looks as though you may be headed for an interesting night with the way you're downing that mood control fluid," she said.

"It has already been an interesting day," he responded.

"As long as you are drowning your sorrows, you may as well pour your heart out. My shoulders are supportive. I've been told on numerous occasions that I'm very receptive to sob stories."

McAlister emptied his second glass and ordered his third. He hungrily reached for it as the bartender extended it to him. Leaning his head back he poured the full contents of the glass down his throat. He returned the empty glass to the counter of the bar and let out a sigh of relief from the burning sensation he felt within his stomach. His body was starting to numb and he welcomed the feeling.

Thinking of all the drinking he had done in his life, he recalled that it had been normal for him to do so for purposes of celebrations. It felt it odd now that his drinking was taking on a new meaning. As his senses became duller, his thought process formulated new ideas in his mind. He reflected the feeling he had experienced when he was released from prison.

McAlister's face bore a smile as he reflected on how he began his life with Kelly. He remembered how vibrant he had felt when letters started coming to him from Kelly as he was serving his prison sentence. During that time he felt empty and without hope when his parents were killed after he had served thirteen months of his sentence.

They had traveled from Statesville, North Carolina after visiting relatives. They had been fortunate enough to make it back to Greenville, but were not fortunate enough to evade a drunken driver who had ventured onto an exit ramp in the direction of opposing traffic traveling south on I-85. McAlister's parents met the drunken driver head on as their cars collided at a deadly speed. News of the incident was delivered to McAlister by the warden of the prison. He was too deep in grief to function. The memorial service for his parents was held without his presence.

McAlister learned three months later of a letter correspondence service with civilians that allowed inmates to enjoy communication with people who lived their lives in freedom. He found that the letters were accepted by numerous types of magazines. He chose to place his letters in a grocery store tabloid called AWARE.

After numerous unanswered letters, McAlister finally heard his name during mail call one evening. His hands trembled as he read the letter enclosed in the envelope along with a photo of Kelly. He thought she was the most beautiful creature he had ever laid eyes on. The letters came consistently three times each week for the remainder of McAlister's sentence.

Kelly visited him in prison on the weekends. They became close to one another, but not as close as they knew they would become. McAlister's mind came back to his new circumstances, reflecting on leaving the club with Natalie.

Natalie walked into the bedroom as McAlister followed her. Once inside, she flung herself on the bed. "Is this were you want me?" she asked.

"The best place in the house," McAlister responded.

"Undress me!" Natalie commanded.

"Your wish is my command," McAlister replied with a smile on his face.

McAlister started by taking her pumps from her feet when he noticed she had exceptionally large feet for a woman. Dismissing the thought, he took her blouse away from her torso. There he noticed that she was extremely flat chested. As McAlister undressed Natalie, he noticed there was a lustful gleam in her eyes. He became more aroused and quickly removed her skirt, receiving a surprise he had never expected when doing so.

Natalie wore no undergarment and had a member that popped to attention when her skirt was removed. McAlister jumped backwards, startled by what had taken place. "What's wrong?" Natalie asked.

"You're what's wrong!" he shouted.

Natalie grabbed him in an attempt to pull his body toward her, but he shook free from her grip, pushing her violently back onto the bed. Her head hit the headboard with a loud thud. She reached for the spot on her head that made contact with the headboard. When she brought her hand away from the spot on her head her eyes widened at the sight of blood. "You bastard!" she shouted.

Reaching beneath one of the bed's pillows she brought out a butterfly knife, flicked it open and lunged towards McAlister with it. McAlister was slow reacting from the shock of the whole experience and Natalie's blade caught the left side of his face. She grabbed him by the top of his sport coat and ripped his oxford shirt. McAlister reached into the right pocket of his pants and retrieved a switchblade. He felt his pants being ripped from his body soon after. He released the blade of the knife by pushing a button on its handle and not a moment too soon.

Natalie had a wild look in her eyes and it was aimed at the private section of McAlister's body. McAlister sensed that Natalie would try to plunge her knife in the area of her stare. A frantic scream accompanied her plunge. McAlister sidestepped her energetic rush and stuck his knife into her chest at a rapid motion. He watched as she fell to the floor. The spot on her chest where his knife was gushed blood on the carpet.

CHAPTER 7

McAlister's stare at the orchids relented as he walked over to Natalie's body and pressed her stomach with his right index finger. The skin was rigid. How long had she been dead? McAlister didn't make an effort to calculate how long he had been there. He knew he had worn out his welcome. How long would it be before someone would discover him? Preferring not to be discovered at the scene he looked about the room for his coat and found it lying on the floor.

McAlister picked up the coat, put it on and walked over to the mirror and inspected himself. He knew that each look in the mirror would bring back a night he cared to forget. McAlister walked away from the mirror toward the vase filled with orchids and took a second look to contemplate their significance in his life. Violently, he grabbed the vase and flung it at the mirror. The sound of glass breaking ended the long silence of lifelessness. He felt the sound restored his sanity.

Reality struck McAlister like a bolt of lightning. All of the flashbacks were over now. There was nothing else to think about except the future, which wasn't going to be rosy. He did not care to think about what was ahead of him. There wasn't a choice, but to think about his next move. He felt as though he had gone through a major phase of his life. For a man thirty-six years of age, he had already experienced a full life.

Disorientation had infested McAlister's mind as quick as a man can pick up a twenty-four hour bug. He wondered why he had allowed himself to spend countless hours in a room with the body of a stiff. He reasoned that most men of logical thinking would have fled such a scene at the moment of blood flow. Now he was racking his mind searching for a victim to lay the blame on. Of course he couldn't blame Kelly for the five-year bit he had spent in the State prison, but he could theorize that she had led him to kill. He found fault with Dane for suggesting that he buy orchids to revive his marriage. What struck him as frightening was that Natalie had been fond of orchids as well. He found it ironic.

The orchids he had tossed at the mirror lay lifeless on the floor just as they were on the lawn the day he went home and found Carolyn. There was a symbolic message behind orchids lying lifelessly uncontained. McAlister could not summon what the symbolism was. His mind flooded with hysteria.

McAlister dressed himself with nervous speed. His hands shook profusely as he tied his necktie. He remembered to pick up his knife that he had dropped beside Natalie's body. When he had finished dressing, he turned the lights off in the bedroom and made his way to the kitchen door. It was one he did not remember with clarity ever entering through. He lifted the bottom edge of curtains that sealed a view through the window of the door and peered out, checking for activity.

Darkness encompassed the atmosphere of the outdoors. McAlister opened the door and stepped out into the night air. The smell of it was refreshing. He felt his lungs expand. The action of this served to psychologically lessen the pain of the headache that he had developed. The headache was trivial compared to the events of the past couple of days. He kind of welcomed it wishing it was the worst of his troubles.

As McAlister walked toward the Honda Prelude parked in the driveway, he reached into the inside pocket of his sport coat for his car keys. He found them, but did not see his Mercedes in sight anywhere. He wondered if he had parked on the opposite side of the duplex. He sped up until he was at a trot.

On the other side of the duplex sat an older model Ford Mustang hyped up with hot rod features. McAlister reasoned that the voices he had heard on the other side of the wall belonged to people younger than him finding it silly that he was trying to deduce the character traits of those to whom the voices belonged. The thought brought an adage to his mind that he wondered if he should have coined. "You can take a lawyer out of the court, but you can't take the court out of the lawyer."

It felt good that he could still think like a lawyer and wondered if he would ever practice law again. The thought jarred him back to reality, causing him to realize that he had no idea where he was. This was not part of the city that he was familiar with. It began to become clear to him that he had not driven his car to Natalie's place. The headache that was thumping at the interior of his skull sent a message that he must have been drinking some time earlier. It came back to him where his car was but he did not know how to get there.

Pivoting himself in a circular motion, McAlister became aware of lights from buildings stretching toward the skyline that he figured to be downtown Greenville. He judged the distance to the lights to be at least twenty miles. Reluctantly, he set out walking in the direction of the mass of buildings and found it difficult to get out of the rural neighborhood. The roads were small and took many turns leading into other roads, just as small. It was agonizing because the neighborhood roads gave no indication that they would lead him into a main throughway that would put him on a beeline to his destiny. After walking the roads for what seemed to be an eternity, he decided to take a more direct approach by walking through the yards of homeowners in the area.

As a small boy, McAlister had once been attacked by the dog that belonged to him. The animal had become rabid, but McAlister was too young to understand the dog's irritability. Grafts of skin from his posterior were taken to replace the skin his dog had torn away from his left calf. The rabies shots were what McAlister remembered most about the encounter. The fact that his mother was there to comfort him through the ordeal was fruitless in the situation he presently faced. McAlister felt fortunate that many of the dwellers of the property through which he walked were still sleeping – at least, he hoped so.

As McAlister walked, he became more relaxed. He thought it reasonable that once he could get to his car, he could drive somewhere secure and sleep until morning. Then, he would try to continue his life, or at least his career. He heard the sound of a deep growl which ended his thoughts. He looked from side to side, but did not see where the sound originated. He heard a bark that proceeded to a growl. The sound was coming from behind him. The four legged creature he saw exhibited long, sharp teeth that he was sure would penetrate his skin with little effort. He was too terrified to move.

The Doberman appeared to be the biggest and most ferocious dog he had ever seen. It looked as though the animal came at him in slow motion. The closer it got to him, the wider his eyes grew. Finally, the leap McAlister anticipated came with powerful force as he felt his body smack the ground and teeth ripping flesh from his upper arm. He tried pushing the animal off with his free hand, but the dog made no effort to back off.

McAlister remembered his switchblade and pulled it from his pocket, but it slipped out of his hand and fell slightly out of his reach. He noticed lights coming on in the house to which the property belonged. Stretching, with all of the strength he could manage, he grabbed the knife, opened it, and sunk the deadly blade into the neck of the crazed dog. It let out a short yelp and fell lifelessly to the ground.

McAlister quickened himself to his feet when the sound of a gunshot rang out. McAlister felt a brief rush of air whiz by one of his ears. It was a sound that signaled to him that he was not reacting quickly enough and he broke into a sprint into the open night. He ran with reckless abandon, crossing yards that had other dogs just as vicious as the one he had encountered, but none of them had such an adrenaline flow as he. Having the instincts of an animal, he knew that he would do whatever was necessary to remain alive. McAlister ran without care of fatigue as the houses began to become fewer and the roads became more like expressways. Finally, he had reached a road that was away from the suburbs. It was unfamiliar to him, but that did not matter.

Walking now felt foreign to him, but he had covered a lot of ground. The thought had never crossed his mind to hitch a ride. He hadn't seen any traveling cars since he left Natalie's duplex. Aware of the dangers of hitching rides with strangers, McAlister thought it amusing that he should even worry about the elements of danger that had once been foreign to him. Now he felt it would come knocking again and he wondered what he would have to do to defeat it when it did.

Lights from a car appeared from a distance down the road McAlister was traveling. The sound of its engine grew louder as it grew closer. Hope began to build in his heart that he would catch a ride. The car lights came closer, and McAlister's hopes became more intense. He offered his thumb from his good hand in a hitch hiker's gesture. His hopes were soiled when he heard the words, "CATCH THIS!"

The sound of wind and the smash of a bottle violated his skull. The impact toppled him immediately to earth. McAlister's head made impact with the grassy ground on the shoulder of the road. The darkness grew thick as he felt small hands pushing against his shoulders. The voice asked if he was alright. It was a female voice – at least, he thought so, but wasn't sure. Slowly, he opened his eyes, making out the outline of hair and a dark face. He shook his head to free the cobwebs and the picture began to become clearer. "Are you okay?" the voice asked again.

Groggily, McAlister felt for the part of his head with which the bottle had made contact. It felt warm to his touch. He didn't have to look at his hands to know there was blood oozing from his skull. There was blood still flowing from the arm where the dog had taken a chunk. He pressed his operative hand to his arm, applying direct pressure to slow the flow of blood. The person with the small hands offered to use rags from the trunk of her car to wrap around his wounds. While she retrieved the rags, McAlister took the opportunity to gather his vision. Obstacles around him became crystal clear.

The stranger came back with the rags as she promised she would. McAlister noticed that she was a petite woman, but very attractive. "I suppose you're wondering why a woman would help a strange man lying on the side of the road when people in the world are so unpredictable and crazy," she said. Without letting him answer, she added. "Well, it's because you looked such a mess lying there on the ground, I knew you couldn't bring any harm to me."

"You should see the other guy," McAlister said half heartedly.

The stranger laughed. "Nice to meet you, I'm McAlister Johnson," he said trying to offer a smile as he introduced himself. "My name is Debbie," she said in return. "Let me help you to your feet," Debbie offered.

"I won't refuse," he replied. "As a matter of fact, I would appreciate it if you could give me a lift downtown. I seem to have misplaced my car."

"I wouldn't dream of leaving you here like this," she replied as she helped him get seated in the passenger seat of her car.

After buckling him in, she walked around the front of the car and took her driver's position. She started the car and headed in the direction of the downtown area. "Where exactly is your car?" she asked.

"Ever heard of The Phoenix?" he replied.

"Who around these parts hasn't?"

"You're quite a distance away from there not to be driving," she stated.

"Well, it's a long story, which I do not care to discuss," he said.

Debbie sensed there was something amiss about his statement, but decided not to follow up on it. She changed the subject instead. "So, how long have you lived in Greenville?" she asked.

"Long enough to know that the city is full of fruitcakes," he answered.

"I've dealt with my share of them, believe me," Debbie laughed at his response and added, "That could be anywhere from one day to fifty years."

McAlister's head was beating thunderously. He wanted to laugh, but he knew laughing would take too much effort, so he decided to flash her a smile instead. They were traveling at a speed that would ensure their trip would be a short duration. They both grew silent, so Debbie switched the radio on to break the silence. McAlister listened to the voice on the radio singing the lyrics, *"I didn't mean to turn you on."* He thought of how many women he had turned on without putting any effort into doing so and felt a surge to his ego.

The buildings from downtown Greenville began to surround them as they neared The Phoenix. The city lights were like pins piercing at McAlister's eyes. They made him feel at home. Soon he would drive his own car and feel a part of the city again.

Debbie slowed down the automobile as they entered the parking lot of The Phoenix. It wasn't difficult for her to determine which car belonged to him because it sat alone in the parking lot. McAlister remembered how crowded the parking lot had been the night before, and was pleased that the lot was empty. It would be very embarrassing for others to see him in this condition.

The gash Natalie had left on the left side of his face was shaping into a permanent reminder. Blood had stopped flowing from his head. His arm ached where the Doberman had taken its toll on it and blood revealed through the bandage there as well. "Well, it's back to normal," Debbie said to him as he opened the passenger door.

"Not really," McAlister reflected in reference to her statement. A solemn expression formed on his face. "I don't think things will ever be normal again."

Stepping out of the car he immediately turned towards Debbie, leaning his body forward so that she could see his face. "Thanks for the ride. You've been more than kind."

Debbie smiled a half smile at him. He saw her as a sincere woman. He closed the door and headed toward his car. Debbie watched as he fumbled for his keys. She rolled down the window and stuck her head out. "I think you should go check yourself into a hospital," she hollered.

"Thanks for the concern – I will!" he shouted back.

McAlister watched her drive away until her tail lights were out of sight. She had made an impression on him. *'Maybe we all aren't devious,'* he said to himself as he opened the car door. There was a folded piece of stationery on the passenger side that he noticed after he buckled himself in. He wondered how anyone could have managed to place it there since the windows had been closed and the doors had been locked. He took the paper and carefully unfolded it. It read, "GO TO HELL!"

It was easy to recognize Kelly's handwriting. He tilted his head toward the sun visor of the car as a person would do if he were asking a favor from God and exhaled all of the air from his lungs. "I already have," he said aloud as if there were someone around to hear.

Looking around at the vacant building, he wished it was happy hour so that he could take in some more rum. He turned the keys in the ignition of the Mercedes and brought his engine to life. As the engine warmed, he tried to determine where he might be able to find a drink or two at 4:23 in the morning. He could not remember anywhere that he had been before that remained open at that hour so he elected to find a secluded area away from the mainstream so that he could catch up on some sleep.

CHAPTER 8

Raven Mountain was a scenic location that McAlister had enjoyed as a teenager. His parents had taken him there on several occasions in their efforts to educate him on the subject of geography. He learned that there were many regions nearby that would allow for privacy and romanticism. Many of his teenage dates learned of his findings as well and became victims of his romantic fantasies.

McAlister parked the Mercedes on the shoulder of a road he knew very well. It was located well away from high traffic areas. Trees and mountainous rock provided tranquility from the hustle and bustle of the city. He reclined his seat and locked both doors, turning the radio until he found a mellow jazz station. After becoming satisfied with a comfortable volume, he let his head lean against the headrest. Sleep came easy.

Only moments after McAlister's snoring began, so did the dreaming. The first image he saw at the beginning of the dream was him lying in Natalie's bed. She was standing beside the bed wearing only a negligee. On the other side of the bed there stood two other women whom he did not recognize. They were dressed in the same fashion as Natalie. Both of them were very sensual looking and tall. "Let us into bed," they all said in unison. We want to please you." They kept chanting their request slowly, and seductively began removing their negligees. "We want to please you," they kept on.

Soon, they were down to their underwear. Bulges printed at the interior of them. McAlister felt compelled to flee, but could not. His wrists were handcuffed to the headboard and his ankles tied. "We are going to please you," they chanted.

McAlister struggled, but it was useless. They removed their underwear, letting their organs spring free. His eyes grew to the size of silver dollars as he wrestled with every ounce of strength within him, but still was unable to release himself. They came slowly toward him.

Suddenly, there was a loud smashing noise against the exterior of the bedroom door. It flew open simultaneously. Kelly stormed into the room. "Get out!" She shouted furiously. Frantically, they retrieved their clothing and left. Kelly closed the bedroom door and locked it. "They are not for you," she said as she began to shed her clothing. Slowly, she undressed. "I want to please you," she began to chant.

McAlister felt the left side of his chest become heavy. He began wiggling to free himself again. "Let me please you," she said. She tugged her panties away from her hips and a male organ jumped out.

"Help!" McAlister shouted at the full extent of his lung capacity as he jerked awake. His breath formed a patch of fog on the windshield of his car and his forehead was wet with perspiration. Now his shirt was soaked and his heart was racing uncontrollably. McAlister's hands trembled steadily. He gripped the steering wheel to stop them from vibrating. Trees and rock slowly came into focus. His heartbeat went back to normal and his hands became steadier. The radio played a tune from Spirogyra that he recognized.

McAlister released his grip from the steering wheel and let his head sink back to where it had been before the nightmare started. He wanted to resume his sleep, but was afraid to do so because he did not want to know what Kelly was going to do to him after all her clothes were removed. He tried to remain awake, but his eye lids felt like there were weights on them. He tried to fight them from closing, but he lost. This time, however, the sleep was uneventful.

Penetrating rays from the sun brought McAlister out of a deep slumber. The heat inside the car began to make his new home uncomfortable. Glancing at his watch, he became aware that he would be missed at his office. It would be unusual for him not to show up for work. Questions would be asked that would raise eyebrows from curious officials. It would make sense for him to report to his office in order to keep questions limited. He summarized that he could make up a story on his drive to the office to cover for his horrifying appearance.

As he drove toward downtown Greenville, McAlister formulated stories in his mind that might explain his physical condition. He theorized that he could explain that he had wrecked his car, but he would have to do damage to the car to make it believable. The story would also not explain how a chunk of flesh had been taken from his arm.

Although he had an astronomical amount of money in the bank, he did know he could not afford to purchase another automobile, especially since he had no permanent place to lay his head at night. Finally, he decided that he would answer any inquiries by telling those interested that he had been attacked by a crew of muggers after hours outside of The Phoenix.

Figuring he could tell them that the gang was accompanied by a dog that initiated the mugging, by taking a bite out of his arm. Then the first human attacker hit him on the side of his head with a beer bottle. He would explain the gash on the side of his face by saying, when he woke up from being knocked out he felt blood flowing down the side of his face.

He would say that he could not understand why his attackers cut his face since the beer bottle had done the job of incapacitating him. That made it easy to get the money they wanted. *'I'd buy a story like that,'* McAlister said to himself. *'I really have a criminal mind.'*

The drive to the Greater Greenville Bank and Trust building took McAlister twenty-five minutes. It was very relaxing and gave him the opportunity to go over his fabrication several times in his head. He felt that the story was the most plausible one he could think of. It would explain why he was beginning to look as though he might be related to a mummy by his appearance.

As he stepped out of the car, he hoped in his mind that those he would tell would buy his story. He felt as though he was walking in someone else's body as he walked toward the elevator in the lobby of the Bank. Patrons in the lobby gawked at McAlister with curious expressions written on their faces. The floor indicator light located above the elevator door reflected that it was held up on the seventh floor. He imagined the extra stares he would receive when it would finally reach the lobby and patrons would file out. The curious minds would just have to speculate.

Finally, the elevator came to the lobby and the occupants did file out and reacted in the way he had expected. He tried not to fix his eyes on anyone, hoping that no one would stop him during his elevator ride. As he boarded the elevator, he turned to face the floor selection panel and found that the previous occupants were still staring at him as they walked away. He punched the button panel that would carry him to his floor.

Irritated by the continuing stares, he forcefully punched the button that read close doors, but they didn't react as quickly as he had hit the button. The doors closed slowly, almost as if they were trying to allow anyone with quick reflexes an opportunity to break the security provided once the doors sealed. To McAlister, the "close door" button was just an added item to make a rider feel he had more control of the elevator than he actually had.

McAlister thought the notion of having control of terrifying vehicles of transport as a stroke of many genius minds working in harmony. The stop of the elevator's motion took McAlister's thoughts away from the operating minds of creative men and enforced the thought that his story had better be able to hold water. Taking a deep breath as he approached the door to his law suite, he paused at the door, reading the label that was fixed to it. Engraved in gold letters on the label were the words, "McAlister Johnson, Attorney at Law." Beneath it was another label that read, "Those who enter this door have a chance."

For the first time ever, McAlister felt he could sympathize with how his previous clients may have felt before entering through the door for the first time. Would there be a person behind it who wouldn't believe any of the words he was prepared to speak? Now, he knew that all of the stories he had heard were well prepared before any words were spoken to him.

He knew that bits and pieces had been left out in some of the stories, and in some cases, he knew that they had been totally changed. He dealt with it for a much healthier than normal fee when he knew his clients were guilty. He had to have some extra incentive for consoling his conscience.

Half confidently, McAlister opened the door and stepped into the reception area. Jeanette greeted him with a startled expression plastered on her face. The look spoke for itself. It shouted out to him louder than her voice could have. Without waiting to hear the words roll off Jeanette's tongue, McAlister answered, "I was mugged."

"My God!" she said. "I hope your attackers are in solitary confinement. You look ungodly! As a matter of fact, I would swear that you are beginning to qualify for becoming a mummy. Have you been to a doctor?"

"Of course I have. That's why I've been out," he replied. "Anyone in my condition would be foolish not to."

"Well you look as though you were patched up by some quack 'wannabe' doctor practicing first aid techniques."

"Actually, I decided to re-bandage my wounds since I know my own comfort zone," he said.

"Well, you are not very comforting to look at right now. Couldn't you have done a better job?"

"Under the circumstances – no! I think I did a pretty good job."

"Well, you have to live with the mess you made, not me," said Jeanette.

"That's a good observation," McAlister shot back.

McAlister walked into his office, hoping to find his usual filled cup of coffee sitting on his desk. Not finding it there, he turned back in the direction from whence he came. Jeanette stood behind him with a cup in her hand. "I didn't know if I should prepare for you today," she said.

"You should always prepare for me," he replied.

Jeanette smiled at him, but her eyes were studying the wounded areas of his body. The smile didn't do much to conceal the look of concern that was on her face. Jeanette turned away from him and walked back to her desk.

On his desk lay his usual morning issue of The Courier Post. He stared at it wondering what the inner contents of newsworthy articles might read. There were always articles on the front page concerning events that were happening with The President or other news relating to movies being made in Washington, D.C. He had grown tired of wasting time reading the front page, deciding to catch up on the major news by watching the 11:00 news on television.

The local section held McAlister's interest and informed him on what was taking place on his home front. Turning to that section, the first article produced a lump in his throat. In bold letters were the words, "Cross Dresser Found Stabbed to Death in Own Home".

McAlister forced himself to swallow the lump in his throat. Instantly, his forehead felt extremely hot. He wiped his index finger across the surface of his forehead and felt moisture. Using the same hand, he grabbed his cup of coffee from his desk and took a long sip. The coffee felt good going down, settling in his stomach before attempting to read the article.

Slowly, he began reading the article. It started out by stating that Nathan Roberts had been found dead in the bedroom of his home by his former wife. The wife told authorities that she had maintained a friendship with her ex-husband and kept close communication with him. She had decided to pay him a visit, but after many unanswered knocks at the door, she decided to take it upon herself to enter the home. In doing so, she was shocked to find Nathan's body lying in a pool of blood. The article did not reveal the name of the former wife, but it did state that she had been cleared due to having an alibi that confirmed it impossible for her to have been involved in the death.

The article mentioned that a weapon was found in the bedroom, but was not believed to be the murder weapon, because the blood on it was not the same type as the victim. Authorities speculated that Nathan had used the same type of weapon to inflict a wound on the perpetrator. They were able to establish that the murderer's blood was type AB negative, a rare blood type that could be helpful in narrowing down possibilities on the perpetrator.

Police also found ashes in the kitchen sink, but could not make any determinations from them. A Captain named David Downing mentioned that they were not fortunate enough to find any fingerprints, because the perpetrator was smart enough to retrace his steps and had wiped prints from anything he may have touched. Captain Downing told reporters that the crime had sexual implications, because the victim was naked when his body was found. He said that he felt the perpetrator may have been psychologically frustrated, but would not comment on why he felt that way.

The article ended by reporting that Captain Downing and his crew had several leads and a lot of investigative work to carry out. "Several leads," McAlister said aloud. He slammed his balled fist down hard on his desk top causing some coffee to spill out of the cup. Jeanette ran into the office abruptly.

"Is there anything wrong?" she asked while casting her eyes downward at the article he had read.

"No, there's nothing wrong. I was just thinking out loud. Continue your typing. I'm sorry I disturbed you."

"Well, if there's anything I can do, Mac, don't hesitate to mention it."

"I'm just irritated by the mugging and all," McAlister said in a softer tone of voice. "I never thought I would become a victim of a crime."

"No one ever does," she said, trying to make him feel better.

Jeanette could sense that he was very troubled. She wanted to hold him so he could know how much she cared for him. "Mac, I may as well level with you," Jeanette said. Kelly was here yesterday."

McAlister gave her a puzzled stare. He couldn't imagine why Kelly would have come to his office. She had already done enough damage. "Kelly! Why did she come here?"

"She mainly came for the sake of Dane. He's been asking about you. She wants me to tell you to stay the hell away from them. She told me about everything that happened. I tried to tell her that I didn't want to know about your private lives, but she insisted. She said that I should be sure to tell you that if you come anywhere near them, she would kill you."

"Is that all," McAlister said blankly.

"That's enough, isn't it?"

"Yeah, that's enough," he replied.

McAlister walked over to the window that exposed an aerial view of the metropolitan area. Down below, he could see other people bustling to get to different parts of the city. He thought of how innocent the majority of them were, cheerful in their own insignificant lives. Most of them had families to come home to that contained virtues of understanding and trust. He felt left out.

Jeanette walked over to where McAlister stood. He was still watching the activity below. She placed a hand on his shoulder. "You can stay at my place, Mac. I need someone to talk to late at night anyway."

"Then you must know that I do, too," he replied.

He turned his face to her. She held a smile of acceptance. She extended her arms and McAlister let his body fall into them. They wrapped in each other's arms and stood swinging in a twisting motion. McAlister pushed slowly away from Jeanette, but looked into her soft eyes. "Do you have a couch?" he asked.

"For guests, but I have known you too long to be a guest."

"I suddenly feel an urge to take the rest of the day off," he said. "I don't have anything important to do today, do you?"

"Only what you have assigned me," she replied. "I had not planned anything special for the evening. I always keep my calendar open. I'm very impulsive, so it doesn't make much sense for me to plan anything," she added.

"There's more to this city than meets the eye," McAlister said. "Let's go out and take a bite out of it."

"What about the office?"

"Office CLOSED."

"Well, I drink margaritas," she said.

McAlister had been walking toward the entrance door of the office suite when suddenly he stopped. "Is there something wrong?"

"No, I just thought I was forgetting something. Let's carry on."

He took Jeanette by her hand and they left the suite. They were quiet on the elevator ride down to the lobby. Both silently anticipated what the remainder of the day would bring. Jeanette didn't want to appear too overly eager about sharing the day with him and hoped that she cared for other drinks besides margaritas.

Seated in his Mercedes, they pondered where they should start their day. Realizing that it was too early for the bars to open, they decided to find a park to waste away some time. As he started the automobile, he thought of how suddenly he was abandoning his law practice. He knew now that his career was going down the drain, but that was part of the unpredictability of the circumstances.

Chapter 9

Jeanette was silent as McAlister maneuvered his automobile through the bustling city traffic. She observed numerous people milling about on the sidewalks. They all looked as if they had to go somewhere in a hurry. Jeanette was happy to have the opportunity to spend her time casually with her boss. She glanced at him as he drove. The glaze in his eyes alerted her that his mind was racing a hundred miles per minute.

McAlister chose to park the car in a convenient spot for inner city parking. He paralleled the auto tightly between two other vehicles. "That's a nifty job of parking," he said to Jeanette after they had exited the car.

"Now all I have to do is feed the meter and we're in business." McAlister put enough coins in the meter to satisfy the two hour maximum. Then, he pointed toward a small scenic park that was situated just beyond Broad Street. He explained to her that they would have to walk a small distance to get to the park. It would have made more sense to drive to Greenbrier Park than walk the distance, but he reasoned that the walk wouldn't hurt them.

They found a bench and seated themselves close together. Momentarily, there were no words spoken between them. Their heads roved about as they inspected the activity taking place around them. Jeanette watched a young couple feed birds that were not bashful being near people. The birds were walking on the grass frantically searching for where the bread crumbs had landed. Some of the geese would attack their competitors in order to have a better opportunity to fill their own bellies. Jeanette laughed out loud, diverting McAlister's stare to her attention. "Did you overhear me thinking something was funny?" McAlister asked.

"I was watching the behavior of those birds over there. Can you imagine filling this park full of people with some insane idiot millionaire throwing money out to them as if he were feeding birds? I'm willing to bet those people would act just as the birds are acting. I think greed is what brings out the animal in humans. Take a look at those birds, some of them are tiny, some are big."

"Notice that a few of them have stopped fighting for the bread but the others are still reacting selfishly even though they have had just as much as any of the others. The only birds that are getting attacked are the one who don't know when to quit eating. They are oblivious to the fact that the next beak pecked in their body could cause their deaths. Do you see the picture, Mac?"

"Boy, you really have a vivid mind, don't you? I never knew you were such an intense person. With a philosophical mind like yours, why are you wasting your talents being a secretary?" he inquired.

"Because I want to be as close to you as I possibly can," she replied.

Their eyes locked and became softer. The tempos of their heartbeats changed as their tongues finally intermingled. They decided it would be exciting to explore the contents of the city together. Strolling through the clothing stores, they shared ideas of what looked tasteful and what did not. Each wanted to know how the other would look in what they thought to be sexy attire. Jeanette thought McAlister would look dashing in a pair of tight fitting leather pants and snakeskin boots.

They chose to try out their fantasies in Maxwell's Department Store at the East End Mall. McAlister vowed that he would reveal to Jeanette what he wanted her to wear when they entered the ladies' department. It was amusing for them once their intentions became evident Jeanette wanted to see McAlister dressed as she desired first, so she convinced him that she should have her wish granted because age should go before beauty. She teased him that if he looked in any mirror, the reflection he would receive would not be one of beauty. "Okay, you win," McAlister said. "I already feel like a freak from all the stares, so let's get this show quickly on and off the road."

They had to search several racks of clothes before they were able to find a pair of leather pants. Jeanette chose a pair that was black and sure to fit him like a glove. She then found a short cut leather jacket to match. "Put yourself into these, while I find the boots to complete the set."

McAlister dressed himself in the dressing room while Jeanette selected a pair of snakeskin boots. She could hardly wait to see his new look. He exited the dressing room donning her leather outfit. She felt a tingle go through her body at the sight of him. The outfits made him look like he was soliciting for a macho male magazine. "Now, the boots," Jeanette said.

"Must I?"

"You definitely must!"

After putting the boots on, McAlister stood and did a few model moves to let her inspect him. "I approve," she said. "Keep those clothes on. It's my turn now!"

McAlister followed her over to the ladies' department. He had no idea what would look sexy on her. He had been used to Kelly shopping for all of her own clothes. He felt that no one knew another's taste in clothing better than the person who wears them. "Well, here we are. It's a man's choice," Jeanette said.

"Where do I start?"

"Anywhere you want to. Take advantage of this opportunity."

"You said it!" McAlister retorted. He decided that if he was going to do this thing, he should go all out. He started by choosing a pair of red panties that were cut very skimpy and a red garter belt and red fishnet panty hose to match. Then, he went to the shoe section and chose a pair of red, six inch pumps. "There you are," he said, handing the apparel to Jeanette.

"You left out a few things, Mac," she said exuberantly.

He thought for a moment with the tip of his thumb pressing against his teeth. "Oh, yeah," he said. "I did, didn't I?"

McAlister raced back to the section where he had chosen the red panties and grabbed an ultra sheer bra from a hanger and handed it to her. He flashed a gleaming sarcastic smile at her. "You're awful," she said while returning a smile of her own that hinted that she could handle his naughty but clever wit. "Follow me to the dressing room, but wait until I give you the signal to come in," she instructed.

"Deal!" he said.

Jeanette inspected herself in the full length mirror and was pleased with what the reflection revealed. Her breasts were full and firm. There was no sag to them. The bra McAlister had chosen for her was just big enough. It squeezed her breasts together and left the top portion unattended to. From her breasts down, were a flat tummy and a waist that immediately tapered where her hips flared into succulent thighs that were well defined. Her calves were muscular, supported by slim, but strong ankles. Jeanette knew that she was the complete package.

"Invitation extended," she said, poking her head out of the dressing room door.

McAlister had been waiting patiently, but jerked his body forward in response to her offer. Opening the door, he found himself becoming intensely excited. He let the door close behind him intentionally. The people who were working in the area were doing other things and did not notice them. "You like?" she asked.

"I love!"

"It's just the lover in you," she said, consciously wanting to make something out of the situation.

Jeanette noticed that he was actually as excited as he sounded by the fullness in the front of the tight leather pants. "Are you going to do anything about that?" She asked, pointing to the front of his pants.

McAlister didn't give an answer, but wrapped his arms around her back and pulled her body close to his. They exchanged a deep tongue searching kiss. McAlister pulled slightly away from her, wanting to take another look at her voluptuous figure. It was enough to make him consider throwing caution to the wind and did so.

Kissing her neck tenderly, his hand rubbed her naked back. He heard her breathing become heavier, which served as a green light to proceed. Slowly, he flicked his tongue toward her naked breast in circular motions. She gripped him firmly by his buttocks and pressed him closer to her so that she could gather his excitement. He fumbled briefly for the clasp in her bra as he continued to lick the top of her breast. He unsnapped her bra and slid the straps away from her shoulders and down her arms until it was free.

Jeanette's breasts were firm and full. McAlister let his tongue work toward her nipples. He took one into his mouth, caressing it with his tongue and pulling on it with his lips secured around it. Then, he found the other nipple and gave it the same attention. Her breath came in short gasps now. Her hands were frantically searching for the button at the front of McAlister's leather pants. She found it and released the pants' grip from around his waist. She pulled them downward until they dropped to the floor. McAlister slipped his thumbs inside her panties and pulled them down along with the fishnet stockings. He took the pumps off and pulled the panties and stockings completely away. He replaced the pumps on her feet, making them the only figure attached to her.

McAlister set his tongue in motion again, licking cleverly around each of her ankles. He worked his way up one leg, then the other, careful not to miss an inch of her flesh. She ran her fingers forcefully through his hair. Her head was flung backward and her eyes were closed. Her short gasps had turned into moans of delight.

The remainder of the store's activity was normal, except that a store detective had been alerted by a female customer that she heard moans coming from the women's dressing room. She was concerned for the customer inside and thought the person may be hurt.

Jeanette began desperately discarding the remaining clothes that McAlister still wore. She reached the point of no return and ached to have his body just as bare as hers. After all of his clothes were removed, she began giving him the attention he had shown her. He was very receptive to her actions. The rest of the world was oblivious to them. They had forgotten that they were in a department store and people were roaming about right outside the door.

McAlister grabbed Jeanette behind her legs and back, gently easing her to the floor. He repeated everything he had done to her before, and then he made a plunge, causing her to let out a shriek. Their motion became rhythmical. Their intensity increased until they simultaneously reached the point that they had strived for.

The door to the dressing room burst open immediately afterward producing shock in both of them. The store detective, a big burly man, gazed down at them, surprised by what he saw. He imagined that this type of thing sometimes happened, but he never figured he would actually encounter it.

McAlister and Jeanette were both speechless. It became apparent to them that they had let their fun go a little too far. McAlister was thinking of how ironic it was that now he was finally with a real woman, a man had to show up and ruin it for him. Suddenly, something about the man caught McAlister's eye. In the lapel of his coat was a small orchid, which McAlister figured a lady friend must have given him. Looking at the flower, McAlister briefed himself on all of his unfortunate incidences. Suddenly, he developed a deep hatred for orchids. "You are both under arrest!" the burly man said in a hostile tone of voice. "You have the right to remain silent. Anything you say can and will be used against you in a court of law."

The rest of the Miranda speech was tuned out by McAlister. He had heard it before and had expected to hear it again. He had no idea that something like this would put him behind bars again. He could hear voices coming from outside of the dressing room. The big detective produced a pair of handcuffs and ordered McAlister to stand and put his hands behind his back. He did so and suddenly, found the familiar feel of cold cuffs secured around his wrists.

The detective reached into the back pocket of his pants and retrieved a walkie-talkie. He turned a knob and spoke into it. Minutes later, another detective walked into the dressing room with a set of cuffs for Jeanette. Her face still bore a shocked expression. The second detective mentioned that someone should bring a couple of blankets from the department store where they were kept. The detective said that he would get them himself, returning to the dressing room once he found them. McAlister and Jeanette were both wrapped carefully with them and escorted out of the dressing room. When the police arrived the detective gave the officer their clothing that they had left in the dressing room. There was a large crowd outside of the dressing room. McAlister lowered his head trying to avoid recognition. He heard his name called, but didn't turn to see who had shouted it. They all walked out of the department store rapidly. McAlister and Jeanette were put in the back seat of the squad car that was waiting for them outside.

There was terror written on Jeanette's face when McAlister looked at her. It was a new experience for her, one that she did not care to endure. McAlister stared out of the squad car window and noticed the rest of the world bustling with activity. The feeling that he felt was familiar. He remembered how helpless he had felt before and also remembering that he had once felt as though the ordeal of arrest was happening to a second person from within him and not his actual self. McAlister wanted to mesh the two people together, making a unified personality so that some kind of sense could be made out of the situation. Looking over at a solemn Jeanette as the car sped along, he wondered if she was going through the same type of ordeal within herself. Jeanette's expression clued him in that she was.

Weirdoes were being brought in left and right at the police station. There were people in purple, green, and psychedelic hairstyles struggling to break free from their blue suited captors. Barely dressed hookers shouted obscene language at booking officers. McAlister noticed that Jeanette and he were the only cooperative people.

The area for booking incomers had been designed with careful thought. Upon entering the detention center, the two big detectives had to stop at a control room booth. A big blond woman who looked to be in her forties occupied the room. She spoke to the detectives as if they were good friends. They exchanged a few words and laughs, and then she pushed a sliding drawer out through the wall that separated them. One of the detectives reached in the drawer and retrieved two keys.

McAlister paid attention to Jeanette watching the exchange. He had been to the facility on numerous occasions as a defense attorney visiting prospective clients, and once as an inmate, himself. He knew that he was very concerned about the functioning of the jail when he was brought there. He knew why Jeanette had paid notice to every move that took place. Beyond the barred door were two, five by eight feet holding cells. Both were occupied by belligerent individuals. As McAlister, Jeanette, and the two big detectives walked by the holding cells, McAlister noticed that the individuals in both cells were stripped naked. One of them was banging continuously on the door. He was also foaming from the corners of his mouth.

To the right of the holding cells was a rectangular shaped room with glass all around it. Inside, were four detention officers working frantically to book the incoming offenders. They were taking photographs, writing information on cards, operating key punches, and typing booking cards. Even more officers were busy assisting in booking newcomers. They would have them place their palms on the booking window. They would then have them extend their lower bodies outward, away from the lower surface of the booking wall beneath the glass.

Jeanette watched intently as the frisk searches were performed. She had seen them done on television, but was appalled by the fact that she was about to become a participant. It was nearing time for Jeanette and him to go through the ringer. A female detention officer came and stood behind Jeanette. "Next!" A woman typing booking cards shouted, motioning for the detectives to bring McAlister and Jeanette to the booking window.

"Well, what do we have here?" asked the woman typist.

The detective who had been making the silly faces at the madman said, "They couldn't wait to get home and decided to make nice in a dressing room at Maxwell's. They're hiding their birthday suits under those blankets."

Jeanette did not speak. She only did what she was instructed to do. McAlister knew that their bonds would only be a couple hundred dollars each. He had seven hundred and sixty-three dollars in the wallet contained in his pants. He also had a checkbook in the inner pocket of his sport coat. Knowing the process he did not worry because he knew that the detention officers would take care of their property, money and everything else.

Once he had seen a close friend tie a small bag of cocaine by a thread to a wisdom tooth. The cocaine was safe in the depths of the friend's throat and went unnoticed by a correctional officer conducting his body search. Unfortunately for the friend, the bag worked its way loose from the thread. He ingested it in the contents of his stomach. Two hours later, the guy died of a drug overdose.

McAlister hoped that Jeanette would take some relief in the fact that she would be wearing a green jumpsuit and would have a lesser degree of problems than the majority of those around her. She had a number of things working in her favor. She was a first time offender, a female, extremely attractive, and had committed her act with a lawyer in town who had friends in positions of tremendous influence.

McAlister let his thoughts drift from his concerns about Jeanette and began to focus on his own. He was taken to a clothing issue room that was in the opposite direction Jeanette had been taken. The officer that had guided McAlister to the clothing room looked to be a mild mannered man. He was no more than five feet, seven inches in height and weighed about one hundred and fifty pounds soaking wet. There was no muscle tone about him, at least none that looked obvious. His hair was fading away from the top of his head. His eyes were squinted at the corners as if he might have been bred partially by an Asian. His lips were full, but his nose was without a bridge. The way his glasses rested on the tip of his nose made him look comical. McAlister tried hard not to laugh at the funny looking man. "Okay. Here is the part I like most. Strip down until you are bare-ass. " said the officer.

'My God!' McAlister thought to himself, 'Are half the people in the world fruitcakes?' Beforehand, the thought of stripping down to the bare essentials was merely a routine. Now he felt hesitant to do so. Becoming nude was lightening fast for him. He simply dropped the blanket to the floor.

McAlister focused his eyes sharply on the officer's name tag. It read, "Robinson, (*Officer Fruitcake Robinson*) McAlister thought to himself. "Run your fingers through your hair briskly," Robinson told him.

McAlister noticed that Robinson was not looking at his head, but his stare was focused on his midsection. "Tilt your head back, and let me see up your nose."

Robinson produced a red flashlight from his hip pocket. He walked up closely to McAlister and shone a light up his nostrils. Confident that there was nothing hidden there, he backed up a few steps and proceeded on with his search. "Open your mouth wide," Robinson ordered.

McAlister stretched his mouth open as wide as it would go. He knew that he would be ordered to lift his tongue so he did so without being asked. Robinson became furious at him for doing so. "I didn't tell you to do that!" he shouted. "You don't do anything unless I tell you to! You understand that?! I'm running the show here, not you!"

The reaction surprised McAlister. He had expected that Robinson would appreciate him making the job easier. *'This guy's not only a fruitcake, but he's about as unpredictable as the weather,'* he said to himself. "Okay, lift your penis," Robinson commanded.

McAlister did so slowly, expecting anything out of the ordinary from Robinson. He watched the look on Robinson's face change from solemn to excitement. "Now grab your balls and raise them." McAlister reacted slowly to the order. "When I tell you to do something, you jump to it!" Robinson snapped. "Quit fucking around or I'll bust you open."

At that moment, McAlister made up his mind that he was being harassed. He decided that when all of this business was over, he would find a way to ensure that officer Robinson would lose his job. "Turn around and face the opposite wall so that I can inspect your backside," Robinson instructed. McAlister maneuvered his body reluctantly so that he could comply as ordered. He felt uncertain turning his back to Robinson, knowing he was unstable. "Bend over and spread your cheeks," Robinson commanded harshly.

At this part of the search, McAlister always felt compelled to ask the person conducting the search if he expected to find a .45 automatic inserted in his rectum. He had never outgrown the humiliation he felt from this particular aspect of the search. McAlister waited for Robinson to proceed with the search, but heard no sounds from him. Suddenly, he felt Robinson touch his posterior. He turned violently around with unleashed fury and landed a strong punch to Robinson's jaw. The impact of the punch made a popping sound that signaled to McAlister that he had probably broken it. Robinson fell immediately to the concrete floor.

A clothing trusty had been watching the search as it had begun. He knew that Robinson was a shaky character. The trusty found it amusing the way Robinson had conducted the strip search. He had seen him perform the search many times before in the same manner, but this time he had taken it to the extreme.

The trusty quickly exited the clothes issue room hollering for detention officers to come and stop the attack. Soon afterward, he came running back to the issue room with three burly detention officers behind him. McAlister had straddled Robinson and was releasing punch after punch to his face. Blood was pouring from Robinson's nose and mouth. McAlister looked like a madman as he wailed away on Robinson.

The officers grabbed McAlister from Robinson as if he were a rag doll. He found himself being slammed hard against one of the walls. The blow to the wall knocked the breath out him. A fourth officer came into the issue room with chains, handcuffs, and wrist cuffs. Two minutes later, McAlister was struggling to free himself from the confines of the chains. Two of the officers picked him up by his armpits, dragging him to a holding cell across from the two occupied holding cells on the other side of the booking office.

One of the officers opened the door. The two officers, who had been dragging McAlister, forcefully threw him into the holding cell. He could feel the wound that the Doberman Pincer had inflicted had opened up and a fresh blood flow had begun. He knew that he wouldn't bleed to death, because the bandage he was wearing minimized the flow of blood and would eventually stop it. With his back to the wall, he let himself slide gently down by bending his knees, letting his body fall on its side. Depleted of energy, he fell quickly to sleep.

CHAPTER 10

Through the fog of sleep, McAlister could see Kelly, Dane, and himself watching television in the den of their home. They were laughing at the events of a sitcom they regularly watched, but were interrupted by the sound of the doorbell. Kelly told Dane to answer the door and to tell any guest to welcome themselves into the den.

McAlister watched as little Dane left the room, turning his focus back to the television. Dane returned to the room followed by three women, all of whom he had dated during the last two years of his marriage. They stood with their hands behind their backs and threw orchids at his feet. Dane ran to his mother and clutched her tightly around her shoulders. He was terrified.

The doorbell rang again. This time, McAlister decided to answer it himself. Opening the door, he found Natalie standing on the other side. She held her hands behind her back as the other women had done. Without warning, Natalie produced a six inch jack knife with a white ivory handle, sprung it open and sunk it deep in McAlister's heart. He fell to the floor like a branch from a tree. Kelly heard the noise of McAlister's body hitting the floor and rushed to the door to find his body spread out on his back with the knife stuck in his chest. At his feet lay purple orchids.

Sweat produced on McAlister's forehead. He jerked quickly back to consciousness surrounded by the stone walls and steel door. He appreciatively welcomed his surroundings. The nightmare had seemed so real. McAlister visualized the dream and questioned his fate. Had he dreamed this because of his experience with Natalie, or was it from memories of part of his childhood that he had tried desperately to suppress. It came flooding back to him.

The hate had been there all along; deep seeded hatred for his father, the father who he had once loved and cared to listen to. His dad had been the ultimate macho disciplinarian raising him. Sports were a must for McAlister. His father worked him out like a drill instructor. As much as he wanted not to do the things he was instructed to do he did them out of respect, but one day everything changed.

McAlister and his childhood friend Derrick Davis had grown accustomed to picking locks on people's houses and going in to spy on them. One day they decided to go in a house in the Raven Creek subdivision. Upon entering the house they both heard what sounded like leather smacking against skin. Unbelievably the door of the room was slightly open and the two of them pushed it open enough to see what was going on.

McAlister saw his dad stark naked tied to the bed. He had a wig on his head with an orchid stuck down the side of it as he had seen women do on occasions. The man with the whip had on all leather clothing and a hat that was too big. Before either of them saw McAlister or Derrick they both ran out of the house and all the way to Derrick's parent's house. McAlister had been crying and started hitting his fist on a wooden shed in Derrick's back yard. He made Derrick vow not to tell a soul or he would kill him, just as his father would do to him if he knew what McAlister had found out. His respect for his father turned to pure hate. He wanted to kill him.

****

Keys rattled outside of McAlister's cell door. A voice was speaking something about how hotshots can get away with murder while the poor and innocent pay for all the wrong doings and burn for it. It was the type of speech McAlister had heard from many of his clients and had grown tired of years ago. He knew that the real reason behind the trend was that the poor were usually uneducated and ignorant about the law. They often had to hire overworked public defenders that couldn't devote much time to their cases. This went through McAlister's mind as the door was being opened. The voice told him that he was free to leave and go home. 'Home where?' McAlister asked himself. He thought of Jeanette and knew that he could live with her. She had shown him a side of herself that he didn't know existed in the many years she had worked for him.

On his way to the clothes issue room, McAlister was stopped at the booking window by one of the sergeants. The sergeant instructed the detention officer who had opened McAlister's holding cell door to take the ankle chains and hand cuffs off of him. While the detention officer followed his orders, the booking sergeant bent his body down for a brief moment and then brought it back up to its original posture. His face lit up with a smile that McAlister could not understand. The smiling sergeant lifted his right arm in the air so McAlister could observe what was in his hand. It was a brown paper bag that had McAlister's full name written on it. "Now, lawyer Johnson, you know that if you try to leave here without what I have in this bag, you will not make it out of the front door of this building," he said and immediately broke into a hysterical laugh.

McAlister had been so intent about getting out of the jail, he had totally forgotten that he had come to jail without clothing. He realized that he was acting impulsively. Impulsiveness, as far as he could remember back, had always caused him some type of conflict. After the sergeant's laughing subsided, he gave McAlister his clothes and explained to him that he would have to come back to the booking window to sign the release paperwork after he was dressed.

McAlister secured the bag in his hands and headed briskly for the clothing room. Inside of the clothing room, he dressed as rapidly as he possibly could and was glad Officer Robinson wasn't there to watch him and wondered if he was somewhere else in the jail trying to molest one of the other inmates. The thought suddenly occurred to him that he could possibly have a new charge for beating Robinson as a result of his misconduct.

The trusty who had witnessed the incident was sitting on a table in the room where the jumpsuits were stored. His head was bobbing back and forth to music coming from the transistor radio that rested on the table beside him. As McAlister walked toward him, he thought how appropriate the song was for the setting. Then, he was tempted to laugh out loud when he thought about it more in depth. He summoned that if they had really been smooth, they would not have been there in the first place. He cursed himself silently for his own stupidity. The head bobbing trusty stood up when he saw McAlister at the half door. "What's happening, man?" The trusty asked.

Without giving McAlister a chance to answer, he abruptly added, "I thought you were going to beat Robinson into oblivion before those damned police came and pulled you off his ass. He's had that coming for a long time. I knew that if I stuck around here long enough, I would get my rocks off watching someone beat the piss out of him. What did you do on the street, man, kill someone?"

The question hit a nerve that made McAlister feel the whole chemistry of his body suddenly change. He remembered that he really had killed someone, but with the rage of violent and negative activity that had affected him, the slaughter of Natalie had almost become totally forgotten to him. He realized that he still had that problem to worry about. He would find the nearest news stand outside of the jail to see what was happening in the case of Natalie's death. "No man, the only thing I'm guilty of is making love to my secretary in the dressing room of Maxwell's Department Store."

"Hell, man, they shouldn't have arrested you for that. They should have pinned a medal on you. Do you know what I mean, pop?"

"Did you see the whole scene with Robinson and me? I mean, before I tried to turn his face into jelly?"

"I saw the whole shebang. I try not to miss anything. I'm no fruitcake or anything like that, but you see it gets quite boring in this place and Robinson provides my entertainment. Watching him is like watching a TV show. You know what I mean, pops?"

"Hey, well, listen. You wouldn't mind serving as my mouth piece would you if it comes down to that?" asked McAlister.

He resented the trusty calling him pops as if he were gray haired and hump backed, but he didn't want to get on the trusty's bad side. He needed him and feared that if he didn't speak up for him, he could get hung out to dry. "No problem, pop," the trusty said.

McAlister shook the trusty's hand and assured him that he would get back in touch with him. The trusty watched McAlister admiringly as he walked out of the clothes issue room. He felt that there were a lot of criminals out on the streets, but there were also people working in the system of criminal justice that were just as corrupt or even more so, and Robinson was one of them. The trusty could tell that McAlister was a man who would not stand still for the misbehavior.

The witty sergeant was waiting for McAlister at the release window with a smile on his face. McAlister's face bore no expression, but inside, he felt lucky to be getting released as quickly as the process had taken place. Knots of stress that had been forming inside his stomach slowly began to unravel. He felt an urgency to have sunlight on his face.

The sun had become a symbol of freedom to him since the beginning of his first incarceration. He relished at the sight of it rising each morning. Looking at the smiling sergeant, he knew that the man didn't hold objects like sun with significance as he had grown to do. "Well, here are your walking papers, Mr. Johnson," the sergeant said. "That was quite a looker you came in here with. I probably would have gotten myself arrested, too if I had a broad like that paying attention to me. As good a lawyer as you are, I'm sure you're not going to have much of a problem getting 'his honor' to see things your way. Hell, you haven't lost but one case in five years, have you?"

"You're wrong sergeant. I haven't lost any." McAlister gave him a cold stare.

The sergeant diverted his eyes from McAlister's stare shortly as if he were trying to recall a bit of the past. McAlister watched his eyebrows rise, which assured him that was the case. "Now I remember," the sergeant said, snapping his fingers together at the recollection. "It was a case about some kid from Marietta that raped a young girl. Hell, the kid was pretty damn young himself. I think his name was Willie Jones. He was convicted, sent to prison, and ended up lynching himself. Later they found out it was a case of mistaken identity."

"Not my case," McAlister said. "I was in a cell thirty feet away watching the kid as he placed the belt around his neck. I'm sorry, but I have not lost a case since I began my practice. As you might be able to tell, when I start something, I go all out."

"I know the guy who defended the kid. His name is Butler Thomas, a bigoted son-of-a-bitch who could care less what happens to his clients as long as they are not of the Caucasian ethnicity. From what I understand about the case, he told the kid to plead guilty to the alleged offense and he would get off with five years. The kid being green to the game went along with the program and bit off a thirty year term in the shitter."

"Such is life," said the sergeant whose face showed awe at McAlister's rhetoric.

"Well, you don't look to be in a big hurry standing here talking to me. All you need to do is sign this release paper and you're on your way. I don't suppose you'll be coming back here anytime soon, will you?"

"I hope not," McAlister replied. "I've had one hell of a week, which I hope doesn't become the trend."

McAlister signed the release papers as legibly as he possibly could. The sergeant looked toward the blond woman operating the control room and nodded his head which McAlister guessed was her cue to open the sally port doors that separated him from freedom. Almost instantly, there was a clanging noise that echoed throughout the booking area.

The barred door of the sally port slid slowly open as if the action of it was like a voice telling McAlister that there was not a certainty about life outside the doors of the jail. McAlister walked in between the barred sliding doors and the solid steel door that provided immediate access to freedom. As he stood waiting, he felt relief that his back was turned to the entire jail and it would hopefully be the last part they would see of him. The solid steel door didn't slide open any faster than the barred doors had, but as it did McAlister saw a number of people who were dressed in ordinary clothing, a signal of welcome for him.

Jeanette had been sitting patiently in a lounge chair outside of the steel door waiting for him. She looked pleasing in her black mini skirt and red sleeveless sweater. The pumps she wore added significant height to her stature and what appeared to McAlister as an extra degree of sexiness. She sprung readily to her feet at the sight of his exit from the jail. She hungrily threw her body into his outstretched arms for the security she had briefly missed. "Everything's going to be fine," he told her.

McAlister put his right arm on the length of her shoulders and began walking toward the entrance/exit doors of the Law Enforcement Center. He wondered what the hour was as he cast his head heavenward observing the stars twinkling brightly. His Rolex indicated that it was 8:45 pm. "What day is this?" McAlister asked Jeanette as they walked.

Neither one of them considered that they would have to catch a cab to get to the location where McAlister had parked his car. "Thursday," Jeanette answered with a shocked expression displayed on her face.

"Today is Thursday, June 16, 1987," she said. "I thought I would add that since you seem to be suffering from amnesia. You do know who you are, I suppose," she added, in an attempt to humor him.

Jeanette noticed that the attempt had failed when she saw the far off look in his eyes. McAlister spotted a cab as they walked across the front lawn of the law enforcement center. "There is a cab on the other side of the street," he said as they approached the road that was bustling with speedy motorists.

"Everyone seems to be in a hurry to get to nowhere, don't they?" Jeanette said as they stood on the sidewalk waiting anxiously for a break in the traffic so they could cross to the other side.

Through the haze of automobile headlights, McAlister could see perimeter lights outlining the shape of a city bus heading toward them. They were both unfamiliar with the schedule of the bus system in the city. They figured they had better try to catch the cab.

There was a slight break in both directions of flowing traffic, and McAlister decided they had better take advantage of it. He cupped his fingers between Jeanette's and tugged her through the seam of traffic until they were both on the opposite side of the street. They were both gasping for air when they opened the cab door.

McAlister noticed that same look from the cab driver that the people had given him on the elevator that morning. He and Jeanette had sat tightly together. The cab ride was relatively quiet. He was quick to notice that his automobile had not been stripped of its tires as he and Jeanette exited the cab. He felt relieved that he wouldn't have to fish out money for damages that could have occurred had he stayed in jail much longer.

McAlister quickened his pace when the notion of his good fortune settled in his gut like burning whisky. Jeanette found it difficult to keep up with him, but was determined not to lag behind. She understood the he felt a reinforcement of his free identity just from the idea of ownership of the Mercedes that sat alone in the parking lot.

There was a plot formulating in McAlister's mind as he maneuvered his automobile through the night traffic. He was sure he would spend the night with Jeanette because his body was crying out from pain and neglect. The scar on the side of his face was healing rapidly, but the pain was definitely present from where the Doberman Pincer had attacked him. A hot shower and warm bed would be a welcome change from how he had spent the last few nights.

Driving to Jeanette's home, McAlister felt a toll on his mind and body from all the extracurricular activity. He could only think of crawling into her bed and cradling himself between the sheets. Jeanette tried to make conversation in order to help him to keep from falling asleep. McAlister fought to stay awake as he drove. A few times, the Mercedes crossed into the fast lane due to his dozing. Jeanette became more concerned and offered to drive, but McAlister stubbornly refused, insisting that he was fine.

Noticing his refusal to communicate or give up the driver's seat, Jeanette turned her head toward the passenger window, letting it fall onto the headrest. Almost instantly, she fell asleep. Shortly afterward, McAlister's head began to bob back and forth. He shook his head profusely in an attempt to free the cobwebs. He became confident he was free from drowsiness and relaxed a bit more.

Eighteen wheelers were frequent on Highway 385 during the night hours. It was unfortunate for McAlister and Jeanette that he dozed off when attempting to pass them. As it rode parallel to them, the Mercedes drifted into the side of the big transfer truck. The sound of the metal scraping metal startled McAlister back to life. Usually a safe driver, his instincts took control causing him to steer the automobile away from the big truck.

The reaction was too sudden. The car left the hard surface of the pavement for the dirt and grass shoulder off of the highway. The change in surface from pavement to grass made maneuvering difficult. Jeanette jerked back to consciousness, aware of what was happening, but panic took over logic due to a selfish desire to remain alive. She grabbed the steering wheel trying to get the car back onto the pavement, but the act only created a more intense response from the Mercedes, causing it to whip around in a violent spin until the tire found a stable surface to grip.

Suddenly, the car began flipping horizontally. McAlister heard Jeanette release a high pitched scream. In addition, he heard metal crush and glass shatter. His head hit something solid, producing a loud thud. It was the last sound he heard.

Chapter 11

Lights were burning hot over McAlister's body as he slowly opened his eyes to the penetrating rays. He was disoriented to his whereabouts. He turned his head from side to side in order to get an understanding of his environment. There were flowers contained in a vase on a nightstand beside his bed. Taking a harder look at them, he noticed they were orchids.

Suddenly, he rehashed the scene with Natalie and the dream he had when he was in the holding cell of the jail. Everything that had been associated with orchids had brought him great misfortune. It was easy for him to deduce from his surroundings that he was in a hospital room. He searched his memory to determine what had led him to end up needing medical attention. All he could remember was driving down I-385 with Jeanette and losing control of his Mercedes after an eighteen wheeler truck had nearly demolished him through his own negligence.

McAlister was stunned to realize that he felt an urgent concern for Jeanette's condition. The last thing he could remember about her was the loud screech she had let out at the beginning of the accident. He fumbled with the bed railing and finally found a buzzer attached for the purpose of summoning a nurse to his room. He pressed it firmly and let his head fall back onto the pillow on which he had been resting.

A rosy faced nurse strolled into his room with a beaming smile. McAlister was given the impression that she was fairly new to the nursing field due to the intensity of her smile. If that was not the case, then he could admire her enthusiasm. Hospitals were generally negative places that housed people when they were in their worst conditions of health. He felt that he could relate to it because the legal profession dealt with a loss of life as something negative. "So, tell me, nurse, what happened to me and how bad am I?" McAlister questioned.

"Well, Mr. Johnson, if you would read this morning's paper, you would find out a lot of things about yourself and that pretty little secretary of yours."

That's what he wanted to find out about: Jeanette. "What happened to Jeanette?" he asked.

"By the way, my name is Laura Blandin. I'll be your nurse while you are with us. Don't worry about your secretary, she's doing fine. It's you we are worried about. The doctor seems to think you had some wounds before you had the wreck that was starting to get infected. "Fortunately for you, you gained his attention. He says he knows you well and has even played racquetball with you a number of times. Dr. Black seems to think quite highly of you. He went on and on in the operating room about how you are a pretty decent lawyer. Is that true?"

McAlister had been regarding Nurse Blandin with wide eyes at the mention of Dr. Black's name. He was sure she was talking about Steve Black. He admired Steve for his values about man and marriage. He also knew that Steve Black played a mean game of racquetball. "Yeah, it's true," McAlister answered. "I have done pretty well so far. You know, win some lose some."

The nurse pulled an instrument from around her neck and shoulders and used it to take McAlister's blood pressure. He watched as she wrote some numbers down on a paper attached to a clipboard. "So, how long have you been practicing law?" she asked without looking at him.

"I'm going on my fifth year now," he answered. He saw the same lined expression form on her face and knew why. "I didn't get as quick a start as your average lawyer. I was in the penitentiary at the age of eighteen without even a high school diploma. When I was finally released, my wife, who was not my wife, then encouraged me to pursue the legal field. She and I both felt that it would be interesting coming from the most negative aspect – that is, being a statistic in the South Carolina state prison system, to studying my way into the positive side of life, so that's what I did. I went to school day in and day out. My wife financed all of the schooling. She could afford it because she was doing pretty well as a lawyer herself at that time. She dabbled in criminal law, but domestic law is her specialty."

"Anyhow, I've got this ego problem that wouldn't allow my wife to outdo me. I wrapped my family into what I was doing and that was my world. It was easy, too. I felt as though life had a reason worth working for."

"Why are you speaking of your ethics as a thing of the past?"

"Because it is," McAlister lowered his eyes, looking into the blankness of the sheet that covered his body.

The look in his eyes clued her in that he was thinking about his family. Nurse Blandin raised herself from McAlister's bed. The action broke his hypnotic stare. "I'll bring you a morning paper so you can see what's happening with yourself. I'll also send you a surprise."

With the ending of her promises, she floated away leaving McAlister with a plethora of thoughts ranging from Natalie, to Kelly, to Jeanette. He was lost when he tried to improvise what the rest of his days on earth would bring on his plotted path. He felt it was obvious that he did not have much of a hand in the plot up until the point of the present. He wouldn't dare to plot as much disaster has he had encountered.

McAlister's head was propped against the pillow as he let his thoughts flow on. Kelly and Dane kept popping up in the mental picture, but as soon as it would happen, he would flush the picture out of his mind. He could not afford any more mental anguish.

There was a short rap on the door of McAlister's room. Looking quickly toward the door, he caught a big surprise. Jeanette was sitting in a wheelchair with a big smile pasted on her face and in her lap was a newspaper. The only thing McAlister could think about was that he was missing his cup of coffee.

Jeanette pressed the top of the wheels downward causing the wheelchair to move toward his bed. She kept the motion until she was parked as close as she could get to him. "Next time, I'm driving!" she said, eliciting a laugh from him. "You see where your driving gets you don't you?"

"Well, you don't have to rub it in," said McAlister.

"So, how are you feeling?" she asked.

"I feel like I am still the same person I was before all of this stuff happened. As a matter of fact, I'm ready to get out of here and continue my life. Being here reminds me of being in prison because of all the restrictions placed upon a person."

"I've had a talk with your team of doctors, Mac, and they say you will be back to normal in no time. You need to relax and take it easy. It's time for you to slow your life down some," she retorted in a motherly fashion.

"Slow down! You must be kidding! You make it sound like I'm getting old or something. I'm just getting started, Jeanette. I'm not about to slow down for any reason. I stagnated myself with a marriage to a wife who doesn't know her ass from a hole in the ground and a son who is not old enough to understand what life really means."

"One day, I'm going to take my son away from that nut, but, that will be after I decide to slow down. I wouldn't want Dane exposed to all this mess I've been through. He will probably get some of its doses without my help once he gets a little more age on him. He'll handle it better than I have. He's a smart kid who rationalizes before action. I don't know where he got that from. Kelly never thinks before she speaks. She just lets her feelings fly out of her mouth in the form of words."

A doctor, tall and clad in white hospital garb, appeared in McAlister's doorway momentarily silent before breaking in on McAlister's speech. "It's time for all good patients to call it an evening. Some of us do sleep around here, you know," he said with a hint of humor in his voice.

"Steve, I should have known it was you. Come on in buddy and meet my lovely secretary." Dr. Steve Black strolled casually over to McAlister's bedside, offering his hand for him to shake. "Steve, it is my pleasure to introduce you to Jeanette."

Jeanette flashed a toothy smile and offered her slender hand for Dr. Black to shake. He took her hand gently in his and raised it to his lips, looking into her eyes all the while. "A real gentleman – they don't come like you anymore," Jeanette responded to Dr. Black's introductory greeting.

"You're a real charmer, Steve. Is there anything that you don't do well?" McAlister asked.

"Yeah, there is one thing that I don't do well at all."

"What's that?"

"Surgery," Dr. Black said with a smile. He then turned and walked out of the room, leaving McAlister with a look of surprise written on his face.

"That Steve has always been an asshole. What a warped sense of humor."

"I thought he was rather cute,"

"Cute with a capital 'A'."

"My, don't we have an attitude this evening. What's the sudden change for?"

"Well, I guess I just need a little reassurance and Steve was the person who could have done that. What if he was serious? What if he feels incompetent about his ability and just shrugs it off in the form of jokes?" McAlister said in a serious tone.

"Mac, you really are being a bit insecure. Relax, I've already heard that your friend Steve is the best there is around here. You shouldn't worry."

McAlister raised his head from his pillow in his distraught disgust at Dr. Black's joke. After Jeanette's reassurance, he let his head sink back into the comforts of the pillow. "Well, I guess Steve is just being his old self. That's the problem with that guy. You can never tell when he is serious. I can say that he has always been very smart, so I guess I am over reacting."

"You sure are, Mac. I have confidence in him and so should you. He didn't have a nervous bone in his body. Just relax so you can get this thing past you. Then, we can resume a normal life."

"A normal life?! What the hell is that? I haven't had a normal life since I left the Pen and you expect me to begin to have one now? To be honest with you, Jeanette, I'm beginning to enjoy all of the crazy things that have been taking place in my life."

"Mac, I have good news for you, baby. Steve was just pulling your leg earlier."

"What do you mean?" asked McAlister with a puzzled expression.

"You've already had surgery, Mac. Steve operated on you when they first brought us in here. We are both going to be released from here tomorrow. So what do you think of Steve now?"

"That Steve never changes," McAlister said exhibiting a look of exhilaration and relief. "I can see that you two are in cahoots together. He is a real charmer. It looks to me like he always has the trump suit in his hand. If I had his hand, I'd throw mine away. Tell me, Jeanette, was he very persuasive?"

"To say the least, he performed all the necessary checks on me. Once he was sure I was fine, he reminisced a bit about his dealings with you. He was so interesting to listen to." She looked at McAlister out of the corner of one eye as if conveying a secret message. "I thought playing a joke on you would be fun, but I can see that you have a tendency to overreact. I must say, though, it was very effective, you have to agree."

"I had no choice," McAlister retorted.

Jeanette flung her head backward as if she were trying to remove foreign debris from the crown of her head. She simultaneously released a hearty laugh from within herself. A happy kind of radiance showed itself on McAlister's face. It reminded him that there had been what seemed like an eternal period of time since he had last laughed. He laughed to the point where he had to hold his sides to diminish the pain.

The laughing eventually began to subside, but as if they were forcing themselves to quit, they held their laughs for a while and then released them again until the sequences became shorter. It eventually stopped altogether. They looked at each other momentarily as though conveying a message. "Well, I'm on my way to my room so you can read your paper. You should get some sleep so you can be fresh tomorrow," Jeanette warned. "I want you in good condition when we go to my place."

Frantically, McAlister reached for the newspaper that had been placed on the night stand beside his bed. He quickly read over the top of it. None of it held any special significance. Toward the bottom of the page was a brief section about his near fatal accident. It described his career accomplishments and then explained the investigation and the officials' version of how the accident had supposedly happened. The last paragraph informed that he had been accompanied in the vehicle by his secretary, but her name was not given.

That article was of little interest to McAlister. He flipped the paper to the local section. There, he found what he had been searching for. The first article on the page at the top left corner concerned him. It was entitled, "Cross Dresser's Murder Still a Mystery." He began to read slowly.

"Police are still uncertain as to clues surrounding the death of a local man suspected of having been killed during a sexual struggle in his home. Thirty-two year old Nathan Roberts was found stabbed to death by his ex wife who had become suspicious of foul play when Mr. Roberts disappeared from his normal sites."

The article stated that there were no suspects in the case, but detectives had found blood samples that were a different type than the victim's, and authorities assumed that the perpetrator had been wounded in the struggle. The hospital room felt like it was beginning to close in around McAlister. There was urgency within him to flee, but he knew that if he did so, it would arouse suspicion. His thoughts became integrated with staying as low key as possible as well as staying one step ahead of the officials investigating the case. He knew that investigators would start checking hospitals for patients who had been stabbed or cut. The patients would be questioned as to their whereabouts on the night of Nathan's death, and alibis would be followed up.

McAlister put the paper to his side. He stared at the ceiling and took deep breaths so that the oxygen could help him clear his mind. Slowly, he began to doze. Before long, his eyes were closed and he had fallen into a deep sleep.

****

Kelly came into McAlister's dream like an apparition in the night. He saw himself standing in the same bedroom with her. She was wearing a skimpy black negligee that clung fittingly to her body. She looked delectable. A candle flickered softly as if it were inducing a romantic interlude. Kelly tilted her head slightly, conveying a silent message in sexual overtones. McAlister was anxious to reconnect with Kelly.

Casually, he brought himself within her reach. His arms went around her as he began to smother her with light kisses. Moans slowly began to erupt from within her as he slowly began to undress her, but passionately he did so with his eyes closed. He let each article of clothing fall to the floor. Upon removing her panties, he became instantly shocked as his hand brushed over a large bulge in her pelvic area. His eyes popped open and looked to the area where his hand had brushed. There was no mistake about it, Kelly was hung.

Before his eyes, her face started to change and her hair slowly started shrinking into her skull until it was cropped close to her head. Her forehead protruded outward as her eyes sunk deep into their sockets. Her nose grew thicker and a mustache grew thick and bushy beneath it. Whiskers formed a shadow around the perimeter of her face. "So, you want sex?" she said in a deep, husky voice.

McAlister jumped backward, stunned by what had taken place. He turned to run out of the bedroom, but a strong hand grabbed him by the waist and pulled him back to the face he wanted to take flight from. "Make love to me now!" the voice commanded.

McAlister tried to pull away again, but this time, he felt his skin gash open. Kelly held a surgeon's scalpel in her hand that emitted a blue reflection from the surgical steel. Blood dripped from the top of it. Before McAlister could react defensively, the scalpel was being jammed into his midsection repeatedly. He gripped his bleeding, wounded stomach. Bursts of red light shot before his eyes due to the anger he felt for what Kelly was doing to him. He wanted desperately to kill her, but the red light turned into white light, followed by glimpses of darkness. He knew he was near death.

After his body hit the floor, the white lights began to fade, and were replaced by complete darkness. McAlister felt something land on top of his hand, which was stretched out in front of him. With the last remaining ounce of energy left within him, he slowly opened his eyes and saw at the tip of his fingers, an orchid, placed there by Kelly.

****

McAlister quickly jerked to consciousness. His breathing was heavy and perspiration dripped from his forehead. He placed his hand on his heart to check its pace. It raced wildly. After noting his heartbeat, he held both of his hands out straight in front of him and watched them tremble. As if frightened by watching them, he clenched both hands into a fist to stop them. The act helped him to gather himself. His heart began to slow to a normal rhythm and the perspiration stop flowing. He opened his hands, watching them carefully to ensure that he had gathered all of his composure.

Sleep was what his mind and body were craving. His eyelids were as heavy as silver dollars. He fought to keep them from closing, scared that he would have another nightmare. When he checked his Rolex that lay on the night stand beside his bed it revealed to him that it was 12:45 am, and a long restless night was ahead of him.

On McAlister's night stand, there was a notepad and some pens. He grabbed them and began writing a letter to Dane. First he started out by telling him that he was sorry about leaving and that much had happened since he'd left. He explained to him that he and his mother were constantly in disagreement with one another and only made each other miserable. He inquired about what activities Dane had been keeping himself busy with and mentioned that they should stay in touch, but preferably keep their communication secret from Kelly if possible. He asked Dane to take special care of his mother.

Checking the time after completing the letter to Dane, he found that he had only taken forty-five minutes and immediately brainstormed on what he could do to keep from falling asleep. He decided to play tic tac toe with himself, but did not do so for long because it was not much of a challenge for him, since he pretended to be the X's and let his imaginary character be the O's. It was no fun because the X's would always win the game. Before the break of dawn, he had played hangman and connect the dots. It had been a struggle for him to stay awake, but there was no reluctance from him to neglect sleep.

CHAPTER 12

McAlister gladly welcomed the candy striper who brought breakfast to his room; not because he was hungry, but out of joy that she was a symbol that everyone should be awake and ready for a new day. He figured he wouldn't have to worry about the nightmares for at least sixteen hours. "I hear you are being released today, Mr. Johnson," the heavy bodied candy striper said as she set McAlister's breakfast tray on the stand beside the bed. "It will be great for you to resume your life as normal again, won't it?"

"It sure will," McAlister responded, but at the same time thinking again about how abnormal his life had become and would remain. He pressed a button on the side of his bed that raised his upper back so he could have easier access to his breakfast. The candy striper turned to leave the room, telling McAlister to enjoy his breakfast as she walked out. "The nurse will be in a few hours from now to do a final check of your vitals and you'll be released shortly after that. Take care of yourself and that pretty little secretary of yours," she said with a smile as she exited.

McAlister gathered all of the upper body strength he could muster and pushed himself from the bed, surprised at what little effort it took to do so. He had expected his muscles to need all of the strength he had summoned to raise himself, finding the floor cold once he did. He pushed himself gingerly from the side of the bed. The immediate sensation his legs felt was that of being supported by jelly. Standing still for a few moments, he feared that if he moved immediately, he would fall flat on his face.

Logic clued him that he would have to move one way or the other before he rotted in the place he stood. Casually, he put one foot in front of the other. With each step toward his destined path, the blood circulated faster and the strength replenished in his legs. By the time he reached the closet most of his confidence concerning his recovery had been restored.

Opening the closet, he found a new suit and pair of shoes. A note was attached to the lapel of the coat. He unpinned it, knowing who had put it there. He was getting used to Jeanette being full of surprises. Written on the note was, "I think you need this," signed with a smiley face. Jeanette had obviously had her sister go shopping to get clothes for him. "I guess she found my credit card," he laughed out loud.

McAlister slipped both feet into his expensive shoes and found that they were going to require practically no breaking-in. Jeanette's taste in clothing was definitely admirable. With the thought fresh in his mind of her attractive qualities, he began to question himself why he hadn't bothered to really get to know her and promised himself that he would.

Slowly, the door of his room opened. Jeanette's walked in. McAlister had already begun dressing when he noticed Jeanette's poster size smile. It was expressive of the way she generally appeared to present herself. There was no way McAlister could reject the beam of enthusiasm she flung around. "Don't you know what it means to knock?" McAlister asked as if he were serious.

"It means that you don't know what to expect from the opponent on the other side of the door," she responded half jokingly. "Since I'm not an opponent, I don't have to knock."

"Well, since you're a proponent of mine, I guess you can come in," he kidded. "Sure was thoughtful of you to buy me these clothes. How did you know I needed them?" he asked as he tried on the sport coat and inspected himself in the mirror.

"Please, Mac, you must be joking; you haven't exactly worn a variety of clothes since coming back to work all banged up. God only knows what became of you. It was easy sending my sister on a shopping trip for you. Oh, and by the way I told her to get something for herself for the inconvenience."

"What! Do you know how your sister shops."

"Do you know how you shop?" Jeanette said. "Trust me she didn't spend that much. She only brought a pair of shoes."

"An expensive pair of shoes," he mumbled.

"What, what was that?" Jeanette said like she was about to slap him in the mouth.

"Nothing, but it's coming out of your check," he laughed.

"Shut up and get dressed," Jeanette said throwing the straw from the table at him.

McAllister looked in the mirror at the scar on his face. Immediately his mood changed. Jeanette could see that he was obviously bothered by something. "Mac, what's wrong?"

"Nothing!" he yelled.

"Mac!" she jumped as if he were going to hit her.

"Jeanette, I feel as though I'm under a lot of stress. I've gone through pure hell lately. I'll be glad when good things start to happen. Please forgive me for snapping at you. You know I don't typically act that way."

"Think nothing of it," she responded. "I guess we all get that way from time to time."

Jeanette started to relax, but watched McAlister with careful eyes that she hoped were not noticeable. "Just do me a favor, Mac."

"Sure, what is it you request, my dear?" McAlister inquired.

"Don't ever let it happen again," she said humorously.

"Sure thing, 'bud'," McAlister replied. "Aren't you ready to get out of here?" he asked.

"Nah, Mac. I've been thinking about staying here for another year. You know how great it is here with room and board, the smell of antiseptic cleaner all the time."

"Well you can stay. I'm ready to get out of here," he said buttoning his shirt

"I've already taken care of that stuff. Actually, my dear man, I've been through the whole nine yards and have been officially released."

McAlister had just put the last of his things away. He quickly turned to face Jeanette who possessed a shy smile. Again he felt outfoxed and outmaneuvered. The smile on her face appeared to him a symbol that she was rubbing it in. He half admired her ability to get things done without giving away a clue. "It's good to see you up and about, Mr. Johnson. You have had a pretty remarkable recovery considering your condition when you first arrived.

"You make it sound as though I was near death or something," McAlister responded.

"Well, how does it make you feel to hear me tell you that you had one foot in the grave?"

"Lucky. I'm a lucky man, I guess."

"You guess?" the nurse said in an excited tone of voice. "Young man, you can guess your sweet ass away and would not have any idea of how lucky you really are. Pardon the morbid straight forwardness, but I encounter people weekly who come in here in the same condition you came in and they never get a chance to experience my services. The Man upstairs must really want to see you entertained by life on earth once more."

The nurse's words struck McAlister with a bolt of reality. When he did manage to gather himself to speak, the shock had already written itself all over his face. He felt flabbergasted and totally consumed by the nurse's striking words. "What's your name ma'am?" McAlister asked, obvious to his sense of being straightforward, but not intentionally so.

A thought flashed through his mind that asking the nurse her name so bluntly sounded childish. He felt as if someone had placed the words in his voice box. He hoped she wouldn't pick up on his impulsiveness. "My name is Gina Lee Brown. I don't understand why you ask, because you know that most people only ask the name of another when they meet people they feel they may want to form a friendship with."

"My point exactly," responded McAlister and thinking at the same time of how lucky he was that the nurse had found a way out for him by ignoring his ignorance. He saw that she merely wanted to carry on a conversation and possibly make his day as pleasant as she put forth the effort to do. "Mr. Johnson, you and your lady friend carry on and I'll return in a few minutes."

Nurse Brown returned to the room walking briskly, carrying a container of water. It was discovered by McAlister first that it was a pitcher for watering flowers that she carried, which she used on the orchids in a pot hanging from the ceiling.

Jeanette watched her perform her chore, but McAlister realized that it wasn't her chore to water flowers. He knew exactly what was going on. The nurse was performing a nice gesture in order to buy time for a chance to get to know him. He knew that because he had showed interest in her that she suddenly felt she had an increased significance in life.

As Nurse Brown walked away from the orchids hanging on the wall, McAlister noticed what they were. Immediately, the pressure of his blood raced coarsely throughout his body. He felt a cold chill run down the entire length of his body. He would swear to anyone that the chill even reached his toe nails if he would live to tell about it. His heart pumped furiously.

The beat of it became irregular within seconds and began to tighten toward the left side of his body. He gripped it to see where it was going. Even through the pain, he had a comical thought flash through his mind. He would later tell friends that his heart went around to his back and kissed his spine.

Jeanette was the first to notice. She screamed loud enough to wake up an entire cemetery of those who slept indefinitely. Nurse Brown dropped the water pitcher from her hand and ran to McAlister as he hit the floor. She went over to the panic panel and pressed the emergency button for assistance. "Send a doctor quick," she spoke into the intercom with exclamation.

Dr. Black reported to the scene accompanied by a young nurse. Jeanette watched the commotion before her with intense fear. She ran from the room, teary eyed and in full stride. When everyone had left the room except for Nurse Brown, McAlister slowly opened his eyes. He looked around in observance that Jeanette had left the room. "What happened to Jeanette?" he asked.

"She left in the middle of your anxiety attack," the nurse responded. "Don't worry. She'll be alright. It's you that we're concerned about right now. I don't understand why you had an anxiety attack. We are going to keep you here for a couple days for more tests and to ensure that you are okay."

"No, you are not!" McAlister said, springing from the bed. "There is nothing wrong with me. I'm sorry, but you are not going to keep me here another day."

"Just calm down, Mr. Johnson, before you have a relapse. I'll make a deal with you. If you check out in good physical condition, I'll pressure

Dr. Black into releasing you today or no later than tomorrow. Is that okay with you?"

"Sounds good to me," answered McAlister. "I'm sure that when you check me out, you will find me in perfect condition."

"Don't feel so confident, Mr. Johnson. You just be sure to get some rest before we start running those tests on you."

Nurse Brown flashed McAlister a genuine smile and wink. He closed his eyes as if he were falling asleep as she quietly made her way out of the room. As soon as the door closed and he was sure she was halfway down the hall, he sprung out of bed. He quickly dressed himself and scanned the room to be sure he was not leaving any of his possessions behind.

CHAPTER 13

With nervous tension, he turned the knob of the door to his room as if it was rigged by a bomb and he expected an explosion. When the latch of the door gave way, he slowly pushed it open and peeked down the hallway. He noticed that his room was the last one on the floor. At the other end of the hallway, he could see a nurse that he had never seen before. He was glad, thinking maybe she wouldn't recognize him. Casually, he walked down to where the nurse stood behind a booth. She greeted him with a mouth full of gleaming white teeth. "What can I do for you?" she asked.

"I need to know which of these rooms you have Jeanette Littlejohn in," he said.

"She's all the way down at the end of the hall on the right."

McAlister offered his thanks and complimentary smile and then briskly strolled down to the room that the nurse had directed him to. He didn't bother to knock, startling Jeanette from her wheelchair. She sprang from it and wrapped her arms around him tightly. "Thank God you are alright," she said. "I thought you were going to leave me here without anyone to love."

McAlister pushed her gently away from his body. He looked deep into her eyes and saw that she was sincere. Silently understanding each other, they brought their lips closer together until they were pressed tightly and their tongues began to dart against each other. McAlister gingerly pushed Jeanette's mouth from his, looking into her eyes momentarily in silence. "Let's get out of here!" he said, breaking the mood and silence between them.

"We can't leave just like that," Jeanette responded.

"Oh yes, we can, and we are," McAlister stated. McAlister began gathering all of her possessions. She already had her street clothes on, which relieved him of his anxiety of leaving the hospital before anyone would discover him missing from his room.

"Mac, what's the rush?"

"The rush is that I'm not staying here for them to run any damn tests on me. I'm doing fine, so why should I let them probe around my insides just to get their jollies?"

McAlister tugged hard at Jeanette's arm, causing her to grimace. "Okay, okay, I'm rushing, but I still don't see what the big hurry is," she said. "Are you in some kind of trouble?"

Reaction elicited itself immediately from McAlister in the form of hostility. He jerked profusely on Jeanette's arm and began to yell at her. "Look, damn-it! Either you are coming or you aren't, it really doesn't matter to me, just make your mind up! I'm outta here!"

Jeanette ran out of the room hurriedly, feeling upset that McAlister had hollered at her like she was a child. When she got to the elevator, which was halfway between her room and the nurse's booth, McAlister was already there punching at the down button, angry with the world.

The door opened slowly, too slowly for McAlister. He placed his hands on each of the doors and attempted to rush them open. When he was satisfied that the doors were open wide enough he stepped into the elevator. Jeanette followed closely behind, panting trying to catch her breath. She did not speak when she was aboard the elevator. She only wrapped a sweater around her shoulders and looked up at the indicator numbers. McAlister had noticed daily on his trips to and from his office how people would never fail to look at those numbers. It always seemed so impersonal to him.

They both were shocked when the elevator reached the lobby, the doors opened, and Dr. Steve Black was standing right before them. A puzzled expression presented itself on his face. He stepped into the elevator as McAlister and Jeanette started to get off.

A man was being wheeled through the entrance doors by a younger man who looked to be older than the older man's son. In McAlister's plight, he nearly knocked the old man out of the wheelchair when he wildly pushed the entrance doors open. The young man pushing the wheelchair yelled, "Hey asshole, why don't you watch what you're doing. You could have hurt my dad!"

Jeanette was tugging against McAlister's grip. She could not understand why he was behaving so irrationally. McAlister could feel her resistance, but he wouldn't allow her to become an obstacle. "Come on," he said, looking at her with a wild look in his eye.

Finally, he reached the street that he had been racing towards and darted down the sidewalk at the corner of an old gas station. McAlister started to laugh. It began as a light chuckle, but in seconds he was near hysteria. His laughing became so intense that he began to cough. His laughing and coughing mixture became so heavy; he nearly choked from lack of air. Tears began streaming down both of his cheeks, causing his face to be become cherry red. When he looked at Jeanette again, she had an angry expression on her face. "When you gather yourself from comedy hour, you owe me a big explanation, mister!" She said with her head slightly tilted and her hands still on her sides.

McAlister's hysteria subsided to mild chuckles. He wiped the remaining tears from under his eyes. Still wanting to laugh, but knowing Jeanette was serious; he pressed his lips tightly together and breathed deeply through his nose to force the remainder of hysteria out of his system. "Look, let's get out of here, and I'll start filling you in some time later on," he said softly.

He turned and started walking away. Jeanette was right at his heels. "Mac, this doesn't make any sense to me, you running out the way you did. No more than three hours ago, you had a near fatal heart attack and now you are out here on the streets running around like some type of criminal."

"Anxiety attack."

"Whatever, it looked like a heart attack."

As they walked, she went right on babbling and flinging her arms in the air from time to time as though she were disgusted with the situation. McAlister began to feel irritated by her nagging. He walked faster in order to alleviate the anger that was building inside of him.

Jeanette, being smaller, found it difficult to keep up with his pace. Her voice became louder as she walked faster and before long, she was virtually trotting in order to keep up with him. Finally, she became disgusted and stopped in the middle of her pace. She shouted at him at the top of her lungs. "Damn it Mac! Will you stop for a minute and listen to me?!"

"Hell no! Either you shut up or get lost!" McAlister replied, never turning his head or slowing his pace.

Jeanette noticed that the distance between them was becoming massive, so her trot became a steady run in order to catch up with him. She ran past him, but only by a few feet and then turned herself so that she was facing him. She put her hands out in front of her to stop him, but the action failed, because he walked around her without breaking stride. "You asshole! You're being totally irrational," Jeanette pointed out. "None of this makes any sense to me. Why are we walking and where are we going?"

"To get a cab."

"There were plenty of cabs in front of the hospital."

"Didn't want one of those," he grunted

She started back after him again. Neither of them paid any attention to the bums and derelicts that loitered on the sidewalks idly. As McAlister walked, he touched one of their shoulders briefly in passing. "Hey, buddy, can I get a cigarette?" the bum asked.

"Don't smoke," McAlister reflected quickly, but almost instantly, he wished he had a pack of cigarettes. He heard the bum ask Jeanette if she had one to spare and she responded just as Mac had, but he knew she wasn't lying. She was the picture of health and a beautiful one at that.

McAlister glanced briefly over his shoulder at her. The bum who had asked her for a cigarette was walking closely behind her. Her arms were folded across her chest as she walked at a brisk pace, looking very upset. McAlister had seen Kelly fold her arms like that as well as other women, including his mother. He thought of it as a universal gesture for angry women. He looked forward briefly, but glanced back over his shoulder because he found her to be sort of amusing with her arms folded, and an angry look on her face. She was walking as fast as she could, her hair stringy from sweat, but worse, the bum maintained a steady pace beside her nagging for a cigarette as if he hadn't heard her reply that she didn't smoke. "Please let me have a cigarette," the bum was begging.

McAlister stopped in his tracks to watch. He knew people well, and knew that Jeanette was being pushed to the limit. He could imagine what was about to happen and he began to wish it would. As if by force of mental telepathy, Jeanette reacted just as McAlister had figured she would. Without warning, she unfolded her arms letting her right hand smack the bum on the left side of his face. The impact sounded like a gunshot in the night. The bum immediately brought both of his hands to his cheek to comfort himself. His mouth flew open at the same time and his eyes grew to the size of half dollar pieces. He stood still for a few minutes, looking at Jeanette with a silly shocked expression.

Jeanette covered her mouth with the same hand she had smacked the man with. She was embarrassed by what she had done. The look on her face was almost identical to his. The whole scene was more than McAlister could bear. He took off running at a high rate of speed laughing all the while as he ran to the end of the street corner and only stopped because cars were crossing the intersection at a high rate of speed, and a crowd of people were waiting to cross.

He reached out for a telephone pole that was near him. Supporting the weight of his body with his left hand, he placed his right hand across his abdomen, practically doubling over in the same process. Tears were streaming down both of his cheeks. He was laughing so hard that he found it difficult to breathe. His sides had started to hurt, but he was enjoying the moment and did not care.

When he managed to partially gather himself, he took the opportunity to look and see what had happened between the begging bum and Jeanette. The man still had his hand to his face, but was walking back in the direction from which he had come. Jeanette was walking behind him in some effort to stop him so she could apologize, but McAlister could tell from the way he was fanning her away, he didn't want anything to do with her.

McAlister figured it would be quite some time before the bum would beg for a cigarette again. The thought sent him back into laughter. The people waiting to cross the street had their heads turned in observance of his hysteria. Logically, he summoned that they were thinking he was a nut case, but he could care less because he was enjoying the moment too much. In the middle of the same breath, he told his onlookers that they had to be there. Fearing him to be a violent man, they turned their attentions from him and proceeded to cross the street. McAllister was grateful when a yellow cab pulled up to the curb.

CHAPTER 14

McAlister motioned for Jeanette to come get in. "Come on!" he said to her in an anxious voice. "Jeanette, we need to hurry before the car dealerships close for the day. We need to get some type of wheels. I still have my check book with me, so we can just write a check for the down payment, or just pay in full, depending on what I decide to buy."

"That's great, Mac, but we could always go back to the complex and get my car, that is, if you don't have anything against Hondas."

"Nah, forget that I need wheels anyhow. The first set of wheels that catches my eye, I'm grabbing. I don't want you to worry about transportation right now. Just worry about keeping pace with me. The first instance I notice you lagging behind, I'm going to speed up and make it harder on you. I'm getting tired of you hurtling behind me and complaining that I'm moving too fast."

"I've got too much to do to let a slow nagging woman keep me from getting it done, so, either you keep up or you get lost. There's a car lot around here somewhere."

McAlister had been on that street many times before and had never known the name of it. He didn't care to know the names of streets unless he had to use them for court purposes. It wasn't unusual that as soon as he would learn the name of a street, he would forget it. Finally, he saw a store on the corner of the next street. He knew for sure that there was a small car dealership only a couple of establishments away.

As they entered the parking lot of the car lot, Jeanette was flabbergasted that McAlister would even consider purchasing an economy car. She had always known him to be the sport car type and was puzzled, because it was totally out of character for him to go after anything other than that. When she noticed that they were going on the premises of the dealership, she immediately thought he would be interested in a convertible Mustang 5.0.

Considering that the lot contained used cars, most of the cars had keys already in the ignitions. McAlister walked around a Ford Escort slowly, carefully noticing all the flaws that marred the car. It was a tan color that appeared to be at the beginning stage of oxidizing. On the right side of it, the back fender was slightly creased.

Jeanette peered through the glass of the passenger window. The seats of the car were the same color as the exterior paint. A pattern of horizontal and vertical stripes in a chocolate color was the décor for the seats. Jeanette was surprised that there were no tears in the seats, although, there was one at the top of the dash. "Pretty nice," McAlister said with a hint of a smile on his face.

Jeanette thought that the smile was one of deception. It was a smile that gave one the impression that something conning was taking place in the mind of the beholder. *'He's gotta be kidding!'* Jeanette thought to herself. *'That car is a piece of junk! I can't believe he's even considering it.'*

McAlister broke Jeanette's thoughts by rapping the palms of his hands down hard on the hood of the car, which made a loud, metallic noise. "Yes, sir, this is the one. We are going to drive this baby right off the lot today."

"But, Mac," Jeanette broke in. "You can't be serious about buying this heap of junk. We would be lucky to make it to the nearest traffic light from here. Surely you must be losing your mind by even considering buying this pile of God knows what. You haven't even investigated whether or not there is a motor underneath the hood. Have you ever heard of at least test driving a car before deciding to buy it? You're acting too impulsively to make an objective decision. Whatever has been bothering you sure have caused you to act irrationally lately. You're beginning to scare me."

"I know what I'm doing," McAlister snapped. "Just leave these types of decisions to me."

He was walking around the car slowly, carefully inspecting the external appearance. Jeanette's words stunned him by the harshness of their reality. However, it was not the time or place to become upset with her. His mind was already preoccupied mostly by thoughts of buying the car. *'This is perfect,'* he thought to himself. *'I can go on my mission and remain inconspicuous. It's such an average, run-of-the-mill car that it would blend into the rest of the automobile population without notice. I'd be foolish to get something flashy, something someone would remember.'*

The office was a trailer that sat squarely in the middle of the parking lot. It was a tan colored trailer that had cinderblocks underneath for stability. The siding of it was so dirty that it needed a major overhaul. The appearance of it raised curiosity in McAlister's mind as to what kind of people occupied it. He was more than sure he would find a man inside with salesman written all over him who would probably talk too much.

McAlister summoned Jeanette to follow him to the trailer and when they reached the top of the steps, he could see a slightly balding fat man sitting behind a desk. He estimated the man to be about forty-eight years old and about three hundred and fifty pounds in weight. As he reached for the door knob, he caught a glimpse of the other two bodies sitting in chairs facing the fat man. Slowly, he opened the door as if he expected someone to be standing behind it that he didn't want to knock down. "Come on in and have a seat," the fat man said with cheerfulness in his voice. "I'll get to you as soon as I finish up with these people."

McAlister located a couch big enough for about four people on his immediate left. It was made of deep green colored leather. The seats of it had cracked in several places.

Once McAlister and Jeanette seated themselves, he briefly glimpsed at the two people who sat facing the fat man. Not wanting to stare, he averted his attention to the surroundings of the room. There were pictures on the walls of autos from a time many decades past. It was evident that the fat man had taken automobiles as a passion in his life.

On the wall, to the left of where the fat man sat, was a book shelf about two thirds of the way up toward the ceiling. McAlister guessed that the books there probably contained something having to do with automobiles. Taking the environment into account, McAlister summoned that the room was simply furnished, yet spoke a bold statement. McAlister felt that if the man was trying to make a statement about the way he had set the place up, it would be something to the effect of, "I know cars."

Jeanette sat beside McAlister quietly, taking in her own thoughts about the surroundings. She felt compelled to talk, but didn't feel comfortable doing so and was glad that McAlister was not making any efforts to strike up a conversation. She noticed that he was in his own mindset and she could relax for a few minutes without being bothered.

At first, McAlister didn't pay much attention to the appearance of the couple in front of the fat man. He had heard the man discussing getting the monthly payments down to one hundred and seventy-five dollars per month. Then, he heard the woman begin to speak. She spoke with a gruff voice and not the legitimate voice of a woman. It sounded cleverly disguised. McAlister frowned and inspected the body from which the voice was coming.

She appeared to be in her mid-thirties, having shoulder length blond hair that was slightly wavy. Her nose appeared broad and her lips were thick. Her shoulders were broader than any woman he had ever seen. She had breasts that were smaller than average and her hands were large, but well manicured. Looking at her large hands made McAlister curious. Without thinking about it, he looked at her feet. She had to be wearing at least a size eleven pair of pumps. Her ankles had veins like a man's.

There was no second guessing, McAlister was sure that he was looking at a man dressed in drag. She had done a good job at choosing her attire. Her black and gray pastel colored dress blended well with her shoes and dark panty hose. She looked very convincing, but McAlister found that Jeanette had taken notice and there was a note of recognition reflecting from her eyes that what she was looking at was not the real McCoy.

Jeanette turned to McAlister with an expression of disbelief tagged on her face. She looked like she was silently saying, "Do you see what I see?" He returned a knowing expression for a few seconds and they averted their stares back to the gender impostor who was talking to the salesman almost pleadingly, trying to negotiate the price of the car down. A couple of times, her voice fluctuated to the point where she sounded like a man.

McAlister and Jeanette exchanged knowing glances again and before long, the couple and the dealer reached the point of agreement and the papers were signed. The fat man gave the woman the keys to the car and the strange couple departed. McAlister watched through the window as the fat salesman showed the couple a few features of their new car. In a matter of minutes, the salesman was back in the trailer introducing himself to McAlister and Jeanette.

"Hello, I'm Ralph Pumpernickel. What can I do for you people today?"

"I'm McAlister and this is Jeanette," he answered, and then almost abruptly, he asked, "How much are you asking for that Escort parked outside?"

"Twenty-four ninety-five, and she's a nice little get around town automobile. That price includes sales tax, by the way."

McAlister whipped out his check book and proceeded to write a check for it. The salesman was looking at him with bulging eyes. McAlister looked up at him and asked, "You will accept a check, won't you?"

"By all means, that is as long as it doesn't react as a center piece in a basketball game."

McAlister did not respond to the fat man's joke, but resumed writing the check. The fat man went behind his desk and produced a bill of sale and title and began filling them out. "Don't you want to drive the car, McAlister?" the fat man asked. "I stand behind all of my cars. That baby out there may not be the best looking machine, but her motor is as sound as you can get."

McAlister slid the check over to him. The fat man picked it up and looked it over carefully. A light of recognition formed in his eyes as he placed it back on the desk. "Say, aren't you that hotshot lawyer?" he asked.

"Yeah, I'm that hotshot lawyer," McAlister answered, then, somewhat disturbed by the fat man's brashness asked, "Can we get on with the business?"

Jeanette was sitting back, quietly observing all of McAlister's actions. She could tell that something had a strong grip on him and it was causing him to act without much foresight. She watched as the salesman gave McAlister the necessary paperwork and the keys to the car. They shook hands and McAlister motioned to Jeanette that he was ready to go. She was also more than ready to leave while she waited inside patiently as McAlister checked the fluids beneath the hood. Before five minutes had elapsed, McAlister slammed down the hood and entered the car. He inserted the key into the ignition and it started almost instantly. The car took a few minutes to warm up, but before long, they were riding along with active traffic.

It started turning dark before they were halfway to Jeanette's home. Neither McAlister nor Jeanette were talking, so McAlister decided to turn the radio on. The dial was set too far left, generally where they played old stuff that McAlister didn't care to listen to. As he turned the dial slowly to the right, he caught a station on which the DJ was reading the news. "Police are still baffled by the murder of a local man found murdered in his home. It is believed that the victim, Nathan Roberts, frequently dressed himself in drag and visited bars to pick up nightly companions. Police speculate that someone picked up Mr. Roberts and went home with him, believing that he was a woman. Once there, the perpetrator discovered the true gender of Mr. Roberts. A struggle ensued and Mr. Roberts was killed in the process. So far, the only clue the police have is the blood type of the killer. The last place Mr. Roberts was seen alive was at the popular nightspot, The Phoenix. Anyone who has any knowledge of this violation, please contact the police department."

"Look out for that car!" Jeanette yelled.

Suddenly, McAlister was brought back to reality, but not a moment too soon. Reflexively, he stomped down hard on the brakes, stopping the car a few inches from a car that had been traveling slower than the required speed limit. "What the hell is wrong with you, Mac?" Jeanette screamed at him. "That's the second time you have almost killed us. I think you need to turn this car around and aim it toward the hospital, because you have been acting weird ever since you came up with the idea of leaving the hospital before you were supposed to be released."

McAlister's pulse raced like a drummer's beat. Jeanette was still yelling something at him, but he was oblivious to it. He was aware that he was turning more paranoid each time he heard or read anything concerning Nathan Roberts. Quickly, he turned his head to the left, checking for traffic and pounded the accelerator when he realized there was none.

Jeanette felt relieved when they were rolling into her apartment complex parking lot. The only thing on her mind was the thought of getting a nice hot bath and some sleep. She was so tired that she almost didn't have enough energy to climb the stairway leading to her apartment. McAlister stood patiently behind her as she fumbled for the door key. After finding the key, she opened the door and reached for the light switch, flicking it on when she found it. Without making any mention of her intentions, she headed straight for the bathroom. "Make yourself a drink," she told McAlister after starting her bathwater.

The living room was furnished with an L shaped crushed velvet couch with a matching love seat on each side of it. There was a mahogany trimmed coffee table with glass set squarely in the middle of it. Across from the coffee table was an artificial fireplace with a mantle above it that held framed pictures of Jeanette's family and friends. To the left of the love seat was an eight foot by nine foot long wall unit that contained mixed drink glasses, brass ornaments, and a host of other trinkets. There were a variety of plants hanging from each corner of the room. Above the mantle embedded in the wall was a twenty-one inch color television set. The room brought a smile to McAlister's face. He liked the warm atmosphere created by the décor.

McAlister heard water splashing around in the bathroom as he concocted himself a rye highball from behind the bar in the kitchen. After he had mixed his drink to the desired taste, he allowed himself the opportunity to inspect the rest of the apartment.

The door beside the bathroom was closed, but so was the door across from it. McAlister figured it was probably a bedroom that was for a guest, or maybe actually Jeanette's bedroom. Opening the door, he found that it was neither. In one corner of the room against the wall was a rack of steel dumbbells. Five feet away from the rack was a universal machine capable of allowing one to perform a full workout. Four bass speakers were suspended from each corner of the ceiling. The far corner of the room across from the universal set was a large bean bag and in front of it along the far wall was a six foot macramé hammock that hung from the ceiling, secured by anchor hooks.

A stereo system was located on shelves about five feet off the floor complete with amplifier, tuner, cassette deck, reel to reel compact disc, and equalizer. In the right corner nearest the door was a small corner bar that held a small icebox and blender. Underneath it was an assortment of fruit drinks, amino acids in liquid form, and a container of protein powder. "Wow," McAlister said to himself, "this woman knows what she wants and is comfortable with home life. Now, I'll check out the bedroom."

McAlister waved his head in a positive nod as he walked toward the bedroom. As he opened the door, he flicked on the light in the same process. The instant he did so, he saw reflections of himself on each wall of the room. There wasn't an inch of wall or ceiling that was not covered in glass mirrors pieced together.

On each side of the bed, was a wine glass top night stand trimmed in brass. The headboard of the bed was as wide as the bed itself. The only ornaments on the headboard were two brass unicorns placed with the horns of each pointing toward one another as if they were about to begin a session of frolicking. "Alright now, this is how it's supposed to be," McAlister said as he threw himself on the bed, but somehow he managed not to spill his highball.

Looking up toward the corners of the ceiling nearest the door McAlister noticed that Jeanette had suspended Bose speakers. He imagined that the music that flowed through those speakers came through the works of numerous jazz musicians. Just as he concluded his thoughts, the sound of a saxophone came through the speakers with the utmost of clarity. He recognized right away that it was Kenny Gogan, somewhat comparable to Pan, the little Greek god who played a flute with enticement.

In the doorway, Jeanette appeared, wrapped from the upper chest to high thighs with a peach colored towel that protruded in all the right areas. McAlister was glad he hadn't drunk more highballs or he might have his reality distorted. Jeanette began dancing a slow, but methodical dance at about the pace a stripper would. In the fluid movement, she made her way to the light control switch. It was the type that could set the lighting from bright to dim and she turned it where the lights were as dim as possible without turning them completely off.

Slowly, she lowered her towel, making a point to spin and dance at the same time. In due time, both eyes of her breasts were revealing themselves to McAlister. The highball did not have any denying effect on the excitement he was feeling. If anything, he felt it gave him a more wild excitement.

Jeanette had managed to get the towel down to her waist to the point where her hips started to flare. All the while, the expression on her face never changed from the seductive smile that she had started out with. Once the towel was to the point where her hips flared the most, she pushed it away until McAlister couldn't see it anymore. Her dance continued, but her dips and sways were closer to McAlister to the point that she was almost within grasp. He wanted to grasp her, but he wanted the show to go on at her pace because he knew that his acting out desire would change the tempo altogether.

Jeanette danced close enough to him that he could almost reach out and touch any part of her. The temptation became so great that he did reach for her a couple of times but each time he did, she would draw herself away from him with a seductive smile planted on her face.

McAlister had reached a peak in his excitement which was becoming hard to contain and Jeanette sensed it. She crawled beside him on the bed and began undressing him. She removed each article of his clothing slowly and agonizingly all the while licking her tongue from side to side between her lips. She knew that she was driving him crazy and loved every minute of it.

After what seemed an eternity to McAlister, Jeanette finally finished undressing him. She pressed her lips to his and darted her tongue back and forth throughout his mouth. The energy between them was growing to dynamic proportions. Jeanette pushed herself away from his face and started kissing him around his neck, moving downward ever so slowly. She moved onward to his chest carefully paying attention to his sensitive zones. She could hear his heart beating faster than normal and his breathing heavier, so she slid further downward on the bed so that she could have access to his inner thighs.

McAlister anticipated what would be next, but Jeanette pulled a sudden surprise on him. Almost like a frog, she leaped forward until her head was parallel with his. "Good night, Mac. I have a headache. Sweet dreams." She said rolling over on her side with her back toward him and closed her eyes for sleep.

McAlister rose halfway up, supporting himself on his elbows. He looked at the back of her head and then at her body. His thoughts accelerated for a reason to rationalize Jeanette's behavior. His first thought was to seduce her, feeling that she wanted it. She must have been playing a game of get the man excited and see how he would react. He decided against seducing her, feeling that it would be low of him to do so. His decision was based partially on the fact that he could hear her beginning to snore, but then, she could have been faking.

His other thought was that she was punishing him for the way she had been treated by him throughout the day. Maybe she wanted him to see what he could have had, but he was not a good boy so he would not get his reward. The last thought he had was that Jeanette didn't feel quite secure with him. Leaving herself exposed to him the way she did might be a test she was carrying out to see where his head was. If he would himself overcome the situation, he probably would give her a better sense of security about him.

Jeanette's snoring had grown intense and McAlister was almost certain that there was no faking to the horrible noise she was making. Careful not to wake her, he slipped gingerly out of the bed and put his clothes back on as quietly as he possibly could. Once fully dressed, he slipped from the room and went to the bathroom. Above the toilet was a two layer shelf. McAlister found on the lower shelf the key to the apartment. Carefully, he eased back into the bedroom and changed the clock from 11:05 PM to 9:30 PM. He tip-toed out of the room to ensure he would not wake Jeanette.

On the way down to the car, McAlister checked his inner coat pocket to make sure his switchblade was still there. He was relieved to find that it was. He pulled it out and pressed the button to test and see if it was still operable. The force of the blade releasing from within the handle almost caused him to drop it from his hand.

CHAPTER 15

The drive to The Phoenix was uneventful. Due to the lateness of the hour, traffic was at a bare minimum. When he arrived at the parking lot he could understand why there were hardly any cars on the roads. Everyone was at The Phoenix. That was good news because statistically, he stood a better chance of accomplishing what he had set out to do. He rode through the parking lot until he reached an area that had cars comparable to what he was driving and found a spot between them.

There was an entourage of weirdoes going into the club. People entering the place were black, white, Asian, short, tall, fat, skinny, long haired, short haired, bald, heterosexual, and homosexual. McAlister thought to himself that he was about to enter a giant melting pot.

As he got out of his car, he could hear a rich bass sound coming from inside. The music gave him a feeling of euphoria as his blood rushed coarsely through his veins. He inspected his attire as he walked toward the entrance and approved of his appearance feeling sure that the odds were good that others would as well.

The bouncer was a tall black guy that looked like he must have played professional football at some time in his life. The guy must have been at least seven feet tall and had to weigh right at three hundred pounds. There was no fat to be found anywhere on him. "Wait right here for a minute," the big guy said. "I've got to get rid of this slime." He had two guys jacked up by the back of their collars.

They both were squirming to break free from the grip of 'Goliath.' Both were bleeding from their noses. McAlister picked up right away that they were both gay and probably had started a fight with each other over some guy who was probably still in the club enjoying himself. A few people had gathered behind McAlister. They all turned their attention to what Goliath was going to do with the two. "What's going on?" McAlister heard some lady ask her date.

"I don't know, but it looks like one of those two guys was fighting." McAlister heard her date respond.

"What's funny is that, I'll bet you, ten to one that they were fighting over which one of them was going to go home with somebody that is probably still roaming around the joint not even slightly aware that he was the subject of their feud. What's worse is that I look around and I see there is an abundance of female impersonators in this joint and I haven't made it past the point of paying my money to get in this place."

Goliath returned to his glass room where he was the recipient of funds that kept the place running smoothly. Disgust was tacked all over his face. It was evident to McAlister and the crowd behind him that the onslaught of patronage for this particular night was taking its toll on him.

McAlister reveled in the idea that the man had brought up about there being an abundance of homosexuals and female impersonators. He felt a sense of relief just hearing that there were transgenders there. At least the night would not be wasted.

Goliath told McAlister that the cover charge would be $7.50 in a gruff voice. At lease the voice fit his body. McAlister produced the money from his pockets without hesitation. The first area of interest for McAlister was directly ahead of him and cluttered with people sitting from one end to the other, already intoxicated to the point that they were open for propositions. There were a few empty seats around, but McAlister happened to find one located directly across from a table where two female impersonators sat.

Knowing female pretenders, as a rule, were almost more aggressive toward hooking a man than an actual woman would be. He acknowledged the fact that he should position himself so that he could make eye contact with them. The rest would come easy.

When the bartender finally made his way over to McAlister, he ordered a dry Martini with a twist of lime. As he waited for it, he turned his body slightly so that he could make eye contact with them. Simultaneously, they returned the stares with smiling faces.

"Three fifty," he heard the bartender say. McAlister retrieved a few crumpled bills from his pocket along with two pieces of silver. A split lime sat on the rim of a four ounce glass containing the Martini. McAlister squeezed as much of the juice as he could into the drink and then dropped the lime itself into it. After his first sip, he turned his body to where he could face the cross dressers.

They must have been watching him the entire time, because they looked to him like they had never moved an inch. One of them took a bold step and came over to introduce herself. She was tall, heavyset and wore a black spandex dress that clung fittingly to her. *'Damn, how did he do that?'* McAlister thought to himself. There were curves there; more than he had imagined. She introduced herself as Claudia. *'It's probably Claude,'* McAlister thought. "My friend and I would like your company. You're drinking a Martini, aren't you? Well, let me order you a twin to that."

McAlister went over and introduced himself to the one left at the table. Fortunately, there was a third chair at the table. He seated himself so that he could be the spotlight of the trio. Claudia returned from the bar with a fresh round of drinks. *'Must be that man thing about her,'* McAlister thought. She had to be the one doing the drink buying. "Have you two already met?" she asked as she placed the drinks in front of each respective owner.

"Partially," McAlister answered. She knows that I'm Bobby, but it's still a mystery to me what her name is." He produced a charming smile that warmed the atmosphere.

"I'm Roberta," she offered, showing all thirty-two teeth. Her voice was smooth, but deep. "Claudia and I like to have fun. We live to have fun."

"Well, fun is the name of the game in this city," McAlister said.

McAlister watched their reactions as they hung onto his every word. "We all have our own interpretations of what's fun," he added. "Myself, well, I find that people are the most intriguing things on earth."

"You are so right about that," Claudia responded. "I find you to be quite exciting."

"You girls go ahead and drink up, the next round of drinks is on me," McAlister said, having no intentions of drinking more than two.

Watching Claudia and Roberta gulp down the drinks made their tongues even looser. Claudia became more aggressive. She pulled her chair close to McAlister's and touched him as she talked. "You know, I'm getting very intoxicated and it's terribly hot in here. Would you care to take me home for a night cap?" she offered.

"Couldn't leave a lady in distress," McAlister answered.

"I'm hanging here for awhile," Roberta told Claudia. "I'll see you at work tomorrow," she winked at Claudia as she and McAlister stood up.

McAlister thought that the two of them acted like school girls. He knew that Claudia would be expected to relate all the events of the evening once they saw each other at work the next day. McAlister held the secret to himself that it would be an unlikely event. "Where are you staying?" McAlister asked as he let the Escort's engine warm up.

"At a hotel across town," she said. Claudia pulled out a pack of Style cigarettes from a little black pouch and lit it as McAlister started out of the parking lot. They exchanged small talk on the way to the hotel. The conversation centered mainly on the topic of positive and negative forces responsible for causing decisions to be made concerning career moves.

McAlister didn't have much to offer to the conversation since he had been pretty stable thus far in his career. Claudia, however, seemed to be experiencing a life of uncertainty, having eleven different jobs in the past three years. It wasn't hard for him to believe since he already felt that she was confused.

As they pulled up to the driveway of the hotel, McAlister rubbed his upper arm close to his side where the switchblade lay idle in his inner coat pocket. He was pleased that he hadn't lost it, considering everything he had been through. "This looks like the place," he said as he shut off the ignition.

Claudia sat in the car patiently waiting for McAlister to open her door. He had not noticed that she was doing this until he had taken a few steps away from the car. He saw that she was looking at him as if to say, "Now, aren't you going to open my door?"

'I swear this son of a bitch is playing the role to the max.' McAlister swallowed the lump in his throat that had formed from the disgust of opening the door for another man. "Well, chivalry isn't dead after all," she said with a smile.

"No, but it's forgotten sometimes," McAlister responded.

"You're so full of it," Claudia said as she locked her arm around his waist.

They went through the lobby to the elevator. The attendant at the desk had his back to them, busy doing paperwork, so he didn't notice them when they entered. There was no one waiting at the elevator. McAlister felt relieved about that as well.

The elevator door opened slowly, inviting them in. "Press 4," Claudia said huskily. She almost lost the disguise in her voice. McAlister did so and the door closed as slowly as it opened. Once the door was closed, Claudia started kissing his neck. A chill ran down his spine, knowing that it was from a female pretender. He kept the signs of distaste of the act hidden from her. 'I'll play this game out until the perfect moment comes,' McAlister said to himself. A couple of times before they reached their floor, Claudia darted her tongue in his ear. He cringed each time she did so.

A bell sounded when they stopped on the fourth floor. Immediately, the door opened. As they stepped out of the elevator, Claudia reached down and grabbed McAlister between his legs. "Save it for when we get to the room," he told her.

Soon after, they were entering her room McAlister could tell that Claudia had been renting it for a while. She had added a bit of her own personal touches to it. "I have you now," she said as she pulled him down on top of her, falling backward on the bed.

She started to undress him, but he stopped her. "No! I want to undress you!" he said. Slowly, he started removing her spandex dress. She had her eyes closed, already enjoying the activity. Once he had it off, he noticed that she had on a stuffed bra. He removed it as slowly as he had the dress, but he did not let on to her that he was shocked because he wasn't.

Another reason was that he didn't want her to open her eyes and see what was about to happen to her. He saw that there was a bulge in her panties. Using the other hand, he removed the switch blade from his inner coat pocket. At the press of the button on the handle, a long glistening blade sprung out. The sound of its spring action was enough to get Claudia to open her eyes. "What…" was all she could say.

"You son-of-a-bitch!" McAlister yelled as he brought the knife down in the center of her chest. The blade penetrated her skin and went deep into the bone of her chest. Blood spurted out like a fountain gushing water. Due to his coat being open, none of the blood got on it, although some blood did manage to catch his shirt. Claudia's body was jerking uncontrollably. "Want me to put you out of your misery?" he asked with a tone of violence resonating from his voice.

McAlister placed the knife at her throat and slid it across until he was sure he had the jugular split in half. She gurgled a couple of times until she moved no more. The bed became a pool of blood, but McAlister did not panic. The first thing he did was went into the bathroom where he cleaned his knife. He removed his shirt, held it over the sink, and set it on fire, holding it over until the heat coming from it was unbearable. He let it fall into the sink to burn to the point where it was unrecognizable. After he was satisfied that it could no longer be distinguished, he took the remains from it and flushed them down the toilet.

There was a towel hanging from the towel rack that he ran scalding hot water over and immediately began cleaning everything he could remember touching in the bathroom. Then, he went to the bedroom and did the same thing, careful not to overlook anything. After ensuring that all of the evidence was gone, he went and stood in front of the full length mirror for a while. Looking into his eyes he searched for an answer to what he had just done. The eyes in the mirror didn't give him any answers. He summoned to himself that everything had sort of naturally taken place without him giving it a second thought.

On his way out of the room, he stopped at the door and listened to hear if anyone was in the hallway. When he was certain it was safe to leave, he reached into his lower outer coat pocket and grabbed the door knob. He stuck his head out of the door slowly checking both ends of the hallway to make sure no one would see him leave the room. The hallway was absent of people, so he hurriedly opened the door and closed it behind him in the same manner in which he had opened it.

Across the hall, one of the rooms had a 'Do not Disturb' sign hanging from the door knob. He grabbed it, still using his coat to ensure that he wouldn't leave any prints, and placed it on Claudia's door. That would keep her body from being discovered, at least for a while, anyway.

He walked swiftly to the end of the hall, avoiding usage of the elevator. He maintained the same pace down the stairway until he reached the lobby where he saw the attendant behind the lobby sitting down and watching television. Casually, he strolled past him and once outside, he picked up his pace again until he reached his car. Fumbling briefly for his keys he remembered that he had put them in his back pocket. Finding them, he opened the door, got inside, and inserted the ignition key and drove off.

As he cruised along, he started laughing out loud about how simple it had been. He thought of how well he had covered his tracks and no one had noticed him. Suddenly, he remembered that someone had seen him. Someone who could easily identify him in a police lineup. "Roberta!" he exclaimed, harshly slamming his palms down hard on the steering wheel. "Damn-it, I forgot about Roberta!"

Now he accelerated the car, knowing that he had to get back to The Phoenix before Roberta had a chance to leave. He raced around the other cars on the road, checking his watch from time to time. McAlister arrived at The Phoenix faster than he thought he would. Pulling into the parking lot, he saw that there was still a line at the door. It gave him hope that Roberta was still there. He chose the first parking space he came to. Moving as quickly as he possibly could, he stepped out of the car and made his way to the entrance.

People seemed to be waiting patiently. McAlister knew why, when he was halfway past the line. Someone had set up a mini bar and drinks were being bought without hesitation. McAlister saw that Goliath still had the same expression on his face that he had when he left the first time.

Once inside, he looked to the area where Claudia and Roberta had been sitting, but there was no sign of Roberta. Instantly he felt panic strike him. 'Calm down,' he told himself. He decided to walk to his left toward the dance floor. Through the thick of the crowd, he squirmed between people constantly moving his head from side to side scanning so that he wouldn't miss her if she was still there.

As he neared the dance floor, he glimpsed at the back of a woman wearing a red wig. She was dancing flirtatiously with a guy about as big as Goliath. As she did a spin move on the dance floor, he saw that it was Roberta. He felt relieved seeing her there having a good time. She and the Goliath look-alike seemed to be enjoying the music.

When the song ended, McAlister watched carefully to see if the Goliath look-alike would follow her off the floor. She walked off ahead of him and he trailed behind her, but once off the dance floor, he went off in a different direction. 'Thank goodness,' McAlister said to himself as he wiped away the perspiration that had formed on his forehead.

McAlister could see that Roberta was making a bee-line for the table she had been sitting at when he first saw her with Claudia. He pushed and shoved his way through the crowd until he was able to walk with ease. Finally, he found himself standing beside Roberta's table. He seated himself before she had a chance to offer him a seat. "Bobby!" she nearly shouted loud enough for everyone standing close by to hear over the music. "What are you doing here? I thought you left with Claudia."

"I did," McAlister answered. "But all I did was seen her to the lobby. I wasn't all that interested in being with her. That's the reason I'm back here, because my real interest is in you. I was overcome by your loveliness when I first saw you. So much so that I envisioned you all the way to the hotel and back and knew I had to come back here to find you."

"I could tell you were attracted to me when you came over and introduced yourself earlier tonight. Claudia has a way of pushing herself on men and it drives me crazy sometimes. Actually, I feel that she turns a lot of men away, like that," Roberta said.

"Well, you won't have to worry about that anymore," McAlister said to himself.

"What are you thinking?" Roberta asked.

"Just how loud it is in here," McAlister answered. "How I would like to see how you live," he added with a seductive smile.

"My sentiments exactly," she said as she started standing up from the table, turning up the rest of her drink.

"Oh, you mean you would like to see how you live, too?" McAlister asked jokingly.

The remark elicited a hearty laugh from Roberta as she walked out ahead of McAlister, overemphasizing her hip action. She waved goodbye to the initial Goliath whose facial expression had not changed one bit. McAlister judged from the look Roberta exchanged with Goliath that either she knew him personally, or she was a regular at the club. He hoped that Goliath hadn't paid much attention to him.

In the parking lot, they discussed whose car would be driven. McAlister bargained hard that they should drive his car and eventually won. Roberta waited for him to open her door. "Boy, those guys sure act out the woman role to the limit," McAlister said to himself.

This time he didn't hesitate to perform the act. "A gentleman, indeed," Roberta said.

McAlister performed all of his functioning at high speed. Before he could catch himself, they were out on the road without him realizing what Roberta was saying. "I suppose you are staying at the same hotel as Claudia?" he asked her.

"I suppose you are right," Roberta answered.

"Damn," McAlister said to himself, "I hope this doesn't get too hairy."

It was almost 1:45 AM when they arrived. Again McAlister didn't hesitate to open the door for Roberta, knowing she was expecting him to do so. Roberta looked at McAlister with a twinkle in her eyes and remarked, "The night is still so young."

On the way inside the lobby area, McAlister told Roberta that he had a phobia about elevators and preferred to use the stairway. "Keeps you in shape, too," he informed.

"Well, I'll go along with the program as long as you promise you won't leave me behind. I might die from exhaustion before we reach my floor," Roberta warned.

'It won't be due to exhaustion, but you're right about one thing – you're going to die!' McAlister thought to himself. "The room is on the second floor, so you won't get too much of a workout climbing the stairs," Roberta said.

McAlister, was influenced by his youthful spirit, and made a dash up the flight of stairs. When he was at the top he stopped and waited for Roberta to lead the rest of the way. "Save the energy," Roberta said as she opened the door.

The hallway was empty and there was no sound. Roberta stopped about a third of the distance down the hallway and inserted her key in room 217. Opening the door, darkness emitted itself, but only briefly because Roberta soon switched on the lights. "I hate trying to get my bearings in a dark room," Roberta said.

She went over to a desk where a radio cassette player was resting. A couple of cassette tapes were scattered beside the radio. She mulled over them briefly, picked one up and inserted it into the cassette player. A few seconds after she pushed the button, the sound of a saxophone became audible. McAlister recognized that it was the music of one of his favorite jazz artists. He had always liked his music, but this was going to be a night that he wouldn't listen.

Roberta started shedding her clothes piece by piece, taking off her dress, slip, bra, and shoes. She left the panties on. McAlister watched in fascination, particularly because she had breasts like a real woman. They weren't exceptionally large or anything, but they were shapely and arousing. McAlister was affected by them and felt ashamed at himself for feeling that way.

Roberta flung herself on the bed and made a few gyrations, motioning for McAlister to join her. He approached her slowly, feeling confused as he got closer to her. Once he was in the bed with her, she wrapped her arms around him and kissed him deeply in his mouth. He felt his stomach turning inside out, almost to the point that he was going to vomit, but he fought it desperately.

Suddenly feeling a need for air, he pushed away from her, not understanding how he felt sick, but aroused at the same time. "Wait a minute," he said. "I have something for you."

McAlister reached inside his inner coat pocket until he found the release button so he could activate the blade as soon as his hand was out of the pocket. "What is it?" Roberta asked.

"This!" McAlister exclaimed as he brought the knife from his pocket in a fluid motion. The blade was sent deep into Roberta's chest. It made a crunching noise as it went in as Roberta's eyes widened from the pain she felt and the shock of what had just happened. She reached for the spot where the knife had entered, trying to stop the bleeding. "That won't help you any," McAlister told her.

He sat on top of her legs so that she could not kick and with his free hand, he placed the palm on her forehead, expending a lot of energy.

Roberta's head was pushed deep into the pillow on which it had been resting.

"Time to say goodnight," McAlister told her as he ran the blade across her throat.

Roberta' eyes grew even wider. She moved her hands from her chest to where the blood was pouring from her neck. Her breathing rate intensified involuntarily as she gasped for air. Soon, the breaths became shorter and the gasping stopped. McAlister watched as her eyes rolled heavenward into her head.

A smile formed on his face satisfied with the job he had done. He went into the bathroom and inspected himself carefully making sure there was no blood on his coat. He then checked the rest of himself over. The only place there was blood was on his face, but first he had to wipe his knife clean.

As he held it under running water from the sink, he noticed that the tip of the blade had broken off. It must be inside Roberta's chest, he thought. Once sure that the knife had been thoroughly cleaned, he folded it away and tucked it inside his inner coat pocket. With the water still running, he cupped both hands together and placed them beneath the flow of water until he had enough to splash on his face. He repeated the effort several times until his face showed no visible signs of blood.

The wound Natalie had left on his face looked healed and aged. It practically blended with his skin. He felt fortunate that it had not welted like cuts he had seen before. It was nothing a little plastic surgery couldn't take care of. He stared into the mirror for a while, thinking of how he had tried to please Kelly by bringing her orchids and felt a certain compulsion. As if suddenly possessed, he grabbed a roll of toilet tissue from the back of the toilet and wrapped several rounds of it across the top of his fingertips until he was certain he had a good safeguard against fingerprints.

McAlister went back to where Roberta's body lay still on the bed. A big puddle of blood had formed on each side of her neck. Some of it started soaking into the blanket. With the tissue wrapped index finger, McAlister dipped into the blood until there was enough on it that it dripped a path as he walked into the bathroom.

Using the same finger, he wrote on the bathroom medicine cabinet mirror, "ORCHIDS ARE DEADLY!" He took a couple of steps back from it and looked at what he had written as if he had never seen it before. "Yep, surely they are," he said out loud.

McAlister looked at his Rolex. It showed the time was racing wildly. *'I've gotta get out of here,'* he thought, *'but first, I've got to clean up this mess.'* He slung the wrapped tissue from his fingertips into the toilet, located a washcloth from the towel rack and wrapped it around his hand in order to flush the toilet. Afterward, he used the same cloth to wipe clean the sink fixtures and mirror edges from the medicine cabinet. He looked around the bathroom to make certain there weren't any other objects he may have touched.

Deciding not to take any chances, he wiped down everything imaginable in the bathroom. Satisfied he went back into the room where Roberta lay, growing colder with each passing moment and proceeded to clean up in the same fashion as he had the bathroom. He placed the washcloth back on the rack after washing it with hot water and soap. "Damn," he said, now I have to do something with the soap. I could have left prints on it."

McAlister picked up the bar and pressed the tip of his index finger hard on it. He held it up close to his face to inspect for a print impression. Sure enough, it was visible. "Can't leave this lying around," he said out loud. "It would be shameful to get busted with a bar of soap left lying around with my prints as evidence." He lifted the flap of his lower outer coat pocket and shoved the soap down in it. "There," he said, feeling smart for not overlooking something so simple.

On his way out of the bathroom, he looked back to where Roberta was lying. He still couldn't believe those breasts. 'Silicone injections,' he thought. 'Has to be!' He was about to open the door leading to the hallway when his curiosity got to him. He turned and slowly started to approach Roberta as if he expected her to come back to life and take revenge for what he had done to her.

He stood at the end of the bed and looked between her legs to see if there was an impression in her panties. There was no male form there. He walked over close enough to the side of the bed where he could just barely reach Roberta's panty line and inserted his index finger inside the elastic panty line and pulled downward. When he pulled them mid thigh, he jumped back, startled by what he saw. There was a red triangle of hair down there and an insertion, but, a male organ hung slightly out of it. It looked slightly like it may have belonged to a child.

'Damn,' McAlister said to himself. "I've heard of this, but I would never have believed it. She's a hermaphrodite.' He inserted his hand into the empty outer coat pocket and used it to open the door after he felt secure that there was no one on the floor out in the hallway. Walking briskly down the hallway, a couple was stepping out of the elevator as he passed. "How are you doing?" the guy asked him.

Without looking back, McAlister answered, "Fine, how are you?" Not breaking his stride he took the stairway down to the lobby and exited the same way he and Roberta had come in. The attendant was checking a couple in and didn't pay attention to McAlister as he left.

Outside, McAlister located his car and quickly got into it and headed back to Jeanette's place. He drove as fast as he could, but not too fast so as not to draw attention to himself. He only hoped she hadn't awakened since he had left. Before long, he was pulling his car into the same spot he had used before he left.

At the door, he stood outside and listened to see if Jeanette was up milling about. When he was sure she was still in bed, he opened the door and crept in silently. He felt like a burglar, slipping into a familiar house at night while they slept peacefully. His confidence rose as he walked closer to Jeanette's bedroom and heard her snoring.

As McAlister walked into the bedroom, he started removing his clothing, throwing each piece on the floor because he did not see a nearby place to hang them. Jeanette had her back turned to the side of the bed, so he would have room to sleep. Careful not to wake her, he gently rolled back the sheets and slid into bed.

Only moments after McAlister fell back into a sound sleep, his dreaming began. He was back at home watching television. Kelly was talking to him from the kitchen as she prepared their supper. He hadn't yet seen Dane. Kelly had informed him that Dane was busy outdoors, but she was unsure what activity he was involved in.

Bored by the television programs, he decided he would go outside and spend some time with his son. As he stepped onto the patio, he looked for Dane, but didn't see him. Instead, he saw two girls sitting over in the far corner of the yard, making mud pies. McAlister figured he would go to the girls and ask them if they had seen Dane. "Have either of you seen Dane?" he asked as he came closer.

"Oh, hi Dad," one of the little girls turned around and looked at him.

"What the hell are you doing wearing a dress?!" McAlister asked. "Get your ass in the house and put on a pair of jeans before I punish you!"

"Dad, there is no need for you to get upset. David and I have already decided that we are going to have our sex changed. Mom already knows. As a matter of fact, she has been talking about me getting silicone injections," He lowered the neckline of the dress he was wearing until a small pair of breasts was revealed. "See what I mean, Dad?"

McAlister rose straight up from the bed, breathing wildly. Slowly, he gathered himself, aided by his surroundings. He realized that it had only been a bad dream. He looked at the clock and remembered that he had meant to set it back. He did so and slid back beneath the sheets. He nudged Jeanette hard in the side purposely, in order to wake her. She turned slowly toward him, opening her eyes. "What time is it?" she asked.

"Go back to sleep," he said. She turned over again and fell asleep minutes later. Many hours passed before McAlister fell asleep. He now felt secure that he had an alibi. He scanned the events of the evening in his mind. He couldn't recall doing anything that would leave the police a clue. Then he remembered that he still had the soap in his coat pocket. By then, he fell asleep, deciding that he would wake up before Jeanette and discard the soap. He sunk into a sleep that was dreamless.

CHAPTER 16

It was around 7:23 am when McAlister rose the next morning. Though it was not in peace and solitude, he could hear a rhythmic bass sound coming from the other room in the apartment. "One, two, three, four, now work it out from all over the floor," a voice was saying repeatedly. He couldn't make out whose voice it was, but he could tell that it was audio from one of those exercise albums that had flooded the market. "Why would someone want to exercise at such an early hour?" he said aloud as he rose slowly from the bed.

It felt like someone had been beating on his body with a jackhammer, he grumbled to himself about how his well planned night turned into a nightmare as he painfully dressed himself. Though he had only had a few drinks, it felt as though he had ten and the loud music coming from Jeanette's exercise room wasn't helping matters at all.

Feeling casual in his tank top and slacks, he strolled to Jeanette's workout. He used the door frame to let his upper body rest as he watched Jeanette perform her religious morning duty. She had become well disciplined to start her mornings out in such a fashion as McAlister could tell from her fluid movements. "Care for a Highball after you finish killing yourself?" he asked her.

"Hell no," she responded, never losing a step in her movements. "You are a sick man to even consider one yourself at this hour. You'll send your body into shock if you drink before eating."

"Hog-wash!" McAlister told her. "That's what's wrong with you health nuts. You structure your lives too much around the crap you believe in. When you take it all into consideration, where do those ideas leave room for fun in your life? You shouldn't do this, you shouldn't do that. What the hell, I figure some things in life are meant to be enjoyed or else they would not be here for us."

Jeanette was still in tune to her workout, but able to maintain conversation with McAlister as the same time. "No, Mac. You have to use discretion about what you take into your body, just as you choose what morals you utilize in your life. I see my body as a temple and I intend to keep it that way. I may drink from time to time, but it is usually very seldom and moderate. It's mostly on special occasions that I do."

"Well, I feel that every day is a special occasion to be reckoned with. I always manage to do something on each one of them that someone will disapprove of, so what the hell is the point of worrying about it? I think I'll just go ahead and mix myself a tall Highball, so that I can get the day started with a different mindset."

Jeanette had neared the end of her workout and was stretching her well used muscles. Her torso was stretched over her legs, and the palms of her hands were gripping her toes. "You know where to find it," she said sounding as though she were stretching her voice as well as her body.

McAlister found the liquor in the same spot it had been when he replaced it the night before. The contents were equal to the amount he had left. It being Saturday, McAlister felt a loss for activity. He located a remote control for the television and pushed the power button as he let his body plunge into the couch. He was past the stage of watching cartoons. Not being a television fanatic he had no concept of the programming available. He had thought wrestling was sort of comical, although he also knew it wasn't real. Watching the wrestlers humiliate one another for a while, before long, he was snoozing on the couch.

The rest of the weekend was uneventful. Jeanette's highlights consisted of her workouts and walks at the park. McAlister preferred to stay indoors. The television weekend was filled with sporting events, which he tried to catch as much of as possible since it had been a while.

It was near the end of the night Sunday when a special news bulletin interrupted a television program that he was watching. "We interrupt this program to bring you a special news bulletin. It has been seven years since Wayne Williams terrorized the city of Atlanta, by killing black youths. It seems that once again, someone has chosen a select group of people to exterminate. Police are baffled by a string of murders that have taken place over the past two weeks. They have failed to come up with any clues as to who has murdered three men who were dressed like women. Law enforcement officials have beefed up their patrol and are using other preventative measures to apprehend the killer."

"...Other preventative measures...?" McAlister asked himself. "What the hell could they be talking about?" Then suddenly it hit him. The most logical thing for them to do would be to send out decoys. He was glad he had been in the legal field for a while and felt sure he could recognize a cop, even dressed in drag. He decided that their preventative measures were nothing to worry about and fell asleep again.

When Monday came, McAlister was awakened again by the "One, two, three, four..." of Jeanette's workout album. He could hear her clap to the beat and he knew that she was in perfect sync to the instructions. Groggily, he dressed himself, inspected himself in front of the mirrors, and left the room feeling confident. "Good morning, little Ms. Workout," McAlister said to Jeanette.

He was standing in the middle of the doorway looking cocky and ready for the world. Jeanette noticed that he was looking rather arrogant and decided to make a comment about it. "So, what's got you looking like you're ready to go out and conquer the world this morning?"

"Well," McAlister said, "I've realized how interesting life actually is. The challenges of life give a man something to strive for. When he overcomes challenges, it gives him a sense of accomplishment and an air of superiority. Not always of superiority over human beings, but simply the intangible of life itself. Do you understand what I mean?"

"Yes and no," Jeanette answered, wiping herself down with a towel. "I understand what you just said. I know what the feeling of accomplishment is like. What I don't understand is you. How is it that through all these years, you are just realizing this? You are a very good lawyer. You're without a doubt one of the best around here. You've practiced, what, five years now and haven't lost many cases? I mean, come on, Mac, you have to have felt the power of accomplishment many years ago."

"Believe it or not, Jeanette, it's true. I'm just now finding out what it's like. Before, I just sort of did things without thinking about them. I guess I'm not like everyone else."

"You can say that again," Jeanette said displaying a look toward him as if she were conveying a silent message that he was strange. "It usually comes naturally to those of us who are normal, but..." Jeanette let him assume what she was going to say. "You know the rest, Mac."

"You'd better get a move on, baby," McAlister said. "We're going back to work today."

"Really, Mac, are you serious?"

"Yes, I am," he responded.

"I'm so glad, Mac. I've been dying to get back to work. I thought you had totally abandoned it altogether."

"Oh, no, no, no," McAlister said. "I just wanted some time to get myself together. I never had intentions of giving up the practice."

"Good, because I've been worried about the Leroy Foster case you've been working on. That boy is innocent and we both know it. There is no way he robbed a convenience store. I'd hate to see that poor kid go to prison for something he didn't do."

Jeanette went to a closet in the hallway and picked out a conservative outfit suitable for office work. She took what she had picked into the bedroom and began getting dressed. McAlister plopped onto the bed as she did so.

"Jen, you know the kid is innocent and so do I. What bothers me is that the D.A. is digging into his past. Leroy's rap sheet is about as long as a dictionary. All he had to do is look like he committed a crime and he's nailed. It's a real shame that the system is like that, but the scum out there don't make things easy on us either."

"Mac, that kid is not scum. He just had a lot of misfortune. It's not his fault that his mother killed his father when he was just a year old. He's been in one foster home after another and doesn't know what the word love means. He's never really done anything that other kids with loving parents haven't done. You have got to make sure this kid doesn't go to prison. He's just a victim of society."

"Look, Jen, I'm not going to get into this with you right now. I know the kid is a good boy, but I see two sides to everything, unlike you."

"Hey, wait a minute, Mac. I'm not going to let you get away with that. You're the one who just came up with a new light on life and you're trying to tell me I only look at one side of things."

"No, I'm sorry, but you don't understand me at all. You see, I do see two sides to everything. I weigh them out and then choose which side I want to defend. That's why I always seem so strongly committed to my emotions about realism. I know what goes on. I just don't speak until I feel certain about what I have in my heart."

McAlister looked at his watch and read that it was 7:43 AM. "Come on, let's go. I have a feeling Leroy is going to be waiting for us."

When they arrived at the office floor, Leroy Foster was waiting in the lobby just as McAlister said he would be. He looked worried and restless. However, he had managed to dress himself conservatively having on a pair of black slacks, a burgundy and black plaid shirt complimented by a nice pair of black shoes. It was an improvement from the ragged jeans and dirty tennis shoes that McAlister was used to seeing him wear. "He must be learning some things about life and the justice system," McAlister whispered to Jeanette as they approached him.

"Oh Mac," Jeanette said slapping him on the shoulder as a result of their earlier discussion.

"How long have you been up here, Leroy?"

"I've been here about a half an hour, sir." He answered in a mellow tone.

The young man was a seventeen year old black kid who stood about six feet, six inches tall. He lumbered over McAlister when he stood up, but looked so humble. Through Jeanette's mind, the notion ran how harmless he looked even with his towering authority. She had talked to him on several occasions and felt a sense of familiarity with him. She knew he was constantly hurting inside. She wished there were more she could do to ensure his freedom and felt confident that McAlister would defend him properly. "Come on in and let me know what's been going on," McAlister told him as he opened the office door.

At first glimpse of the office, it looked foreign to him since he had broken his habit of being there every day. The atmosphere of the office set his frame of mind for dealing with legal matters. Jeanette opened the file cabinet drawer, retrieved Leroy Foster's file and placed it on McAlister's desk. The spot on his desk that she had placed the file reminded her of the time of day that it was. It hit her suddenly that she was forgetting something.

'*Oh, sure,*' she thought. "How can I forget something as ritualistic as bringing him his morning paper and cup of coffee?"

Jeanette took enough money from a large container on her desktop to pay for a newspaper. McAlister had taken his seat behind his desk and Leroy had taken the client's chair. Jeanette left the two talking as she went for the morning paper. When she returned with it, McAlister and Leroy were still engrossed in conversation. She poured a strong cup of coffee from the coffee maker and placed both the paper and coffee on McAlister's desk. "Mr. Johnson, I'm scared," Leroy said, sounding like he would break free from the strength of his emotion. "I don't want to go to prison for someone else's crime. I'm trying to straighten my life out and now I have this to contend with," he hung his head.

"Look, Leroy, you aren't going to prison," McAlister assured him. "God, and myself, will see to that."

"But, I don't have anyone who can vouch for me," Leroy said. "It's just my word against theirs and who is going to believe me?"

"A jury will," McAlister replied. "We have to convince a jury that you weren't around at the time of the crime. Leave that up to me. It's my job. I'm going to find out the real truth in the matter."

"I feel better knowing that," Leroy told McAlister. "I could use all the security I can get. It seems like there isn't a judge in the court system who hasn't seen my face at one time or another. I'm afraid that they are going to get tired of seeing me."

"Leroy, I've got to get busy on your case," McAlister said. "There isn't much you can do here. What I would like for you to do is try to remember everything that you possibly can about the particular day in question. If there is anyone you may remember, get their names if you can, and I'll summon them to court so they can testify on your behalf. Stay in touch with me, okay? As a matter of fact, give me a call tomorrow, even if it's just to let me know how you are feeling."

"Thank you, Mr. Johnson. I feel better having you on my side. I'm just worried about how I'm going to pay you," Leroy said, looking stressed all the while.

"Don't you worry about that, Leroy," McAlister said, appearing sincere. "We'll cross that bridge when we get to it. I'll work something out that will be easy on you. Just stay employed and you won't have anything to worry about. As long as I know you are trying, I'll go to the mat for you."

McAlister stood up and extended his hand for Leroy to shake. They looked each other squarely in the eye as they shook hands. As Leroy passed Jeanette at the typewriter, she stopped him. "Now, Leroy, you don't worry about anything, alright? Everything is going to go fine.

You've got Mac on your side and when you've got him, you can't lose," she told him. Jeanette made sure she said it loud enough for McAlister to hear her. He looked up from the paper he had begun reading only briefly.

After Leroy left, McAlister looked up from his paper again. "Hey, Jen thanks a lot," he said.

"For what?"

"For putting the pressure on thick."

"Look, Mac, that kid is scared he's going to go to prison for something he didn't do. I've talked to him and I know he's sincere about trying to put his life together for himself. I just want to make sure you put forth your best effort in defending him."

"Jen, the police claim they have a witness who identified Leroy in a lineup. On top of that, Leroy seems to have developed a touch of amnesia about where he was and what he was doing the day the store was robbed. He's going to have to help himself just as much as I can help him. I told him to relax as much as possible and then try to remember whatever he can about that day."

"You're right, Mac. The poor kid is frightened. I think he is so scared that he has blocked just about everything in his mind. Hopefully, he will be okay in a couple of days."

Jeanette then decided to change the subject. "So, what's going on in the world?"

McAlister folded a couple of pages and began to speak. "Oh, nothing out of the ordinary. Just your usual killings, robberies and politicians making asses of themselves."

"So what else is new?" Jeanette reflected.

McAlister became quiet again. He found an article in the local section of the newspaper concerning the transgender murders. It stated that a string of murders had been taking place in the city, but police were no closer to finding a perpetrator than they were when the murders had started. He put the paper down after reading the article and began looking over the Foster file.

Leroy Foster had a checkered life that McAlister attributed to the pangs of having grown up as a foster child. He had been shipped from home to home throughout most of his life. His parole officer described him as being a rebellious young man. Most of Leroy's brushes with the law started when he was in middle school and carried over into his high school years. The start of his trouble was truancy. Other charges included several counts of simple possession of marijuana, trespassing on private property, reckless driving, and the one that got him a year in reform school: joy riding.

From looking over Leroy's file, McAlister noticed that there were no violent crimes associated with his record. In fact, all of his offenses had been rather minor with the exception of joy riding, for which he had serve one year. McAlister, himself, had engaged in most of the same offenses and he figured that most kids had as well. He gathered that most of the things Leroy had gotten into were probably in the company of other kids, most likely for the purpose of acceptance.

McAlister picked up the receiver of his desk telephone and placed it against his ear. He dialed Thomas Dash, a big robust and aging detective who had worked privately for him since the beginning of his practice. Dash generally spied on suspected adulterers and was fast and efficient. He answered the phone in a gruff voice. "Hey, Tom, what are you still doing in bed at this hour?" McAlister asked, checking his Rolex simultaneously. "You can't catch any worms by lying around in bed all morning."

"So give me something exciting to do," Dash said in an unenthusiastic tone.

"You bet," McAlister told him. "I'm working on the Foster case. You know, the kid that's suspected of robbing the convenience store? Well, it seems he needs an alibi. How about you checking into it and see if you can come up with a witness."

McAlister paused a second and then added, "Any way that you can, you know what I mean?"

"Yeah, I know what you mean," Dash answered, sounding a little more pepped up.

After hanging up the telephone, McAlister sat still for a few minutes, letting his thought pass. In the beginning of his practice, he wanted to believe it was only fit and proper to play the law by the books and rules of due process. Before long, he saw all of the injustices built into the system, it became discouraging to watch the guilty walk and the innocent victimized. At that point, he decided to do whatever it took to ensure the injustices did not take place. "Hey, Jen," McAlister half shouted, "What other appointments do I have for today?"

She looked over his appointment organizer. "Well, you've got Betty Batson at 11:00 and David McIntyre at 1:30. Both of them should be pretty quick. Mrs. Batson had been complaining that she hasn't had much of an opportunity to talk to you about her divorce, and Mr. McIntyre just wants you to notarize some papers for him."

"Good!" McAlister replied. "I need as much time as I can get to do some research. I think I need to hire myself a paralegal."

"Mac, I don't see how you have gone all these years without one. You could have your work cut in half."

McAlister did not reply. Jeanette looked back and saw that he had his head already stuck in one of his law books. She continued her work as though she had never been interrupted. After reading, McAlister began jotting down notes from his books and correlated it with what information he had on Leroy Foster. The ring of the telephone startled both McAlister and Jeanette after the long period of silence due to their diligent work. McAlister watched as Jeanette replaced the receiver on the telephone base. "Mrs. Batson, right?" McAlister asked.

"Yep, that was her. She's on her way up."

McAlister put away the books and notes and had Jeanette retrieve the Batson file. He familiarized himself with her case and finished as she was coming into the office. "Come on over and have a seat," he told her.

Mrs. Batson was a plump woman, but had a cute face. McAlister figured Mr. Batson ran off with another woman because of her obesity, but he wasn't foolish enough to mention those thoughts to her. He could hear her breathing as she sat there in front of him and hoped she wouldn't die in his office. The sad thing was she looked uncomfortable. "Mr. Johnson, I've been trying to catch up with you for weeks now. Where the hell have you been?" she asked.

McAlister could see that she was upset. He remembered from last speaking with her that she was in a hurry to get her divorce over with. She had met a younger man who she said was crazy about her. The word 'crazy' stuck out in his mind. McAlister looked at her squarely for a moment before he spoke. "You haven't been reading papers lately, have you? I was in an automobile accident and I was laid up in the hospital for a while. I'm sorry I haven't been in touch with you. Fill me in on what's been going on."

"I've been watching Fred carry on with that little teenage girl he thinks he's hiding from me. I can't believe a grown man can have such a childish mind. I have tailed him on several nights. It was no surprise that each time I did he carried that bambino to a hotel."

"Did you take pictures?" McAlister asked her.

"Why, no I did not! That's your job! I'm paying you my hard earned money, so you do your damn job!" she demanded.

McAlister leaned forward in his seat as though he wanted to make sure that Mrs. Batson could hear what he intended to say. "Look, we need evidence to make this divorce work in your favor. Since you took the time to play a special agent, you should have also taken along your equipment. You could have easily blown your cool by tailing your husband. If he didn't spot you, you can be certain that he is going to be careful. You may have blown it for my guy snooping around him. You should have used your head and helped yourself."

"Hey, you look here, Mr. Hotshot, what kind of lawyer are you? I hired you to handle my divorce, but so far, I haven't received any results from you. I could have hired a fly-by-night lawyer to do something as simple as to handle a divorce, but I figured, why not employ someone who is a sure shot to get it done right? Boy was I ever wrong about you. You haven't got a damn thing done yet, have you? There's no excuse for that! You're a lawyer! You're telling people, 'Hire me to take care of your legal problems.' Do you know what that means, Mr. Johnson? That means you are supposed to work as an assassin would if he were hired to get rid of an unwanted. Your intensity should be one hundred percent toward completion of all your missions. I think you get the picture. Well, what do you have to say for your absence of mind?"

"Mrs. Batson, how dare you to call me an idiot. That's what you just did, you know. What has happened with people's consideration of man's mishaps along life of uncontrollable circumstances? I am a man, Mrs. Batson. I'm only capable of handling my controllable circumstances. Do you understand where I'm coming from? Bad things happen to me, too. Negative forces capture my being just as yours does.

Mrs. Batson wiggled in her seat as much as space would possibly allow until she became comfortable. She cast her gaze down, but only briefly. Squarely, she looked him in his eyes and offered her apology. "I guess I did get carried away, Mr. Johnson. I just want this damned man out of my life. My new boyfriend has been feeling intimidated and wants me to hurry my dog husband out of my life. Right now, we're unable to have the full secure feeling of a healthy relationship while I legally belong to someone else. So, could you please do something?"

"Yes, I will, Mrs. Batson," McAlister said, standing up from his chair. He reached for a cigarette contained in his inner coat pocket and lit one as he began pacing across the space of the floor. "About your boyfriend," McAlister started.

"Right now, you are in a race with your husband to secure a new life, but both of you are so caught up in your own personal lives that you can't even see through the clouds of smoke you have created. Neither of you are playing the game of divorce right. The idea of suing someone for divorce on the grounds of adultery is to make the court think you have abided by the laws of marriage all along. It means you have to practice celibacy until you are divorced. Now, since there is only a small percentage of the American population that actually does that, it means that you have to at least appear as though you are abiding by the rules of the game. Visibility has to be very minimal. You don't want to be photographed together. Keep your telephone conversations down as much as possible. Just be aware Mrs. Batson, that he may have a good lawyer, too. Whichever party proves the other has committed adultery will be the winner, and the winner takes all."

"Now I see the big picture," Mrs. Batson said, sounding as if a light bulb had switched on in her head. "I need to slow my life down considerably, don't I?"

"Exactly," McAlister agreed. "Not only that, but you need to help me handle your situation with one hundred percent of my abilities, just as you mentioned. That means you have to take a look at yourself every day."

"I follow you," she said, sounding as though the energy in her voice had been completely expended.

McAlister could tell from her demeanor that he had broken her down to the level he needed prior to dealing with her. "Now, what I'm going to do is put my hard case man on the job. If your husband likes to be seen with his pretty young thing, then I'll just have to make sure our Mr. Dash captures the two of them all snuggly on paper. He'll jot down times and places."

"Excuse me a minute, Mr. Johnson. Who is this Mr. Dash you mention?"

"Thomas Dash, my private investigator," McAlister answered. "He's been with me for years; very productive, too."

"Why didn't I think of that?" Mrs. Batson asked.

She had an astonished expression on her face. "Because you don't get paid to think of those things," McAlister answered. He replaced himself in his seat at his desk and extinguished his cigarette in the ashtray atop his desk. "Mrs. Batson, Jeanette will be getting some correspondence in the mail to you informing you of our progress. Just be patient and smart, and trust me to handle it in my own fashion. Can you do that for me?"

"I can do that," Mrs. Batson said. She maneuvered her pocketbook up onto her shoulder and stood up. McAlister figured that there must be at least three hundred pounds of her. She shook his hand and proceeded out of the door waving good-bye to Jeanette as she left.

Jeanette looked at her watch. It was 11:30 – lunch time. She pushed herself away from her typewriter and went into McAlister's office. He was still sitting at his desk so she walked around behind him. She massaged his shoulders and whispered in his ear. "Where are you taking me for lunch?" she asked.

"Hummm," McAlister purred from the pleasure of the massage. "I thought it was your turn to treat," he said, eyes closed.

His voice sounded as though he would fall asleep if she kept it up. "I took care of the last one," Jeanette said.

"Well, if you insist," McAlister said as he stood. "Let's go down to the sub shop for sandwiches," he suggested. "Sound good to you?"

"That'll work," Jeanette answered. She grabbed her purse from the closet and they left the office and McAlister made sure the office was locked. In the elevator, they decided to walk to the sub shop since it was close and that parking situation was horrendous. On the way there, they walked past a man playing jazz on his saxophone in front of Dexter's department store. They both thought he sounded very close. The sound of his saxophone faded away as they got closer to the sub shop.

McAlister felt like rejoicing as they walked through the doors. Jeanette ordered a turkey sub with all the fixings along with a Pepsi to wash it down. McAlister seemed to fret over what he was going to have, but eventually decided to have a meatball sub.

They chose a window seat so that they could see the city go by them. They discussed office procedures and practices common to most others, marriages gone sour and the crazies that infiltrated the city. McAlister agreed with Jeanette that there was a lack of trust among the people in the city due to the high rate of crimes.

As they were finishing the last bites of their sandwiches, McAlister saw two female impersonators about to walk past the restaurant. Quickly, he jumped from his seat and reached for his wallet pocket. "I've got the bill," he said, sounding as if he were suddenly in a hurry.

He grabbed Jeanette by her hand and started pulling her toward the cashier. The two transgender men had just passed the establishment as McAlister was paying the bill. He kept his eyes glued to them as they walked slowly by as though they were excited. They were lurking about the sidewalks staring at the people who went by them. McAlister was sure that they were female impersonators, because they were paying a little too much attention to the men.

As he and Jeanette walked back to the office, she became more talkative. She was leaning on McAlister's upper arm as they walked. As she talked, she allowed herself to check her surroundings. McAlister was transfixed by the movements of the two men. He observed the way they walked and their over emphasis of femininity and almost wanted to laugh out loud at how stupid he thought they were.

As he watched them turn onto a perpendicular road, he allowed his thoughts to diminish and tried to focus on what Jeanette was saying. "So, what do you think about that?" Jeanette asked.

"That's just great," McAlister answered.

Jeanette shoved him in his ribs. "What do you mean, 'That's just great'?" she asked while looking at him like he had just committed a cardinal sin. "I mentioned to you that Leroy could spend a lot of time in prison and you respond, "That's just great!'"

"I was sarcastically speaking," McAlister answered, almost admiring his answer.

As soon as they were back in the office, McAlister went back to his desk and jotted down more notes from his law books. At certain moments, he would reread particular codes, pondering how they could be interpreted or twisted in favor of the suitor. He wrote down his interpretations based in favor of Leroy Foster.

Jeanette positioned herself at the typewriter. As she was seating herself, she said to McAlister, "I can't wait much longer for what I want you to have in store for me tonight. Too many strange circumstances have been standing in the way of what I want to do to you."

Her words hit McAlister like a prizefighter's punch. It was not because of his satisfactions of her desire, but more out of fear that she was not considering that he had plans of his own that he intended to carry out. The two transgender men he had seen earlier during lunch had wet his appetite. "Jen, I'm overwhelmed, baby, that your hormones have become so hyperactive for me, but I'm going to have to spoil some of your plans because Jake Robinson, from Robinson and Brothers Law Firm, and I have an engagement this evening so we can plot legal strategies. There will be other nights that will be just as interesting for us."

"I won't come between you and your business," Jeanette said. "Like you said, there will be plenty of nights." She flashed her radiant smile before seating herself, but felt deflated, as though her emotions were a balloon and someone had suddenly poked a pin in it.

After some considerable time had passed, McAlister put down the paperwork he had been going over. From inspecting his watch, he realized it was nearing time for Mr. McIntyre to pay him a visit. As he concluded the thought, the office telephone rang. Jeanette replaced the receiver and without turning her head said, "David McIntyre is on his way up. He has the paper with him that he wants notarized. I think all he has are some papers for purchasing a new car, so it won't take you long."

McAlister could tell from her voice that she had picked up a bit of an attitude. "See that he gets in okay," McAlister told her.

He decided to play with Jeanette and see if he could make her even madder. "I know my job!" she told him. "You just concentrate on yours!"

"Boy, you sure have gotten a little hot under the collar," McAlister said. "What's bothering you?"

He knew what was bothering her, but he did a good job of pretending that he didn't. He remembered his first evening at her apartment, how she had strip teased him and left him hanging. He thought of his little ploy with her as a fun game of revenge.

David McIntyre was in the office soon after Jeanette had announced the he was on his way up. He offered his hand for McAlister to shake and approached him at his desk. As they shook hands firmly, McAlister inquired about how David had been doing. "I'm staying out of trouble," he replied. "It's just a matter of keeping the numbers straight."

David was a CPA who had at one time come close to getting a federal prison bid for embezzlement. With McAlister as his lawyer, he ended up beating the case, but only marginally. In David's spare time, he worked toward restoring cars, old ones mostly. He was constantly searching for and finding old cars that were beat up to the point where people normally disregard them. He managed to find an old '57 Chevrolet for which he had great ideas for restorations.

McAlister looked carefully over the bill of sale. The seller had already signed his paperwork. After careful inspection of the papers, McAlister looked at Mr. McIntyre who looked as though he was hanging on whatever McAlister's next move would be. "Where did you buy the car?" McAlister asked.

"Chi-town, Illinois," Mr. McIntyre answered, sounding boastful. "I've found other beauties up there before, and great deals, too."

"Isn't $3000 an awful lot to pay for a car like that?" McAlister asked.

"By heaven means, no," he answered. "I've seen beat up '57s go for as high as five G's.

"Well, for tax purposes, that is an awful lot of money to pay for one," McAlister said. "Why don't we say you paid $200 for it?"

"Sounds good to me," Mr. McIntyre answered.

McAlister reached for one of his desk drawers in which he kept bills of sale. He gave the paperwork to Mr. McIntyre and instructed him to fill it out, making sure to sign the seller's signature with his left hand. When he had done so, McAlister notarized the papers and accepted an extra hundred dollar bill that Mr. McIntyre slid across to him. "It's always a pleasure doing business with you," Mr. McIntyre said as he reached for the papers McAlister was returning to him. They embraced hands once again and very quickly, Mr. McIntyre vanished.

McAlister shuffled through the stack of papers that had managed to pile up on his desk since he had seen Leroy Foster earlier that day. When he found Leroy's file, he opened it and re-inspected the information he had gathered on him. After he felt confident that he could retain what he had learned from the file, he replaced it in the file cabinet. He checked his watch, and it was nearly 3:00 pm.

The telephone rang. It was his private detective working the Foster case. He told him that he managed to find an alibi for Leroy Foster and he would give him the details when they would meet. Satisfied with the news, he decided to call it a day. Jeanette was still busy with her secretarial duties, oblivious to the time of day and what McAlister was doing. She jumped when he touched her shoulder. "You scared me, Mac. I could have had a heart attack!"

"Quickly, put away what you are doing, Jen. We are knocking off early today," McAlister told her.

She glanced at her watch and saw that it was a couple of hours before the normal quitting time and wondered what was so important that McAlister wanted to leave work early. She decided not to inquire out of fear that she would irritate him. It was noticeable to her that he had been acting sort of strangely, but she was not going to push the issue.

Jeanette worked as diligently as possible to put away the paperwork where she could find it in the morning. Generally, she hated being rushed by anyone, but she tried to bear with the uncomfortable feeling as much as possible. McAlister had seated himself on the couch and busied himself reading the latest issue of a magazine. Jeanette could tell he wasn't totally into it, because he was sitting on the edge of his seat as if her were ready to dash off somewhere. "All done and ready to go," she told him as she walked toward him with her pocketbook swung across her shoulder.

McAlister put down the magazine he had been reading as if he had never had any interest in it at all and grabbed his sport coat off the corner coat rack near the door. He looked around the office once more before leaving. Certain that they were not forgetting anything; they locked the doors behind them.

McAlister did not bother to explain why he had decided upon an early departure as they were leaving the building. Once they were in the car, he told Jeanette that he needed to pick up some equipment for racquetball before the sporting goods store closed. All of his other equipment was either at Kelly's or in the back of his trashed Mercedes. He didn't feel like going through the trouble of getting the old equipment. "Jeanette, I would like for you to drive your car to work from now on. I have a lot of running around that I normally do each day after I leave the office and I don't want to hold you up from doing anything you might want to do or vice versa for that matter."

"Okay!" Jeanette reflected, "You're the boss. Mac, I have a question for you, and please don't get jumpy when I ask you about it."

"What is it, what do you want to know?"

"Well," Jeanette started, almost as if she didn't want to ask. "Why the hell have you been acting so weird lately? I'm beginning to think you are losing your mind."

McAlister thought about the question for a moment. He started laughing aloud. "You think I'm going crazy, huh? Now, Jen, you see, I was worried about Leroy Foster all the time I've been acting strangely."

Before long, they were at the apartment complex. Jeanette changed into her workout attire and put on some upbeat music. McAlister wished he had a change of clothing, but that was something he had intentions of spending the day doing something about. For the past couple of days, he had been feeling very inconvenienced due to not having a regular change of clothing, his personal brands of deodorant, toothpaste, soap, and other items. "Well, I'm outta here," McAlister said to Jeanette, who had just begun her workout.

"Okay, take care," she said as he had already started out the door.

Before closing the front door, McAlister stuck part of his body back inside and yelled to Jeanette, "Don't wait up for me, but I may wake you up when I get home," he departed without a response.

The first place McAlister had on his list of stops was the shopping mall. His love for fine clothes was in good taste and it had been driving him mad to go without them. His favorites were Blass and Armani. As he entered the department store he caught glimpses of sensual women that browsed through the store as though they had nothing to do for the rest of the day. He regretted that he could not spend the remainder of his day feeling casual. What little amount of time he had allotted himself seemed to be rapidly dissipating.

McAlister found that the men's clothing section was vast in variety. Carefully, he mulled over different suits that were in his taste range. He stuck mostly to dark colors, aware that they enhanced his physical appearance more than bright ones. He was also careful in his selection of neck ties realizing that the right one could do wonders for a suit, but the wrong one could ruin its appearance entirely.

It took nearly an hour for him to pick out ten suits he felt completely sure would satisfy his selective taste. That would practically take care of his office attire, but he needed casual clothing as well. He was partially fond of wearing designer jeans with oxford shirts and penny loafers. The fitted jeans were among his favorites. He made it a point to check to see it the store stocked before he would buy any other type of jeans.

When he had chose five pairs of jeans that fit well the only items he could think of that he would needed were socks and underwear, which he wanted to be sure he had an abundance of. His mother drilled into his head at a very early age that he should always have clean socks and underwear in case of emergencies. He picked up twenty-five pairs of each.

On his way to the sporting store McAlister decided that racquetball had become somewhat boring since he had become the South Carolina State Champion a few years back. He had now mastered the game to the point that he cared to take it to when he first became interested in playing. The time had come to take on a new challenge in sport.

As he was walking into the sport shop, he was mentally preparing a list of items he needed to play his new sport. He told himself that he would need a mouthpiece, knee brace, and a damned good pair of basket-ball shoes because of his weak ankles. While at the counter, paying for his products, he reacted as if a light had come on inside of his head. A pretty young lady was operating the cash register at the time the light went on. "Oh, yeah, that's right. I need an extra large jock strap."

Before he started walking toward the area in which he supposed them to be, he cast the cashier a sarcastic smile of humorous acknowledgement. Her response to his slight overture was as she had caught on to his wit. He knew deep in his gut that he was a very effective person. He was thankful for having an open mind. When he returned to the counter with the jock strap, he could see the young lady was doing her best to contain her laughter. "Will this be all?" she asked.

"Sure thing." McAlister answered.

The response sent the cashier into hysterics. She laughed almost uncontrollably until she managed to regroup. "You're hilarious," she said, wiping tears from underneath her eyes.

"You should see me when I'm funny," McAlister said. The statement brought more laughter. McAlister double checked the contents of his bag to ensure that he would not have to return to the store if he had thought something else he would need during his drive after leaving. "Do you have strapped goggles?" McAlister asked.

"Yes, they are right over there," the cashier answered and waved a finger in the direction that the goggles were kept. She checked out his body as he walked over to get the goggles. By the time he returned to the counter, the cashier had written her name and telephone number on a little piece of paper.

"Okay, Deanna Peterson, we will do dinner sometime soon, how about that?" McAlister said.

"Sounds great," she responded. McAlister grabbed his bag and left the store. On his way out to the car, he slipped Deanna's telephone number into a compartment in his wallet. Finding the sports club was no problem for McAlister. Although he had never been a member, he had passed it on numerous occasions and had always promised that he would one day join it and let his membership at the racquet club expire since he could play racquetball as well as other sports there. He was very pleased to find that it offered almost any recreation imaginable and the facility itself was in extremely good condition.

Since his primary interest was basketball, he ventured back to the location where the employee who handled the memberships had shown him the basketball courts. When he got there, three games of full court basketball were in progress. Having already dressed in his new clothes, he sat alongside a few other guys on the bench who were waiting to play the next game. "Who has the rise," McAlister asked the guy next to him.

"I do," the guy responded. You can run with me if you want to."

The guy went right back to talking to his buddy. "Yeah, man, somebody is wiping those cross-dressers out slowly, but surely," he said to his buddy. "If I knew who was doing it, hell, I'd probably join him," he added as he and his buddy laughed.

McAlister did his best to remain emotionless after hearing the kids talk. He felt like he had some allies. The talk made him feel almost like a vigilante, cleaning up the city of its undesirables. The buddy of the guy who had been doing all of the talking said, "Look at it this way, wiping them out definitely has to have an effect."

"Amen to that," the first guy answered.

"Good point," McAlister said to himself. "I didn't think of that."

A finger tapped on his shoulder. He looked up and saw that it was the guy who had offered to let him play the next game. "Hey, man, we're up."

Both teams that had been playing were exiting the floor. The other four players who were to be members of McAlister's team went out and started practicing jump shots. McAlister tried his best to shake the feeling of being the new guy on the court. He knew that they wouldn't readily accept him until he proved himself by displaying his ability.

When the ball fell from the rim into his hands, he dribbled it around a bit and took a jump shot which caused the net to make a snapping sound. One of the other players returned the ball to him as he stood at the top of the key. As if he were playing a game, he immediately took the ball down the middle of the court and slam dunked it through the basket with a fury of strength. "Damn," he heard one of his teammates respond.

McAlister knew that the slam had earned him a few brownie points with his teammates. "Let's play," one of the players from the other team said as they were returning. One of the players from McAlister's team told him to take his shirt off. Hurriedly, he did so, making him the fifth player out of ten who had no shirt on. 'Good idea,' McAlister thought. Soon, the game was underway at a pace that McAlister hoped would slow down a bit. He blended in well with the other guys on the team. He grabbed five rebounds, stole the ball once, gave three assists, and hit five points before the game ended.

As they were running down the court at one point, he asked one of his teammates what final score they played to and the guy told him they play to eleven by ones. The score of the game was tied at ten. One of his teammates pulled down a defensive rebound and McAlister made a fast break for their basket.

The guy threw the ball to him and as he caught it, he dribbled the ball between two players in the middle of the court, broke free, and slam dunked it hard to win the game. "YES!" he heard his teammates say. They all slapped him five after the game. His debut on the court was a success. Satisfied with his performance, he gathered all of his possessions and headed for the shower.

After the shower, he was on his way to The Phoenix to take his dosage of alcohol. The alcohol, he felt, would totally relieve any extra stress he didn't desire. Over the past couple of days, he had noticed that his stress level was higher than normal. There were a couple of methods he was sure would rid the stress. Drinking was one, wiping out cross dressers was another.

CHAPTER 17

Goliath was still working at the entrance when McAlister got there. His face was expressionless. McAlister wondered if the man ever felt any emotions. He seemed almost robotic in his movements as if he were a cyborg on a mission.

A glimmer of recognition showed itself in Goliath's eyes as McAlister paid his admission fee. McAlister felt his heart skip a beat. Maybe Goliath did remember seeing him leave the club on the night he had committed his last murders. Then, again, maybe he was just feeling paranoid. He let the eeriness of it pass as he walked away through the crowd.

The music was pumping out loud tones that sounded good to McAlister's ears. Casually, he strolled around, checking out the faces of those around him, hoping he would spot a female impersonator. For a moment he felt like he was wasting his time when he heard a voice behind him resonate a slightly masculine tone. It was a tone that he'd come to recognize as a man trying to disguise his voice to sound like that of a woman.

Almost abruptly, McAlister changed his direction. As he turned around he saw that on his left was a couple engrossed in conversation. The person doing the talking was the same person he had originally heard disguising his voice. McAlister instantly plotted a way to break up the conversation of the two. He aimed his walking direction to the female impersonator, but he turned his head away from her just before bumping her hand, knocking her drink to the floor. She gasped at the sound of the glass breaking. Some of its contents splashed back over her pretty white shoes. She stepped back as though the action would prevent what had just happened.

The guy she had been talking to stepped back a couple of quick steps to prevent the liquid from splashing onto his pants. McAlister took advantage of the distance he had created between the two and stepped between them turning to face the transgender. "I'm so sorry, sweetheart," he said. "I should have been paying more attention to where I was going."

"You sure as shit should have," she reverberated. "You idiots never watch where the hell you're walking. You see a piece of ass and you lose all of your senses, including your sense of direction."

The words she spoke registered lightly with McAlister. He had mentally prepared himself. "Oh, come on now, baby doll. It's not the end of the world. You'll be alright. Those pretty little pumps of yours will wipe clean and I'm on my way to buy you another margarita at this very moment."

His smile enlightened her as she fell in behind him as he directed himself toward the bar. The guy she had been talking to drifted off into the darkness of the crowd. McAlister scanned the bar for empty seats. Far to the right end of the bar, he spotted two seats that looked cozy. He grabbed his guest by the hand and ushered her toward the empty seats. "Bartender," he shouted, loud enough to get the bartender's attention. "Two margaritas, please."

McAlister turned and looked at his companion. "These will taste twice as good as the one you were drinking. Just wait and see." He winked at her with a flare that sent her erotic vibes. "So, what am I going to call you, other than clumsy?" asked his new date.

"Ronnie," he said. "Call me Ronnie, but don't call me late for dinner."

McAlister elicited a laugh from her. "I like you, Ronnie," she said. Flashing her with a smile, "Feeling's are mutual," he said trying to sound sincere. "How long are you going to keep me in suspense?"

"What do you mean," she asked.

"I mean, like, what is your name, Baby Doll?"

"Oh, shit!" His date exclaimed. "You're ever so right. I am sort of holding you in the dark on that. I'm so sorry. Normally, I state my name right when I meet a person, but I guess under the unusual circumstances, I simply forgot to introduce myself. My name is Norma Freely."

She extended a long hand for McAlister to shake almost forgetting her strength, because she squeezed McAlister's hand harder than he would expect any female to. Automatically, he figured that real name was Norman Freely. *'Very convenient,'* he said to himself. *'All she had to do was drop the 'N' from her first name.'* He thought about his name and what female name it could closely resemble, but nothing came to mind. *'Good,'* he thought to himself.

McAlister looked at Norma straight faced and asked, "Pardon an old cliché, but what's a nice girl like you doing in a place like this?"

Norma batted her eyelashes several times rapidly. "Oh, I don't dispute the fact that I'm a nice girl, but this is a nice place, too. I come here a lot and I have to admit, I do enjoy it here. What do you find wrong with it?"

Trying to think quickly and feeling that he had offended her, he said, "Oh, just that I don't come here often enough to find the likes of women like you."

Feeling somewhat relieved that he had saved himself with his answer he was glad that her response was a radiant smile. She sort of half cocked her head sideways and looked at him out of the corner of her eyes and asked, "What do you mean?"

"I mean that you are one sexy lady as well as you have some brains to go along with those lusty looks of yours."

"Well, I feel very lucky you should notice and it really speaks well of you perception."

McAlister laughed to himself at her arrogance but he admitted that he was fond of her tactfulness. Too bad this isn't a real woman, he thought to himself. "We could really have some fun."

Norma looked at her watch that read it was still quite early: only 9:30. She thought about how she would like to leave and go to a hotel with Ronnie. She wanted to force the issue, but knew that it wouldn't be lady like doing so. She would have to wait for him to eventually ask her home.

McAlister decided that he would soon make a move on Norma, but he wanted to wait until Goliath was preoccupied with something that would keep him from noticing when they left. He listened to Norma talk about how nice the people who came to The Phoenix were and how she had made a lot of friends there. All the while, he looked for Goliath to leave the entrance area.

Finally, the moment that he had been waiting for had arrived. One of the other bouncers had walked briskly over to Goliath and summoned him to help remove a drunken patron who was staggering at the far end of the establishment. Quickly, McAlister grabbed Norma by the hand and said, "Come with me. I have something to show you."

Norma had gone through a few more drinks by then, so she was giggly and receptive. She tagged along behind him. "Baby, aren't we in a big rush," she said sarcastically but also still giggly.

McAlister wondered how far gone this one was psychologically. He had long ago, since first dealing with Natalie, reasoned that all of the cross-dressers were mentally screwed up. They had gone past the point of being closet gays and had balls enough to try to pass themselves off as women.

Norma was practically being dragged by McAlister in his frantic rush out of the club before Goliath could see him. Quickly, he opened the passenger door of his car and pushed her gingerly into the seat. A few seconds passed and he was seated next to her starting the car Norma had a bewildered look on her face. One that said that the alcohol she had consumed was taking its toll.

As McAlister drove, she talked about how men could sometimes be assholes, but at other times sweethearts. She just didn't understand men, so she preferred to just deal with them as they were. McAlister looked for a hotel out away from the hustle of the city night. He decided upon one he found in Spartanburg County. Norma was still giggly as she and

McAlister crossed the threshold of the hotel room. McAlister had been careful when checking into the room to use a phony ID with a fake name. He never left home without it.

Inside the room, Norma had made her way over to the dresser where she stood in front of the mirror casually inspecting herself. She kicked her size twelve high heels off. *'What masculine looking feet,'* McAlister thought. At least he hoped that there weren't any women who had feet like that. McAlister walked slowly through the room and visually inspected it. He wanted to make sure that there was nothing amiss about the room other than the murder that was going to take place. When he went into the bathroom he found it to be clean enough.

When he went back into the room, Norma had stretched out across the bed with her arms flung in the back of her head. "Come here, Big boy," she said while motioning with her index finger for him to come join her. McAlister approached with caution as he strolled toward her. He let his arm brush against his pants pocket to make sure that his trusty blade was still with him.

The lump of it made him feel secure. "You rang?" he asked as he climbed on top of her trying to tell himself that it was only temporary that he would have to be so close to her. He did an academy award winning performance pretending that he wanted her sexually. Norma was puckering her lips expectantly for a kiss at about the same time McAlister was retrieving his blade from his pants pocket. The clicking sound of it opening must have been a familiar one for Norma, because her eyes widened in terror. The blade was inserted in her neck before she could do anything defensively to save herself. Blood spurted from her neck like it was a fountain.

McAlister was barely able to avoid the spurting of blood on his clothes. It was soaking into the bedspread like a sponge. Norma was gasping for air, but it became harder to do so with each passing second. McAlister waited until there was no sign of life emitting from her before attempting to remove her genitals.

Reaching underneath her skirt, he found her, large member pinned back toward her anus, clad by the tight nylons and panties she wore. He pulled the nylons and panties down near her knees until he was free to cut Norma's penis off as close to his balls as possible. Once he had removed it, he forced its length headfirst into Norma's mouth.

Looking at her, he thought the look of terror in her eyes was in congruence with what he had just done to her. It was a very fitting stare. Satisfied with what he had done, he set about cleaning the dwelling of everything he had touched and did not touch just to be certain. He worked around Norma's body as if she were not there. Pretty soon, the whole place was glistening clean, as if the room had not been occupied all that day.

McAlister was careful to keep his hands off of the doorknob as he was leaving the room. He placed his hand inside his pants pocket and turned the knob. Slowly, he opened the door, cautious enough not to alert anyone. Expediently, he moved off of the floor and down through the lobby, hoping that no one would see him or get a good look at him. He was sure not to look at anyone directly in the face. That way, he would only be remembered at a glimpse.

As he started his car, he let out the air that had built up in his lungs. It felt better now that the hard part was over. He drove toward Jeanette's at a speed that was legal, careful not to be stopped for speeding. The lights were all out at Jeanette's when he arrived there. There was a note illuminated by way of a corner light in the living room. It read, "Sorry, Mac, but I couldn't wait up any longer. Love, Jeanette".

He tiptoed into the bedroom over to the alarm clock and looked at Jeanette's stillness before adjusting the clock back a couple of hours. Silently, he removed his clothes and slid into bed, hoping to awaken her so that he could make her aware of the time. She rolled over until she bumped his body. Groggily, she opened her eyes, which looked fireball red from the deep sleep she had been engaged in. "What time is it?" she asked.

"It's only 10:00 p.m. Go back to sleep, Jen." McAlister answered. She lowered her body back to the bed after observing the digital clock beside McAlister on the end table; it did indeed read that it was 10:00 p.m. After she was comfortably snuggled beneath the comforter, he waited for a few minutes to pass. Once he was sure that Jeanette was sound asleep, he reached over to the end table, grabbed the clock and reset it to the time it should have been.

Satisfied, he put it back where it had rested before. Then, he dropped the back of his head to his pillow and began to review the occurrences of the evening. It was as if he were watching a movie in which the actor was due an award for a performance of top caliber. He had set the stage as any good actor would reviewing the final moments at the hotel with Norma.

The proper steps had been taken according to how he had planned things. He recounted the cleaning of the dwelling and how diligent he had been in making sure that the entire place was spic and span. He was satisfied with the evening as he closed his eyes and rested peacefully.

Chapter 18

The following morning, he woke to the sound of rhythmic dance music emitting from Jeanette's aerobic room. It was loud enough for the neighbors to hear the lyrics distinctively. McAlister threw the comforter away from his body. As though he were rejuvenated by way of electrical charge, he sprung from the bed and onto his feet before the rest of his body could make adjustment to the suddenness of the act. He almost toppled over, but caught himself before he lost momentum.

As he felt his body circulation even out, he gathered a few bathing items and headed for the shower. Inside the shower, he scrubbed himself hard, hoping to rid any fragments of blood that may have settled on his skin. He scrubbed so hard in some areas that they became tender. Finding baby powder and oil in the medicine cabinet he used them to soothe his body. It was a ritual he had been practicing since childhood and was not about to stop just because he was staying with Jeanette. He had missed a couple of nights doing it since he had been there and already it had begun to get underneath his skin.

It was as if his soul had been cleansed as well. He knew that the day would feel airy and invigorating. It made him relish life itself. He didn't think of the madness that had taken place since his wife had discovered Carolyn. He had come to a point of acceptance of the acts that he had engaged in and made up his mind that he would not dwell on them.

He began dressing himself as meticulously as he always did, careful to make sure his tie was straight and his shirt was neatly tucked. His hair had to be neat or else he would feel as though he looked like a bum. Finally, he was satisfied with what he saw of himself in the mirror.

The music stopped blaring from Jeanette's pump room. McAlister reckoned that she would come into the bedroom within a few minutes and begin her preparation for a day at the office. He patted her on the butt in passing on his way to the kitchen. "Good workout, champ?" he said to her.

"Just a daily thing," she responded. "Something you need to start if you ever plan to be healthy," she added.

"Oh, no, don't you start that trip with me again. You already know how I feel on the subject, so go easy."

Already he had made it to the kitchen where the drink glasses were available. He took one from the cabinet and followed up the action by removing a tray of ice cubes from the freezer. After he had broken the cube free from the tray, he put a few in his glass, and poured in two thirds of gin. He didn't bother to mix it with anything because he did not care for the heaviness of a sweet drink. He took a healthy gulp, almost emptying the glass.

Jeanette poked her head in from the bedroom door. "Having another all liquid breakfast again, aren't you, Mac?!"

Before he could answer, she disappeared back into the bedroom. With his drink in hand, McAlister strolled into the bedroom. Jeanette was taking off her leotard. He noticed how full busted and firm she was as he marveled at her sculpted body. Her tapered waist and gently flaring hips were almost too much to bear, which was evident from the tent in his trousers.

McAlister didn't care to comment on her looks, but favored relishing the delightful appearance of her body. He was throbbing in solitude as she began to dress herself slowly and with great care not to overlook anything that may be out of place. The pride Jeanette held for herself was exuberant. It overwhelmed McAlister. He had to admit that she always managed to make him feel good.

They were both silent when he walked up behind her. She saw him approaching her by the reflection of the mirrors, but did not try stopping him because she desired him just as much as he did her. As she was about to snap her bra together, McAlister's hands cleverly prevented the action. Her bra fell to the floor and his hands began sensuously massaging her breasts. He pressed himself snugly to her behind, enough so that she could feel the size of him, approvingly so.

Her moans started at low and guttural tones that became more pronounced as McAlister's hands became more exploratory. The remainder of clothing Jeanette had on quickly found their place on the floor along with her bra. Shortly after, McAlister's clothes occupied a spot on the floor beside hers. She turned to face him and began softly kissing his lips. She moved her lips over to his ear and nibbled for a moment, and then started working her lips down his neck to his chest. She took extra care on his nipples, kissing and licking them until he thought he would burst with excitement.

Trembling as she moved her way downward, she took his member into her hands and began to work it with expert skill. He silently thanked God for giving him such a perfect woman. She was everything a man could ask for in a woman. Pulling her up to his lips once again he decided to return the favor. He moved his mouth downward until he was at her nipples. He took them gently between his teeth and began to run his tongue over them softly.

Jeanette moaned with delight and couldn't stand it a moment longer. She felt a throbbing sensation between her legs and knew she was ready. From the rock between his legs, she knew he was just as ready as she. So she climbed on top of him and began to swivel her hips around and arch her back until they both exploded with delight. They fell to the bed apart from one another, enjoying the moment after the climax. Instantly they fell asleep exhausted.

The next morning McAlister turned to face Jeanette and smiled softly at her. "It feels so good, lying here, just basking in the glow of the morning sun."

Jeanette rolled over close to him and wrapped her arms around him. "Mmm," she moaned. "It sure does. It would be delightful if we could lay here like this the remainder of the day," she assured him.

"Don't ever get too comfortable, Jen. We definitely need to go into the office today. We have been pretty slack lately and I feel rather guilty about it."

McAlister thought about other things that he probably should feel guilty about, but didn't allow it to affect him. They lay in bed staring at the ceiling and exchanging small talk as McAlister patiently smoked his cigarette.

Jeanette felt spent and ready for dreams, but found it was too late when McAlister struggled to his feet and began getting dressed. She knew that was her cue so she joined him. She found it imperative to start each morning by downing a ten ounce glass of V-8 before leaving the apartment. McAlister waited anxiously as he watched her consume two full glasses of it.

The drive to the office was smooth, due to following traffic that didn't get bound and gagged by a mar of red lights. McAlister and Jeanette's conversation was about the things at the office that needed to be attended to. They were behind on everything that needed to be taken care of. McAlister hadn't heard anything from Detective Dash for affirmation on the witness testifying for the kid.

As soon as they got situated at the office, McAlister looked at his calendar to see what would take precedence for the day. The biggest item on his agenda was a 2:00 p.m. court appearance to finalize the bankruptcy proceedings for one of his clients. Jeanette had already begun her daily routine by the time McAlister got around to calling Detective Dash's home to see if he had left for the morning. Dash picked up the receiver on the fourth ring and spoke into it with a gruff tone that clued McAlister that he must have been drinking heavily the night before. "Who is it?" Dash asked as he was not use to receiving a phone call so early in the morning. He looked at the clock that clung to his bedroom wall. It showed that the time was 8:23 am and he should have been out of there some time ago.

"It's me," McAlister answered.

"Oh, *Mac*, how are you doing?" Dash asked, relieved that he had recognized McAlister's voice immediately. It was important to have the quality of rapid identification if one was to go far as a detective. "Doing fine!" McAlister answered.

"Let me guess," Dash said quickly before McAlister could say anything more, "You called me to find out if I have secured our witness, right?"

"Absolutely! You have the mind of a psychic. Don't worry about a thing," Dash told him, "I'll be by your office as soon as I get dressed and the morning traffic permits."

"Roger that," McAlister said, satisfied with the progress. "I'll see you soon."

They exchanged goodbyes and hung the telephones up. By the time McAlister was off of the telephone with Dash, Jeanette had managed to place the morning newspaper and a freshly brewed cup of coffee on his desk. It surprised him because he had not noticed her come in. He swiveled his chair around with his back to the door when talking to Dash. As he sipped his hot coffee, he scanned over the headlines to see if there was any news about the recent murders. Surprisingly, there was none.

As Jeanette pecked away on her typewriter, a scrawny looking man walked into the reception area and stopped at her desk. He stood about five feet seven inches tall and looked as though he weighed about one hundred fifteen pounds soaking wet. He had jet black hair and apparently didn't take much pride in keeping it washed or combed. Wisps of hair hung across his forehead almost touching the rims of the thick lens glasses he wore. His face looked greasy where his hair touched it. His eyes were deep brown, almost black in color and he had a thin nose and a thin upper lip, but his bottom lip was oversized. As for his chin, it was almost nonexistent. His jaw protruded back toward his neck and almost tapered to a point.

McAlister could see from the distance what a pitiful looking man he was in appearance and he instantly felt sorry for him. He thanked God simultaneously that he wasn't cursed in that way. He saw the guy reach inside the corduroy coat he wore and remove a wallet. He already knew what was on the inside. The motion alerted him that the character was a detective.

McAlister's heart sank as he heard the man ask for him by name. Soon afterward he watched Jeanette get up from her desk and walk toward him. When he looked up at her, she was standing in front of his desk silently. A look of fear showed itself on her face. It was almost as if the look was saying, "Oh no, now they know you are the one who murdered those people." It was a look of understood recognition.

"What is it, Jen?" McAlister asked while trying to sound as ignorant as he possibly could to the events taking place.

She looked straight into his eyes, but with horror in her own. It was almost as if she were looking through him. She turned her head and looked in the direction of the detective and then back at him and said, "There's a man here that wants to see you. He's a detective."

McAlister nervously rubbed his palms together trying to relieve the tension that had accumulated there and said, "Well, send him back here so I can relieve his curious mind."

Jeanette turned and walked back toward the detective. McAlister cleared his throat so that he could be prepared to answer some questions. It was his reaction that he was sure the detective would take notice of. So he kept quickly reminding himself to be as calm as he possibly could and maybe the detective wouldn't form any negative opinions about him.

The detective approached him with his badge extended in one hand and the other hand extended to shake. "Mr. Johnson, I'm Detective Gene Foley, of the Greenville Police Department, Homicide Division."

As McAlister shook his hand, he gave the man a quizzical look. "Oh, you are here to ask my advice about something concerning one of your cases, aren't you?" McAlister said with more certainty. "Go ahead and ask anything that you would like," he added.

Gene scratched the top of his head and used the same hand to push his falling glasses back onto his nose. "Actually, I'm not here to get any advice from you, Mr. Johnson, but I am here to get answers from you."

"Answers about what?" McAlister asked. He noticed that Gene carried a pesky air about him that he knew would irritate him if the man was in his presence for long. "Do you own a knife?" Gene asked.

"I own plenty of knives," McAlister offered.

"No, I mean do you own a pocket knife?" the detective asked, scratching his head and grimacing at the same time as though he smelled something displeasing. McAlister realized that he had better be careful of his answer, remembering that the tip had broken off inside the body of his last victim. "I did have a pocket knife at one time, but I lost it some time ago," he said.

McAlister never did offer Gene a seat, although he stood next to a chair in front of his desk. Gene finally took it upon himself to take the seat and made himself comfortable. Watching him do so, McAlister became slightly uneasy about the detective as the motion meant that there were more questions to be answered.

Gene spoke up, "Mr. Johnson, we found a victim with a blade tip stuck in him. We decided that since there are many knives available, we would start by checking with stores that offered catalogs. Stores that offer catalogs generally take information from their customers for the purpose of sending out those catalogs. Your name was one of many that appeared on our lists, Mr. Johnson, so you see how we know how to get in touch with you. Your wife wasn't very cooperative in helping us find you."

"So you spoke with Kelly, did you?"

"Yes. She said that it's been a few weeks since she has seen you and that you left in kind of a hurry because you had been spooked. I asked what she meant, but she would not elaborate."

'Good,' McAlister thought, 'this asshole doesn't need to know my personal business.' As a matter of fact he wondered why Kelly had not visited him at the hospital and reasoned that she was done with him just as much as he was done with her. They had spent many days and nights arguing throughout the years. "Where did you go when you left your wife, Mr. Johnson?"

"That's none of your business," McAlister said angrily.

"Need I remind you, Mr. Johnson, that I'm operating at the capacity of the law and I can ask you anything I damn well please." He gave McAlister a long hard stare until he managed to make him uncomfortable enough to cause him to sink into his chair.

McAlister decided that he had better try to maintain his control as much as possible. "I'm sorry, Gene, that I reacted that way, but when you brought up the subject of my wife, it did not sit right with me. You understand that, don't you? Besides that, I have every Tom, Dick, and Harry wanting me to perform some type of service for them. I can barely keep track of my own life anymore. Will you forgive me?"

Gene scratched his head again, but in a different spot this time. 'Got to be lice,' McAlister thought. "No problem," Gene answered. "Just try to refrain from flying off the handle. I'm going to get to the bottom of these murders and when I do, I'm going to crucify whoever is responsible. My boss wants answers and so do I. Now let's try to continue where we left off. Where did you go when you left your wife, Mr. Johnson?"

So expected, McAlister figured he would come back to that question. He cleared his throat and said, "I went to my secretary's place. I moved in with her."

"Did you do so the very day that you left your wife?" Gene asked.

"No," answered McAlister. "I went to a bar after driving around the city for quite a while."

McAlister suddenly thought about the fact that Gene's next question would be, "what bar did you go to?' which meant that he would follow up on the information he was given and would possibly talk to someone that would remember his face from the bar. Someone who would remember him sitting with Natalie and leaving with her. He reasoned that Gene was pretty smart and would go as far as getting a photograph of him to show around. That would nail him.

"No, I'm sorry, I'm wrong about that. I didn't go to a bar. After I got tired of driving, I pulled my car off to the side of the road and caught some shut eye. The next morning I returned to the office and discussed with my secretary that I had left Kelly and needed a place to stay until I could get myself together. I've been living with her ever since."

"I read about you having an accident that hospitalized you for a while," Gene said. "Was it your secretary that was with you?"

"Yes, Jeanette was with me," McAlister answered.

Gene squinted and looked back at Jeanette who wasn't paying any attention to them. "She's a real looker," Gene exclaimed. He stood and offered his hand again for McAlister to shake. "Nice meeting you, Mr. Johnson. It's a shame we couldn't have met under more pleasant circumstances."

McAlister did not respond immediately because he was still thinking about what Gene had said about questioning Jeanette. "Oh I'm so sorry," McAlister said, gripping the extended hand and shaking it firmly.

Gene turned and headed for Jeanette. McAlister sat down again and looked to see whether Gene would indeed stop at Jeanette's desk and question her. Through the glass window he could see that he was indeed questioning her. He was standing over her as she looked up from her chair. From time to time she would nod her head and speak a few words. After a matter of minutes, Gene departed. No sooner had he left Detective Dash entered.

McAlister watched as Dash exchanged a few words with Jeanette. They laughed and giggled, but only for a few minutes. Dash entered his office with an air of superiority that he had exuberated since McAlister had known him. He was wearing a grey, two piece double-breasted suit that looked as though it were tailored to fit him the way all his suits did.

"Macaroni, my man, how the hell are you feeling this morning?" Dash asked.

McAlister hated when he called him that, but was too concerned about Gene to let it bother him. "Why was the weasel here, Macaroni? I was surprised to see him. You aren't looking to replace me with a new Private Dick, are you?"

"No, Dash, I'm not." McAlister answered. "What can you tell me about 'The Weasel'?"

"I can tell you that he gets all the high priority stuff down at the station and that so far, he's had a one hundred percent success rate. He started out three years ago on patrol, mostly with traffic diversion because the chief and other higher powers thought he was so geeky looking that he must have been somewhat retarded."

"The Weasel started complaining a lot that his talents were going to waste, but at first, no one would listen to him. Finally, the higher powers decided they would give him a chance, just to silence him. They figured he would screw up and be sent right back to directing traffic. He worked the Vice Squad for a while, but as far as he was concerned, his talents were still being wasted. He was interested strictly in working homicide.

"After the higher powers became fed up with his complaining, they gave him the shot he was looking for. Since he has been working homicide, he has twice been offered a promotion to head up the division, but each time turned it down. He's one of those types that have to be out in the field working on a case."

McAlister had lit up a cigarette before Dash had entered his office. He relinquished the smoke from his lungs and smashed the butt in the brass ashtray atop his desk. He clasped his hands together and gave Dash a stern stare. If he could trust anyone in the world, it was Dash. They had grown up together and knew one another like the backs, and fronts, of their hands. "There's something I want you to do for me since you've taken care of our other little problems," McAlister said. "By the way, you did inform our witness of the court date?"

"Taken care of," Dash said.

"Well, what I need concerns 'The Weasel'."

Dash squinted momentarily curious about what business McAlister could possibly have with 'The Weasel.' "I want you to keep tabs on him for me. Don't worry about any of the other things we've been working on. Keep a list of the places he goes and the people he talks to. I want you to call me every night at 9:00 p.m. for a report. Do you understand?"

"Got it," Dash answered. "I'll get started on it right away." Dash turned and started to leave, but before he could make it through the door, McAlister yelled, "Hey, Dash, this one pays double!"

Dash flashed an approving smile and turned to exit. He dropped a few lines on Jeanette and left after a few minutes had passed. "Jeanette, I need to see you, sweetheart," McAlister called out.

She abandoned what she was doing and came to him. As she stood before his desk, she fidgeted with her hands. "Jen, what did that Gene fellow ask you?"

"He asked me when it was that you moved in with me."

Jeanette could see McAlister's anxiety. "Don't worry, I told him that you moved in the night you left Kelly."

McAlister swallowed the lump in his throat. "He also asked me if I'd ever seen you with a switchblade knife with a broken tip."

"What did you tell him?" McAlister asked.

"The truth," Jeanette answered. "That I haven't. Mac, are you in some kind of trouble with the law?" she asked.

McAlister stood up and began to walk around as though he were in a debate with himself. Jeanette swiveled her head around, watching him pace. Finally, she spoke up. "I figured you must be in some type of trouble. You have been acting extremely strange since leaving Kelly. At first, I thought that was the reason, because you missed Kelly, that is, but now I think it's a lot worse than that."

"Jen, right now I need to keep my confidences to myself. Soon, you will know answers to everything that's in question in your mind, but right now, I can't tell you anything. You did the right thing by telling that detective that I moved in with you right after leaving Kelly. You will have faith in me that I will eventually let you know what's happening, won't you?"

"Yes Mac, because I love you."

Suddenly, as though undaunted by Jeanette's comment, McAlister stopped in his tracks. "Shit," he said out loud.

"What's wrong, Mac?" Jeanette asked.

"I told Gene that I moved in with you the night after I left Kelly, and you told him that I moved in that same night. Our stories don't jive, and I'm sure that Gene picked up on it. Shit! Did he ask you for the exact date that I moved in?"

"No, he didn't," Jeanette answered.

McAlister's mind began to race. He was trying to find a solution to take care of the problem that he was facing. The only thing he could think of was to get Jeanette to contact the detective and tell him that she made a mistake about when he had moved in with her. She could tell him that she had mistaken because it was so sudden to her, but after he had left the office, she remembered that it had been the night after.

The Weasel would probably know that she had changed her story to suit McAlister, but there was nothing that he could really do about that. Oh, he was sure the detective would make a note of it, but Jeanette was also human, and prone to make mistakes. McAlister decided that he wouldn't lose any sleep over that. He had Dash out playing hound dog.

If The Weasel would happen to talk to anyone who could be damaging to McAlister, he would at least have an idea of how close he was to cracking the case. He put the worry out of his mind, confident that Thomas Dash's assignment would be well executed.

He looked out to see if Jeanette was busy doing anything and saw that she was steady at work. Instead of asking her to call Leroy Foster, he picked up his telephone and dialed the number himself. It rang for a good while before anyone picked up the receiver. The voice on the other end sounded as though it probably belonged to an elderly woman. That observation was reinforced when he had to raise his voice several times before the person on the other end could understand what he was asking for. "Yes, Leroy is here," the voice said, "hold on just a minute." She summoned for him several times before the receiver was picked up by Leroy.

"Hello?" Leroy said.

"Leroy, this is McAlister; how are you feeling this morning?"

"Fine, considering the circumstances," answered Leroy, sounding quite mellow.

"I have some very good news for you," McAlister said, "Something that may put you on a cloud for the rest of the day."

"Oh, yeah? What's that?" Leroy asked.

McAlister could tell that Leroy's voice perked up a bit sensing his excitement. "We have a couple of witnesses that can testify that you were not responsible for the convenience store robbery. My private detective, Thomas Dash, is the man responsible for that. I think what he did was took that photograph you left of yourself back to the attendant of the store who claimed you were the one who stuck him up. He still insisted that it was you. He found that there were a couple of his regular customers who had been there on the day in question, tracked them down and showed each one your picture. One was certain and the other was almost certain that it wasn't you. He said that the man who hit the store was of a darker complexion and had a big mole on his forehead.

"Then how does that help me?" asked Leroy. "If the store attendant says that I'm the one, then won't that nail me?"

"No!" answered McAlister. "Dash said that the man also told him that all blacks look alike to him. Don't you see? He says that it was you, but then he also makes a statement like that. He was not consistent with his statement. I will have no problem ripping his testimony apart on the stand. Don't worry; we have this one in the bag. Relax, Okay?"

"Okay," Leroy said. "I trust you."

"We go to court Friday, remember so get there early enough that I can go over some things with you. See you then."

McAlister checked his watch. It was congruent with what his stomach was telling him, lunchtime. He saw that Jeanette was putting aside her work so that she could prepare to go to lunch as well. She entered his area and just stood there, looking at him. He exchanged the look with her and reached for one of his cigarettes.

After lunch, Jeanette returned to her tasks, which had already kept her busy all morning. She was always busy during the morning. She would pull files, check information in them, add information to them, replace them, type memos, send out letters, and numerous other tasks that kept her occupied each day. She was also responsible for reminding McAlister of his court dates and gathered any necessary paperwork that needed to go into court with him.

Shortly after 1:00 p.m., she began searching the files for the one with the name, "Andrew Davis" on it. It was needed for the 2:00 p.m. bankruptcy proceedings that were scheduled that day. She handed it to McAlister, who quickly read over the contents. She informed him that Andrew had called before lunch and said that he would meet him at the courthouse.

Andrew Davis was a middle aged ex-business entrepreneur who had managed to piss away all of his money by letting a cocaine addiction get the best of him. He had once been considered very handsome and desirable to many women, but the cocaine had managed to whither him down to practically a skeleton.

When McAlister entered the courtroom, Andrew was already there, waiting for him, wearing a suit that hung from his thin frame as though it were hanging from a pole. His cheeks were sunken in and his eyes had receded back into his head. He looked horrendous to McAlister, who was glad that bankruptcy proceedings were usually quite simple and quick as long as everything was well prepared, which it was in this case. The proceedings went favorably for them and they were out of court within a short period of time.

On the way to their cars, Andrew told McAlister that he would be back on top some day. "Sure you will," McAlister retorted sarcastically. He knew that Andrew was still using, even after he had lost everything. Andrew followed McAlister back to the office complex so they could settle up. At the office, McAlister found that Jeanette was still busy with the paper chase. He felt good about the fact that he couldn't have found a better and more loyal employee. He left instructions for her to write Andrew a receipt to the tune of $300. Andrew asked if it would be alright for him to write a check for the amount. McAlister was leery of the idea, but agreed to accept it on the basis that he was sure Andrew had at least $300 in his checking account.

The remainder of the day at the office was pretty much routine. Both McAlister and Jeanette felt exhausted by the time the work day had ended. Jeanette told McAlister that her first priority once they got home was to catch up on some sleep. She ended up falling asleep during the drive home. McAlister was very proficient in maneuvering his car through the mad traffic that engulfed Greenville on a daily basis.

Jeanette began stripping her clothes as soon as they entered the apartment. She left a trail all the way to the bedroom. McAlister found the items he needed in order to make himself a stiff drink. Turning on the television he removed his sport coat, and sunk down on the couch. After taking a few sips from his drink, he began dozing off without cognizance of doing so. Before long, he was in a deep sleep. Unknowingly, his drink slipped out of his hand and down to the floor.

Chapter 19

McAlister may have slept the remainder of the evening if it hadn't been for the telephone ringing loud enough to wake him. He looked at the clock on the wall and saw that it was 9:00 p.m. before picking up the receiver. He knew who would be on the other end of the line. "Yeah," he said groggily into the receiver.

"Big Mac, wake up," Thomas Dash said.

"What you got for me?" McAlister asked.

"Well, Mac, by the time I was able to catch up with our boy, the only place I could follow him was to your wife's house."

"How long was he there?" asked McAlister.

"About fifteen to twenty minutes," answered Dash. "From there, he went back to his office. There has been no other activity from him other than that, except that he went home to his wife."

"He has a wife?" asked McAlister, sounding incredulous.

"Yeah, as sickening as it may sound," answered Dash.

"The generosity of women never ceases to amaze me," McAlister said. "Thanks for the info, Tommy, and keep me informed."

"Sure thing, bud," Dash replied.

McAlister reasoned that The Weasel had gone back to talk with Kelly to find out the exact date that he left her, as well as the time he left. He wondered what other miscellaneous information he would ask her about, unless they had been shooting the breeze for ten or fifteen minutes. He could not believe that it was already 9:00 p.m. As he stood up, he noticed the glass he had dropped on the floor earlier when falling to sleep. After picking it up, he washed it and created another concoction in it. The television was still going, but after flipping through the channels, he decided he would rather listen to some music. He turned on the stereo, satisfied with the radio station that was already on, then returned to his seat after turning the volume down on the television, but did not turn it completely off.

McAlister had almost finished his drink when Jeanette came into the room. She was wearing a thin negligee. Standing before him, she extended both of her arms in the air and let out a lengthy yawn. After the stretch, she sat down on the couch beside him and smiled as she looked into his eyes. "Old habits are hard to break, huh, Mac?" Turning up his glass and gulping the contents down, he pushed himself away from the couch. As he headed over to mix another drink, he said, "Who says I want to break any old habits?"

"What's bothering you, Mac?" she asked.

As he returned with his fresh drink in hand, he tried to appear unaffected by Jeanette's inquiry. "If I told you that nothing was bothering me, would you believe me?" he asked.

"No, I wouldn't believe you, Mac, not with the way you've been acting lately."

"Oh? And how's that?" McAlister asked.

"Like, you're carrying the world on your shoulders. You haven't been very good at hiding whatever it is that's eating at you. I wish you would open up to me. I could be of some help to you, do you know that?" Jeanette asked.

McAlister downed half of the liquid in his glass, batted his eyes several times as though he were contemplating something. "There are some things that have happened recently. I want to tell you about them, but I don't think the time is right."

Jeanette ran her fingers through his hair and kissed him on the cheek. "My dear man when you're ready to spill the beans, I'm here for you and you can trust me with whatever it is." She stood up and took his hand into hers, in an effort to pull him up with her. "Come on, this apartment is getting stuffy. Let's go out somewhere to dance," she suggested. "Maybe it will help get whatever has been bothering you off your mind for a while."

"I don't know about that," answered McAlister. Jeanette let go of his hand and returned to her bedroom. McAlister continued to sit on the couch and think about the events of the day, mainly about The Weasel. He would not take him lightly. As long as he knew how much progress The Weasel was making, he would know what moves he should make.

Jeanette returned from the room, but this time, she wore a skin tight, glittery party dress that just barely covered her rear. It did a great job of highlighting her assets. All of the workouts had proved worthy. She tried not to be arrogant, but it would have been understandable if she was.

McAlister downed the contents of his glass and started for another before Jeanette cut him off from doing so. "Put your coat on, Mac, so that we can get out of here."

"Can I put this down?" McAlister asked, holding up the glass so that she could see what he was talking about.

"Yeah, you can get all the drinks you want once we get to The Phoenix. I don't go out much at all, but when I do, I happen to like that club the most of all."

"Then, The Phoenix it is," he said. During the drive to The Phoenix, Jeanette talked about how when she was younger, she rarely ever went out to clubs. All of her friends thought that she was a square because she hardly ever hung out with them. She explained to them that partying wasn't the most important thing to do in her life. There were other priorities that took precedence.

McAlister wasn't concentrating on what Jeanette was saying. His thoughts were centered on maintaining his cool at The Phoenix. He wondered if Goliath was there tonight and if he would be recognized by him. He was also thinking about The Weasel, who bothered him more than Goliath did. "Earth to McAlister, earth to McAlister, come in please."

"I'm with you, baby, sorry about that," he said. "I was sort of in outer space just then. There's so much on my mind that I find it hard to pay attention to anything other than my own thoughts. What were you saying?"

"I don't care to repeat myself, Mac. If you don't want to listen, then I don't care to waste my breath"

"No, no, go ahead…I'm all ears," McAlister said.

"Well," Jeanette said, somewhat reluctantly, "I was just talking about how when I was young, I was so much different from the rest of the kids from my age group. Many of them thought I was a square because I didn't go out much or do drugs. I just had my priorities in order and they didn't. Many of them today are unhappily married with a bunch of unwanted kids, and others are in prison. It really didn't pay off for them to try to live adult lives when they weren't really adults, you know what I mean?"

"Yeah, I know exactly what you mean. I've been in prison before, remember?" With that, they both rode the rest of the way to the club in silence.

Goliath was still the doorman at The Phoenix. There was a crowd at the door, as usual, who were anxiously waiting for the good times that were part of the activity inside. The music was loud and rich in bass. Bodies were moving rhythmically to and fro. It was one big party that would extend well into the night if one dared to stay there long enough.

McAlister grabbed Jeanette's hand in his and shoved his way through the crowd with her trailing him. Finally, they reached the bar that was surrounded by patrons pouring a variety of liquids down their throats. Half of them looked plastered, but seemed to be in no hurry to give up their seats at the bar. "So what will you have to drink?" McAlister shouted to Jeanette, although she was close enough to whisper.

"Gin and tonic," she shouted back. The bartender who was at their end of the bar looking frantic trying to please all of the customers waiting for his service. Many of them were leaning over the bar in efforts to get his attention. McAlister held out a crisp twenty dollar bill high enough in the air to get the bartender's attention. "What will you have, Buddy?" he asked.

"One gin and tonic and a Margarita," McAlister answered. The bartender was quick in his action of putting the drinks together. McAlister recognized that he was the same bartender who had tended to his needs the night he got sloshed with Natalie. Shortly after his order was placed, the drinks were placed in front of him. "That will be seven bucks, buddy," the bartender said.

McAlister paid for the drinks and dropped a dollar in the tip jar. Jeanette began sipping on her drink immediately. Looking around the club, McAlister saw that most of the seats had already been taken. He spotted an empty table that had a perfect view of the dance floor. Hurriedly, the two of them rushed over, just beating out another couple who had the same idea.

Jeanette was bobbing her head back and forth and rocking in her seat. "Do you want to dance?" McAlister asked.

"No, not until I've had a couple of drinks," Jeanette replied. "I usually like to get wound up before I hit the floor." She continued to bob her head back and forth moving in her seat as though she were ready to tear the floor up at that very moment. McAlister remembered an instance when he was in high school, before he got in trouble, that the school had a dance one night after a football game.

Being an avid dancer, he was pretty excited about showing his goods. The girls at the dance were all sitting in their seats, moving back and forth as though they were anxious to dance. He asked the prettiest girl there to dance, but she rejected him. Not one to give up, he asked every girl in the place to dance and was turned down each time. He became so frustrated that he left the dance.

Jeanette reminded him of those girls from the dance that night. He pushed himself away from their table. "Then you won't mind if I dance then?" he said.

"Mac," Jeanette started, but before she could get any more out of her mouth, McAlister was halfway across the room asking some other woman for a dance. Jeanette laughed to herself and continued sipping her drink. McAlister found another nice looking woman that accompanied him to the dance floor. To Jeanette's surprise, McAlister moves were pretty smooth. She could see him from where she was sitting. He was moving so well that she began to regret saying that she wasn't ready to dance with him.

On the dance floor, there were people dancing to the beat of the music and occasionally, McAlister was bumped by them, but he didn't let it bother him because he was having too much fun. As he danced, he glanced at the people around him. They all seemed to be normal, with the exception of one person who was halfway across the dance floor.

Suddenly, McAlister became transfixed with the presence of a man dressed in women's clothing. He was sure it was a man, but the transgender had done a great job in disguising himself. An intense hatred replaced the good feeling McAlister had felt prior to seeing the transgender. He forgot all about the woman he was dancing with, although he kept moving to the beat of the music. "See something you like?" the woman who he had been dancing with asked.

"No, I just thought I saw someone I hadn't seen in many years," he answered. "I didn't mean to make you feel like I had forgotten about you." He tried to return his attention to her and the rest of the people in the club, but the transgender was like a magnet luring him in.

After the song was over, he thanked his dance partner and escorted her off the dance floor. He rejoined Jeanette at their table, but watched to see which direction the he-she went before doing so. He thought about making up some reason to take Jeanette home, but he knew she wouldn't go for it. "Boy, you sure do have some nice moves," Jeanette said to him as he sat down. "Where did you learn to dance like that?"

"It just comes natural," he answered. "I've always enjoyed dancing, so when I do, I put myself into it."

"I just ordered another drink for myself," Jeanette said. "Would you care for another?"

"No," McAlister answered. "I think I'll finish up mine." He picked up his glass and took a healthy gulp of the now watered down contents.

"You're going to get ripped if you keep gulping 'em like that," Jeanette warned.

"Takes too many to get me drunk," McAlister said. "I'll be alright. If you don't feel secure about me drinking, I'll let you drive."

"I trust you," Jeanette told him. The waitress brought over Jeanette's second drink. McAlister could tell from looking at her eyes that the first drink had affected her. He didn't know many women who could really drink. He figured that Jeanette was good for four at most. She was still writhing in her seat as though she wanted to be dragged to the dance floor.

McAlister paid little attention to her. Instead, he focused on the tranny who had returned to the dance floor with a new dance partner. She was slinging her lady in all directions with a big happy smile plastered on her face. McAlister reasoned that the cross dresser had done a good bit of drinking and was ready to be picked up. He thought that whoever picked her up sure would be in for a surprise – an unpleasant surprise at that. He wondered if whoever that person would be would react the same way he did with Natalie.

Jeanette seemed to be drinking her second drink a lot faster than the first one – at least twice the original pace. McAlister knew the pattern well. You start off slow at first and pick up the pace as you become more inebriated. If you mix your own drinks, you usually start off mixing a small amount of liquor with the mixer, and as you drink more, you end up with at least half and half portions. He knew that was the way it worked for him.

Jeanette discarded the straw from her glass and began taking swallows from it. McAlister knew that he would have a drunken woman to reckon with if he continued to let her drink that way. Her smile broadened as she drank more. Impatiently she looked around for a waitress. As one walked by, she stopped her and ordered another drink. "Now I'm ready to dance," she said.

"I'm not." McAlister told her. Before the waitress could get far from their table, McAlister stopped her and ordered another drink for himself. "I'm waiting for a good song to come on," he told Jeanette. "I won't dance to just anything. I have to feel good about the music before I can dance to it."

A tall young guy who had been sitting at the bar, staring at Jeanette came over to their table and asked her to dance. She looked at McAlister as though she were waiting for his approval. "Go ahead, enjoy yourself," he told her.

She sprang to her feet enthusiastically and led the young guy to the dance floor. McAlister watched as she weaved her way into the middle of the crowd. He was unable to see them after they were engulfed by the crow, but he wasn't interested in them anyhow. He refocused his attention to the tranny who was still on the dance floor, but closer to the edge where he was more visible.

The waitress brought their drinks to the table, momentarily breaking McAlister's gaze from the transgender man. He reached deep into his pocket to retrieve some change that he needed to pay for his drinks and made sure he gave the waitress an extra dollar for her efforts. The drink he ordered was stronger than the first, but it suited him well. He wouldn't have to spend so much money if they continued to make them like that. Economically, it would be more reasonable to order the next two as straight up double shots.

Before the song ended the he-she and her dance partner left the floor and took a table beside McAlister's. He could see more of the man behind the drag as close as he was to him. He was surprised that the guy couldn't tell that the person he was talking to wasn't a real woman. At that instant, he conceived an idea that could provide an interesting outcome.

Confident with what he was about to do, he poured half the contents of his glass down his throat and let it register. The more he thought about what he was going to do, the funnier he found his idea to be. Once the warm feeling settled into his gut and he felt himself getting excited, pushing himself away from his table and casually strolled over to the couple of interest. There was one empty seat at their table where he took it upon himself to sit in. "Hi, Leroy, how have you been?" McAlister asked as he slapped him on his back.

The transgender squinted her eyes and drew his head back in surprise. "Excuse me, there must be some kind of mistake," he told McAlister. "My name is Samantha," he added.

"No, Leroy, I don't know why you're trying to fool this dear man by telling him your name is Samantha, but we both know the real deal, don't we?"

"What the hell is going on here?" the guy who had been sitting at the table, looking flabbergasted asked.

"What's going on here is that Leroy is Leroy, or Sam maybe, but not Samantha," McAlister answered. "Here, let me show you what I mean." Swiftly, he reached up and pulled a wig away from Samantha's head. It was clear that the perpetrator was a man. He tried to retrieve his wig, but McAlister held it tight with a big smile plastered on his face. The guy sitting at the table with them sat there with his mouth open in total shock. The next thing that happened was the exact reaction that McAlister had hoped for. It was the whole reason he had decided to pull the prank.

The shocked man gritted his teeth and grimaced at the he-she. "You son of a bitch!" he said, right before punching him in the face. It was a hard punch with his body behind it. The punch knocked him out of his seat and onto the floor, making a loud thud that captured the attention of at least half of the people sitting near them. McAlister began a hearty laugh. The guy who had punched the transgender then kicked him in the gut which made him fold his knees up to his torso.

Blood was pouring from his nose. As two bouncers ran to the guy who had elicited the violence and lifted him up underneath his armpits until his feet were dangling off the floor. He didn't struggle as they took him out of the club. "Damned cross-dresser!" the guy was yelling as they carried him out.

Jeanette made it off the dance floor before McAlister returned to their table. A disoriented look came over her face when she got there. "Mac, what are you doing over there? This is our table here, isn't it?" she asked.

McAlister was still giggly about the incident. "Did you see what happened over here?" McAlister asked.

"I came over because I saw trouble brewing and wanted to stop it, but I was a little too late. What was it all about?" Jeanette asked.

"Oh, just that a guy and girl were sitting here and the guy told her that she looked an awful lot like a man. That's when I stepped into the picture and said, 'Let's see.' I lifted the wig away from the girl's head and we found out that the girl was actually a guy. The other guy got mad and knocked the piss out of the pretender and there you have it."

"Wow!" Jeanette said excitedly. "Imagine what might have happened if you guys hadn't made that discovery. The guy that they kicked out might have gone home with the transgender. That's scary," Jeanette said as she took her seat. McAlister rejoined her at the table.

Jeanette fumbled with the straw in her fresh drink and then brought it up to her lips for a sip. She must have remembered that she had discarded the straw from her last drink because she quickly got rid of her new one. "What's wrong with the straw?" McAlister asked. "Too slow for you?"

"Yeah," Jeanette answered, "too restricting."

The disc jockey put a slow song on the turntable and Jeanette agreed to dance with McAlister. On the floor, he held her very close, causing each of their hormones to flourish. "Think you can down that drink fast so we can get the hell out of here?" McAlister asked.

"We can leave now if you want to," she replied. They danced the rest of the dance in silence. On the way out, Jeanette told McAlister that she wanted to stop and talk to the doorman.

McAlister figured that she meant Goliath. "I'll go to the car and let it warm up while you talk to him," he said.

McAlister didn't look at Goliath as he walked past him on the way out. He sat in the Escort with the engine idling for about ten minutes before Jeanette came running out as though she were in a hurry. She had a big smile on her face as she got into the car. "I had a pretty good time tonight," she said. "I want to thank you for bringing me out."

"I enjoyed it, myself," McAlister said as he placed the car in gear.

Back at the apartment, Jeanette was still in a good mood. She was humming a tune that McAlister didn't recognize. "Why are you so pepped up? He asked her as they got undressed.

"I've got a date with Robert," she answered.

"A date with who?" he asked as if he had not heard the name, although he did.

"Robert Sullivan, the guy working the door," she told him. "We were classmates in school, but I never really got to know him well. We're just going to go on a friendly lunch date one day next week."

So Goliath's name was really Robert Sullivan. McAlister preferred to refer to him still as Goliath. The name had already soaked into his mind and it was there to stay. "Was Goliath that big when you guys were in high school?" he asked her.

"He was just a wee bit smaller," she replied. She spread her thumb and index finger just barely apart and held the gesture up to emphasize that it was only a wee bit.

"I'd hate to run into him in a dark alley," McAlister said. "He looks like he doesn't take any prisoners."

As Jeanette took off her primary clothing, she inspected her eyes up close in the bedroom mirrors. "Robert was pretty quiet in school," she said. "He didn't hang out with anyone in particular when I knew him. I don't think he would harm a fly," she added.

"He probably wouldn't," McAlister said in response to her statement. "You know, though, that it's the quiet types that you have to be careful with," he added, sounding as though he were an authority on the subject. He also offered, "You know that when a person generally keeps things bottled up inside, it's like they're a time bomb capable of exploding at any time."

"Robert is level headed as far as I can tell," Jeanette said, already down to her bra and panties.

McAlister started taking his clothes off as well. "He told me that he works as an engineer during the day. The club is just an outlet for him. He gets to meet people that way, and he finds it very relaxing as well."

"Enough about him," McAlister said. "I want to focus all of my energy on you." He had managed to shed all of his clothing with the exception of his underwear. Jeanette still had her back to him, inspecting herself in the mirror. McAlister stepped up close behind her and wrapped his arms around her waist. The way her waist tapered felt good to him. His erectness felt good to her backside.

McAlister flicked his tongue and maneuvered it slowly around the sides of her neck, causing her to fling her head back in a wanting way. "You like that, don't you?" he whispered in her ear. He licked the same ear that he had whispered into, along the edges. "You like that, too, don't you?" he added.

"Yes," she moaned. Slowly McAlister caressed her breasts, still contained in her bra, feeling her nipples harden between his fingers. Her head began to swing slowly and methodically from side to side. As he started maneuvering his tongue along the small of her back, he reached up with his hands and unsnapped her bra. He pushed what was hanging loosely away from her shoulders and paid little attention to it when it hit the floor.

Jeanette felt her legs begin to weaken and supported herself by placing her hands out in front of her against the mirror she was looking into. McAlister cupped his hands around the front of her thighs and gingerly gripped them for a few seconds before sliding them along the length of her thighs. He had dropped down to his knees and found himself accessible to the area just below the bottom of her panties stretching to lick the back of her thighs. Jeanette was writhing back and forth, just barely in control.

Removing Jeanette's panties was aphrodisiacal to McAlister. He could feel his prowess rising to a new height. Jeanette planted herself more firmly as McAlister's tongue roved back and forth over the entire length of both of her legs. Not able to take anymore, he removed the only garments left between them then picked her up and placed her on the bed where they had captivated the electricity and turned it into a united explosion.

Fortunately, McAlister had been wise enough to set the alarm slightly before dozing off to sleep. The suddenness jolted him to consciousness the following morning. Jeanette lay undaunted by it. The drinking they had done made it difficult to pull away from the bed, but unlike her, McAlister had grown accustomed to it. She was mildly snoring when McAlister's feet touched the floor.

Before getting dressed, McAlister shook Jeanette to life, which wasn't easy. She had been sleeping very soundly. When she finally woke up, she moved about the room unenthusiastically mentioning that her head was pounding. McAlister assumed that it was logical because she did not regularly drink.

McAlister prepared a Highball and turned on the television to the morning news while he waited for her. On the television, one of the city reporters held a microphone in front of The Weasel. The topic was the transgender murders. The reporter interviewing The Weasel asked if the police department had been making any progress in the case. The Weasel told him that they were stymied at first. Now a few things had begun to develop just a little, but nothing that would merit having a locked up case.

Jeanette came into the room just as the interview ended. She looked a little better than when she first got out of bed, but she still wasn't all smiles. "What was all that about?" she asked.

"Just about those murders that have been taking place recently," he said calmly. "Are you ready to go?" he asked.

"Not really, but I guess we must," Jeanette answered. "I could probably use about eight more hours of sleep, but let's go if we must."

At about the time that McAlister's feet hit the floor, so did The Weasel's. He was very systematic in everything he approached. A product of a military father, it was instilled in him that the early bird catches the worm and nothing comes to sleepers but a dream. He even made it a habit to rise early on his days off as well as holidays. It generally drove his wife crazy.

CHAPTER 20

Thomas Dash had set his watch alarm to go off at exactly 5:30 a.m. He figured that doing so would allow him enough time to rise before The Weasel did. Trying to sleep in his car had been difficult because it had gotten quite cold during the night, surprisingly so. Now he was glad that he had set his alarm so early because there was a light on in The Weasel's house.

Dash looked in his rearview mirror and then glanced around in all other directions before opening his car door to dispose of the urine in a milk container he had used to relieve himself before falling to sleep. He shook the container hard to rid as many excess drops as possible before replacing it under the seat of his Chevrolet Blazer. After checking his appearance in the inside visor mirror, he hoped he didn't look as bad as he felt. He wished that McAlister would have given him some idea of how long he wanted The Weasel tailed.

In The Weasel's bedroom, his wife lay snoring away in bed as he showered himself awake. He had already made his stop in the kitchen to turn the coffee maker on before doing so. As he showered, he thought about the murders. They had to be stopped. It was obvious to him that whoever was killing them had a hatred for them. What bothered him was that there wasn't much consistency in the time between the killings. If there was, he would try to set the killer up by planting decoys.

He didn't take much care in picking out his clothes for the day. In his closet, he had pants hung in a section together, shirts together, coats next, and then ties and accessories last. The clothes in his drawers were all folded neatly and ordered by item as well. He grabbed a pair of Christmas green slacks and a striped blue shirt to accompany it. The tie he retrieved from the closet was a paisley design of green and blue. It would have looked good with a carefully chosen outfit.

After getting dressed, but neglecting to comb his hair, he went into the kitchen and prepared his coffee with sugar but no cream. Once it was to his liking, he left the kitchen and took a seat in the den after turning the television to news. There was nothing he cared to hear about reported in the news. After downing his cup of coffee, he returned to the bedroom and planted a kiss on his wife's cheek as she slept soundly. He figured she would probably be asleep when he returned home since she spent most of her time sleeping, watching soaps, and spending his hard earned money on clothes for herself. He felt she deserved it for being with him as beautiful as she was. There wasn't anything he wouldn't do for her, but if he knew that she had two other lovers, he might have thought otherwise.

Dash ducked low in his seat as The Weasel exited his home. He wasn't too likely to be seen, but he had made it a point early in his career to always be extra careful. It was a priority that had helped him stay alive up to that time. Dash wished he had the cup of coffee he was sure The Weasel carried in his thermos to his car. What else would anyone drink so early in the morning?

While they drove he was careful to stay a good distance behind The Weasel so that he would not alert him to the fact that he was being followed. A good detective could usually feel when he was being followed because he generally tailed people himself. It wasn't hard for Dash to keep an eye on The Weasel because it was hard to lose track of a beat up faded lime green AMC Gremlin.

Dash thought it was appropriate that The Weasel drove such a car. Everything else about him said second rate. Everything except his success at his job, even if he did piss nearly everyone off whom he came in contact with. He was not surprised that The Weasel's first stop was at the station. He waited outside while The Weasel was briefed. As time passed, he watched the city come slowly to life. Traffic increased minute after minute.

Chapter 21

McAlister opened the office and let Jeanette through first. "Would you care for some coffee?" he asked her. "I know you feel like crap this morning and I don't expect a whole lot of production from you. We all have our moments when we indulge in more than we can handle. I don't fit into that category, myself, but I do understand," he joked.

McAlister managed to illicit a laugh from her. "What do we have going on today?" he asked.

"Not a whole lot," she answered. "With today being Friday, I don't feel like doing anything anyhow," she added. "I suppose, since Leroy Foster's case is next Friday, we should call him up and have him come by so that you can rehearse with him for the trial. I'm sure he's going to be a little frightened.

"Good idea," McAlister said in response. "Call him at about 9:00 a.m.; he'll probably be up by then. I'm sure he hasn't been sleeping so well these days."

McAlister paused for a moment. "Guess what you forgot to get from downstairs?" he asked in realization.

"What?" Jeanette asked, sounding groggy.

"The morning paper, how could you forget?"

"I wasn't in the mood to remember," she answered, sounding almost resentful. "If you have to have it, I'm on my way downstairs to get it," she told him.

She started to head for the door. "Get back here," he said. "I'll get it myself. I had no idea that you were feeling as bad as you are."

"Mac, I feel like my head has been run over by a train. Now I know why I don't drink – it's not worth it."

While McAlister made the trip downstairs, Jeanette turned on the coffee pot and let the coffee brew and then plopped her body down on the office couch. It only took a few seconds before she started dozing. Rest, she was sure would make it better. She was sound asleep when McAlister returned to the office. He shook his head upon sight of her. "Looks like I have it by myself today," he said out loud. There was no response from as she slept silently.

****

Dash followed The Weasel to McAlister's former address where he had once lived with his wife, Kelly, and son, Dane. Dash parked his vehicle on the opposite side of the street, a few houses up from Kelly's. He watched as The Weasel knocked on the door several times before returning to his car at a brisk pace. Dash could see from where he was that The Weasel picked up his radio and made a call. After he finished his call, he replaced the receiver and started the car. Dash started his simultaneously.

From Kelly's house, Dash followed The Weasel downtown. Once they were there, The Weasel drove slowly observing the people who walked about the city sidewalks. Dash wondered what he was looking for, but he quickly found out when The Weasel pulled his car to the side of the street and got out. He stopped a passerby, who had been walking down the sidewalk.

The person he stopped quite apparently was a tranny. The transgendered man shook her head "no" from time to time. The entire interview lasted five minutes. The Weasel returned to his car and looked for an opening in traffic. Dash closed his notepad after jotting down an insertion and started behind The Weasel.

****

It was quiet in the office, except an occasional snore from Jeanette as McAlister scanned over the newspaper, but there was nothing of real interest in the paper. He sipped his coffee and pushed thoughts through his head as to what he could do to relieve the boredom. He was startled when the telephone rang. "Mr. Johnson, this is Brenda downstairs. There is a woman down here that says she would like to see you if possible."

"Send her up," he told the receptionist. As an old habit, McAlister pulled his pen from his inside coat pocket and began tapping his desk with it. It was a reaction customarily due to anticipation in his case. He wondered what could be so urgent and was surprised to see the woman who walked through the door was not a woman at all.

McAlister could see that the person was somewhat confused that there was no one available to receive her at the front portion of the complex. "Back here!" McAlister yelled out to her. The person extended her neck as if looking to see where the voice was coming from. She made her way back to him. "May I help you?" McAlister asked her, his voice almost shaky due to the overwhelming circumstances.

"Yes, you may," the woman said, still standing.

McAlister offered her the seat in front of his desk, which she gladly accepted. She sat down and crossed her legs in a very feminine way. She had to be at least six feet, four inches tall. Her jaw line was very pronounced and she had a strong chin that accompanied it. McAlister could make out a few whiskers starting to protrude from the chin of the woman who sat across from him. It was absurd that anyone would mistake her for a real woman. "Do you mind if I smoke?" she asked.

"Go right ahead, I smoke so I don't see why you shouldn't." She reached into the purse she had been carrying over her right shoulder and retrieved a cigarette from its pack. As she stuck one into her mouth, McAlister lit it.

"My name is Barbara Davis," she said relinquishing the smoke after a big draw. "I think I may need some legal help. Well, as a matter of fact, I know I need some legal help," she corrected. "You see, I killed a man, but it was in defense."

McAlister tried not to show any sign of shock. He excused himself to get another cup of coffee. When he returned to his seat, the woman was bouncing her crossed upper leg nervously. "How did this happen?" he asked.

"You have to excuse my forwardness, but you see, I make my living from the streets," the big woman said. "I'm a high priced hooker. I know that what I do is dangerous, but it pays the bills."

McAlister doubted that she was high priced. There was nothing special about her that he could see would make a man want to pay a high price. She was just pumping herself up to be sure. "I get all kinds of strange men that proposition me. It would be crazy of me to be with all of them, so you see, I'm very selective about who I spend my valuable time with. I can usually tell who has money and who doesn't."

"One night, I was standing out on the streets and this good looking gentleman pulled up to the curb where I was, driving a dark colored stretch Lincoln Town car. He rolled his window down and summoned me. He told me he was looking for a lady to spend the evening with back at his place and flashed some big bills at me and told me that it would be worth at least three hundred dollars if I would go along. Of course, I got in the car with him. "Before long, we were at his place. He had a nice bachelor pad, well furnished. While I made myself comfortable, he put on some sort of music and poured us a glass each of cognac. I sipped mine slowly while I listened to him talk about growing up in a rough neighborhood, but overcoming the odds by educating himself and working hard. I admire good rags to riches stories…"

The Weasel waited in his beat up car outside of McAlister's building. Thomas Dash waited across the street from him, wondering why he was paying so much attention to McAlister. Surely, he didn't suspect him for the transgender murders. Why else would The Weasel put so much time into investigating McAlister. Dash hoped that McAlister was clean.

He would eventually have to give up his gravy job working for him if he wasn't.

Dash figured that by The Weasel sending the tranny up to McAlister's office, he was setting him up. He was definitely one smart cop. Dash had seen through the years that a lot of cops waited for results. The real good ones produced results when the heat was on. Dash realized that The Weasel was one that could be learned from.

The hooker continued her story. "My gentleman began to explore my body with his hands, but I kept him at bay by slapping his hands from time to time to keep him from touching me where I wasn't ready to be touched. He told me that I was trying to play hard to get, which I was, but only to add to the excitement. Well, he must not have found it exciting to be brushed off that way because he got pissed off, which amused me even more."

"So, what happened next?" McAlister asked.

"All of a sudden, the excitement changed for me. A dangerous expression came over his face. There was a mad look in his eyes. He started reaching into his pocket and I sensed that what he was going to pull out would not be a banana – I was right. It was as long as a banana though. He had one of the largest switchblades on him that I have ever seen."

McAlister's heart was racing madly within his chest. He was trying his best to be cool, but was afraid that Barbara could hear his heart beat at an unusual pace and intensity. What he was being told was so familiar to him. It was like a play in which he had been the lead actor on several occasions. "I keep a little .25 automatic on me at all times," Barbara said. "I rely heavily upon it to rescue me in bad situations. I never had a need to use it until my gentleman pulled the surprise on me," she added.

'You were going to pull a surprise on him,' McAlister thought to himself. *'He was just ahead of you at the game,'* he added to the thought. "I know my little .25 caught him by surprise," Barbara continued. "The shocked look on his face told me that. I felt very powerful, surprising him. In a sick way, it felt very good."

'You're a sick person,' McAlister thought. "I didn't expect things to go any farther than that. I figured that the gun would make him nervous and he would high-tail it out of his own place, but he didn't. I guess he had his pride."

"He looked at the gun for a long time while I pointed it at him. Neither of us said a word. I looked at him while he looked at the gun. Then, he tried something very stupid."

"What was that?" McAlister asked as he lit a cigarette, shuffling around in his seat as if his butt were getting sore.

"He reached for the gun," Barbara said. "The dumbass reached for my gun. I had to waste him."

"McAlister tried to imagine how he would have reacted if he had been the other guy in the situation. He probably would have tried to get the gun, too. He reasoned that he probably would have gotten killed as well. The idea of the transgendered men he had killed having guns had not even registered to him before. McAlister realized that in the future, he had to account for his victim being partially prepared by having a gun. Better yet, he assumed that he had better buy a gun for himself.

Barbara was silent, looking at McAlister, awaiting a reaction. He took a couple draws from his cigarette and then extinguished it after it was only halfway done. He stood and began to pace the floor. He stuck his hands in his pants pockets as he did so. "We do have a case of self defense here, but we also have a problem," McAlister said.

"What kind of problem?" Barbara asked.

"The gun," McAlister replied, "You were carrying it illegally. Besides that, you were engaging in an illegal activity at the time of the act. Prostitution is illegal, you know."

"I'm well aware of that," Barbara said. "I have something that I must admit to."

"Which is?"

"My real name is not Barbara."

"Then what is it?"

"It's Bob," she said.

"Bob!" McAlister repeated his eyebrows rose as if he were half shocked. He was somewhat surprised, but not at the name. He was shocked that she came out and gave her male name, her true name. "You mean Bob like a man's name?" he questioned.

"Yes, I mean Bob like a man's name!" she exclaimed. "I'm really a man."

McAlister stopped pacing the floor and stood directly in front of Bob with his mouth open wide enough for something to enter it. He was doing a good job of pretending. Bob felt better that he had done such a great job of hiding his gender. McAlister closed his mouth and stuck his bottom lip out. He quickly tilted his head to the side and then back to its original position. "Oh well isn't this a trip,' Bob laughed. "You sure had me fooled," McAlister lied. "I thought you were a woman all along. You're one of those transistors… I mean, transgendered," McAlister said correcting himself. Bob laughed at his little joke.

The Weasel sat in his car, marveling at how innovative he was. He realized that McAlister could find out that the woman he had sent up to his office actually had not killed anyone at all. He was interested in what McAlister's reaction would be to Bob, figuring that he was right about McAlister being the murderer. The Weasel actually expected McAlister to make some type of attempt on Bob's life.

Dash was patiently sitting in his Blazer, keeping his attention focused on The Weasel. He kind of liked the fact that he was being paid double for such easy work. Whatever reason he was assigned to keeping tabs on The

Weasel must be an important one. Dash could tell that from the way The Weasel had his head tilted down and was writing notes on a pad.

In the office, McAlister had quit pacing the floor and retaken his seat. He pulled a personal information form from his desk drawers and sat it atop his desk. He wrote down Bob's full name on the form and then began asking him questions pertinent to completing the form. The main thing he was interested in was Bob's address.

Bob gave him the information as he asked for it and upon completing the form, McAlister located a blank folder in which to file it and stuffed it inside. He then placed it on an empty spot atop his desk. He explained to Bob that it would be wise for him to turn himself in to the police. He instructed Bob to only tell the authorities about the crime and no one else and to give him a call when they were ready to interrogate him and he would come down to the station to accompany him. With the understanding between them, Bob left the office.

Bob stood outside The Weasel's car and spoke with him briefly. Dash observed The Weasel passing some currency off to him and wondered how much money it was and exactly what services had been performed. He was sure that whatever had been done had to do with McAlister.

Bob walked away from The Weasel's car content with how he had carried out the assignment. The Weasel started his car and drove off after Bob walked away. Dash duplicated The Weasel's action. They drove at a normal pace, but Dash noticed that The Weasel was not heading for any particular course as they made turns from street to street and gave no clear sense of direction. Dash figured that either The Weasel must have spotted him or he didn't have any specific place to go at the time. The latter was correct. The Weasel simply had no particular destination in mind.

McAlister called down to the morgue to find out if they had found any dead bodies recently. No one had been found that would fit the identity of the person Bob had killed. He had a weird feeling about Bob and felt that something was amiss about him. There was nothing that he could put his finger on, but he didn't feel secure about the conversation they had shared.

Jeanette began to groan back to consciousness. Her head was pounding uncontrollably. The light in the room made her head hurt even more, but she was finished sleeping. She decided that after a few cups of coffee, she would feel much better. Her first cup didn't help much, but it was a definite start. "Well, well, it's alive," McAlister said. "It's about time. I've been pretty busy this morning. I even have a new client, a very weird one though," he told her. "The guy came in here in drag."

"You mean a man came here dressed as a woman?" Jeanette asked, shocked, but expressionless.

"Sure did," McAlister answered. "Supposedly, he murdered someone in self-defense, but the police don't know about it yet. I called down to the station and they haven't had any report of a body found. How are you feeling?"

"Like shit," she answered. "I think I'm going on the wagon for about a year," she said holding her hand to the side of her head momentarily to support it.

"There are a few things that you can do to help yourself recover," McAlister advised.

"Oh yeah and what's that?" Jeanette's tone of voice was sarcastic.

"Well, if you want to, you can run out and buy yourself some eggs."

"What for?" she asked, her eyebrows rose.

"Drinking raw eggs will help restore the nutrients to your brain."

"Oh, and what other bright ideas do you have?"

"Tomato juice is always good."

"For some reason, I can go along with that," Jeanette said as she prepared her second cup of coffee.

"Jen, remind me when we leave today, I need to run by Kelly's place and get some clothes. I kind of miss them, you know? My clothes, that is."

"You don't miss your son?" she asked.

"Of course I miss my son. What do you think that I'm heartless or something?" McAlister exclaimed. The expression on his face was serious.

"It was just a question; don't jump down my throat about it. Aren't we getting a little bit sensitive?" Jeanette said, her eyes bulging. "Mac, I think I'm going to gather myself and go through all of the files to make sure they are updated."

She left the area and started her work. On her desk, she saw Leroy Foster's court date and hoped the best for him. According to McAlister, it would be a pretty simple case. In her opinion, there were no simple cases. Anything could happen. McAlister thumped his desk with his fingers as he sat thinking about everything that was going on in his life. "What a mess," he said to himself. "I'm married, separated, a murderer, sometimes a crooked lawyer, and I haven't tried to do much to change any of it. I've got people depending on me to help get their lives straight and I can't even find the time to get my own life together."

He pulled another cigarette from the pack and lit it. The first drag on it helped to calm his thoughts. He held the lit cigarette out inspecting it, watching the smoke evaporate into the air. "What a disgusting habit," he said out loud, but didn't extinguish the cigarette.

"Well, let's see...What do I have going on that takes priority? The Foster case!" He said out loud as if a light had come on in his head. He grabbed the legal pad that was in the corner of his desk and pulled it closer to him so that he could write on it. He wrote "Leroy Foster" at the top of the page.

First, he wrote biological information about him, including everything he knew about his family history. "No prior serious criminal activity," he wrote in parentheses. Through investigation by Dash, he had found out that Leroy was an extremely hard worker. His former employers praised his work performance.

Then, McAlister wrote down the crime that had been committed and why it was speculated that Leroy committed the crime. Next, he wrote that the store attendant had said he was sure that it was Leroy who had robbed him, but to him, all blacks looked alike. McAlister placed an asterisk beside that note as an indication of a strong point in the case. Lastly, he wrote down that there were a couple of witnesses that could testify that Leroy was not the person who had robbed the convenient store.

After McAlister finished writing his notes, he read over them to be sure that he was satisfied with what he had written. He was confident that he didn't omit anything. He held his pen to his temple for a while, contemplating whether or not he should call Leroy and have him come into the office so that he could tell him the truth about the method by which the witnesses were gained. Dismissing the idea, he decided that it was not smart to let innocent people know his methods.

Jeanette popped her head into his space and alerted him that lunchtime had arrived. She told him that she wasn't going to lunch because she still had a massive headache. McAlister pushed away from the desk and headed for the door. When he passed Jeanette, she had a book in her hand and was sitting down at her desk. "Still reading that romance novel?" he asked.

"Every chance I get," she replied.

"It will probably help soothe your head," he told her.

McAlister was out in a flash. The destination he had in mind was the convenience store that Leroy was accused of robbing. The traffic during the lunch hour was always frustrating. He had learned some time ago to just enjoy the sights along the way and remain patient.

The store was in a heavily populated area. McAlister could not believe that anyone would have the guts to rob a store in such a visible area, but there wasn't much that criminals did that made much sense to him. He parked his Escort in front of the door of the store. Arrogantly he approached the store attendant and could tell from first sight of the man that he was the person Leroy had described to him as the accuser.

The guy was tall and dingy looking. It looked as though he knew nothing about showering or combing his hair. His skin on his face was oily and pimply. The first thing McAlister thought of when he approached the man was the comment he had made about all blacks looking alike. 'What a real jerk this guy must be,' he thought to himself as he extended his hand for the man to shake.

McAlister introduced himself as Leroy's lawyer. The man slowly backed away from McAlister as though he had just been told the man had hepatitis. "So you're the lawyer for the guy who robbed me?" he said roughly.

"No!" McAlister said, "I'm the lawyer for the kid who you accused of robbing you. By the way, I never did catch your name."

"It's Robert Reiner," the man answered gruffly, not looking at McAlister.

"Mr. Reiner, I'll bet that if I did a credit check on you I would find your credit is messed up pretty bad, wouldn't I? As a matter of fact, I probably should investigate you. You know, check to see if you have a police record."

Robert looked nervous at the mention of being investigated. "You know Leroy didn't rob this store, don't you? I think what really happened is that you have a dire need for money, so you decided to take money and report the absence of cash as a robbery, didn't you?"

Mr. Reiner was silent. There was nothing he could think to say right away. McAlister sensed from the silence that he had struck a nerve. He had only wanted to rattle the man, but he could see that his speculation held some weight. This was an angle that he wished he had considered earlier.

Robert turned his back to McAlister and started fiddling with items on the shelf behind him. He was extremely nervous and McAlister could tell. "Nobody robbed this place at all, did they? You took the money and told the cops you had been robbed by some black kid that you just happened to see walking by the store. That kid just so happened to be my client, Leroy Foster. Admit it! You did it, didn't you?!"

The clerk just kept fiddling with the items on the shelf. "Look," McAlister said. If you admit it, you will probably get off with probation if you've never been in any kind of trouble. But if you don't, I'll see to it that I nail you for it. You did it, didn't you?!"

"Yes, damn-it, I did it!" Robert said, spinning around quickly, looking infuriated. "I did it because my family needed things! They needed food and clothes. I'd do it again if I had to! You probably never had a want for anything, have you?" Robert said as though he really knew all that McAlister had been through in all of his life.

McAlister thought about the time he spent in prison and wanted to tell Robert about what it was really like to want. He decided it wasn't a proper time to do so. "Yes, I know what it's like to want and need," he told him. "I know well what it's like."

Robert calmed down some. He hung his head and said, "I only have an eighth grade education. I can't get a job making good money. I have a wife and four children. All I want for my kids is that they get a good education – a lot better than I got. I want them to go to school wearing good clothes and not have to worry about whether they will have dinner or not. I know what it's like to go to school wearing ragged clothes and hungry. It doesn't feel good."

"Where does your wife work?" McAlister asked feeling a bit subdued.

Robert took a seat on a high stool he had set up behind the cash register. Time elapsed after McAlister's question. "She doesn't," Robert answered, looking up into McAlister's eyes.

"Why not?" McAlister asked.

"Because I don't believe that my woman should have to work," Robert answered. The sympathy that McAlister felt for Robert's situation quickly vanished. *'How stupid can this guy be?'* he asked himself. *'His wife has a royal idiot on her hands.'*

"Do you think that you make so much money your woman doesn't have to work?" he asked.

"My woman will not work as long as she is with me," Robert boasted.

McAlister realized that if he got heavily involved in a conversation with Robert, he would be wasting valuable time. He picked up the telephone beside the cash register and started dialing the number to the police station. "I'm calling the police, okay? They will come get you and book you. You may be able to sign a recognizance bond since you have never been arrested."

"Wrong," Robert said. "You were right when you said earlier that I probably have a police record."

"Well, you'll find a way to have bond posted – maybe a bondsman or something."

A female voice answered the other end of the receiver. "Police department, may I help you?" the voice said.

"Yes, you may," McAlister said into the receiver.

Quickly, he asked Robert what the store number was. "It's 56," Robert said, looking remorseful.

"You need to send a car down to the convenience store number 56 on Arlington Road to pick up the store attendant, Robert Reiner, who is turning himself in for embezzling store money. How soon can you have a car down here?" he asked the woman.

"Within five minutes," she told him.

During the five minutes that they waited for the squad car, Robert called the store manager and explained the situation to him. He told McAlister that the manager would get there as soon as possible. A squad car pulled up with two policemen right at the five minute mark. McAlister recognized both of the policemen from court appearances. He knew them both by name and joked around with them when he saw them. "Well, look at what the cat dragged in," he started, laughing all along. Now I feel safe."

"You're just jealous," the youngest looking of the two said, smiling and showing a mouthful of pearly whites.

"Yeah, why don't you give up all that money you're making and come do some real work?" his partner said.

"Well, what do we have here?" the youngest cop asked.

"Do you remember when this store was robbed about nine months ago and a young kid whose name is Leroy Foster was fingered for it?" McAlister asked.

"Yeah, I remember," said the older cop.

"Your true perpetrator is the man behind that counter," McAlister said, nodding his head toward Robert. "He is going to cooperate in return for a deal."

Reaching into his coat pocket, McAlister pulled out one of his business cards and gave it to Robert who approached the policemen with his hands out in front of him in a motion that offered them a chance to place handcuffs on him. "Put them behind your back for me," the youngest cop said. He retrieved a pair of handcuffs from his belt and put them around Robert's wrists.

CHAPTER 22

The loud ring of the telephone startled him to consciousness. It was lying at the end of the couch on which he sat. He picked up the receiver on the third ring. "Mac, how are you?" the voice on the other end asked.

Glimpsing at his watch, he saw that it was 9:00 p.m. exactly. Dash had always been prompt. "I could be better,"

"You and I both," Dash answered. "I've been tailing The Weasel all day and to tell the truth, I'm beat."

"Where is he now?" McAlister asked.

"I'm sitting out in front of his house at the moment. I hope he's in for the night. I need some shut eye. I'll probably take a nap after I get off the phone with you."

"That's a good idea. Fill me in on what's going on with our man."

"Well, I tracked him this morning to an area downtown. I watched him observe the pedestrian sidewalks briefly, and then he got out of his car. He stopped some weirdo who had been walking down the sidewalk. I don't know if he knew her."

"What do you mean weirdo?" McAlister asked.

"The woman he talked to looked like she could have been a man. They talked for about five minutes."

Suddenly, McAlister understood the visit he had from Barbara at the office. He was sure that if he did a follow up on Barbara, he would find out that her story had been fabricated. "What else did you observe?" McAlister asked, feeling sure that he was right about Barbara.

"What I tell you next may piss you off," Dash said.

"Why is that?" McAlister wanted to know.

"He picked the lock on the apartment door that you are living in."

McAlister's heart thumped hard. His thoughts became disoriented as he tried to figure out what it was that The Weasel could have been interested in finding. Then, he remembered the knife. "Mac, are you still there?" Dash was asking into the telephone.

"Yeah, sure, I'm here," McAlister said, snapping out of the train of thought he had been in. "Is there anything else, Thomas that you can think of?" McAlister asked.

"Not right off the bat," Dash answered. Then, he suddenly remembered that The Weasel had given the stranger some money after he had left McAlister's office. "Wait a minute - yeah I witnessed The Weasel give your stranger some money after she left your office. How much? I don't know."

"How tall was this weirdo that you saw him talk to?" McAlister asked.

"About six foot three or four, somewhere around there," Dash answered.

'Bingo,' McAlister said to himself, he was sure that The Weasel was trying to set him up. "Are you sure that The Weasel is at home?" McAlister asked.

"I'm sitting outside of his house right now. I doubt if he will be going anywhere."

"Good," said McAlister. "Very good work, stay on top of him. I'll talk to you again at the same time tomorrow night.

Jeanette, who had been reading her book, could not help but overhear McAlister as he spoke with Thomas Dash. She folded the corner of the page she was reading and closed the book. "Mac, what's going on?" she asked. Her face looked inquisitive.

"Do you remember that weird looking detective that came into the office a few days ago?" He waited for her answer.

"Yes, the very strange man. How could I forget him?" Jeanette said.

"Well, it seems that Mr. Weirdo has been a very busy man. For reasons I don't understand, he has been very concerned about me."

"What do you mean?" Jeanette asked as she sat up straight in her seat.

"Thomas informed me that he was here today checking the apartment out."

"Do you mean to say that he broke into my apartment and searched around for something?"

"I mean exactly that."

"He has no right breaking into my apartment. I'm going to call the police. She stood up and started for the telephone. McAlister stopped her before she could get to it.

"Now just cool out. Don't go calling the police. I can handle this. There's no need to get the cops involved in this thing."

Jeanette took her seat back, feeling somewhat squelched about getting upset. "What do you suppose he was looking for?" she asked.

"I have no idea," McAlister lied. "Don't get too worried about him coming back in here. I don't think he found what he was looking for. I'm going to go out for a few drinks. Care to join me?" he asked, hoping she would say no. He almost wished he had not asked the question the moment after he asked her. If she said yes, it would destroy his plans for the evening.

"No, I'm pretty wrapped up in this book and there's not much left of it for me to read. I'm just over my hangover anyway. Go ahead and enjoy yourself."

McAlister downed the rest of his drink and remembered that his sport coat was still lying on the bed. He returned to hang it up in the closet and exchange it for one that matched the clothes that he was wearing. Before hanging it, he reached inside the hidden pocket and removed his switchblade. He put the knife in his pants pocket. A dark brown coat that hung in the closet matched the clothes he was wearing well.

On his way out of the apartment, he saw that Jeanette was still reading intensely. She did not look up as he walked by. "Don't wait up for me," he told her.

"I'll be out like a light when you return." He shut the door softly behind him so that he would not disturb her. Stepping out into the night air, he found that it was a beautiful night. Not too extreme either way as far as temperature went. As he started his car, he debated as to where he would go. He was frequenting The Phoenix way too much, he thought, but it was one place that he was sure to find a date. He felt as though he was pushing his luck. He would try it there if he could not find a date by cruising the streets downtown.

McAlister found the streets to be quite busy for as late as it was getting to be. Cruising the streets slowly, he saw that there were all sorts of activities taking place. He saw drug deals in mid transaction, a drunk being rolled, and street corner hookers soliciting their goods. The type of woman he was looking for, he saw sporadically from time to time, sometimes by themselves, and at other times, they were hanging together. His best bet, he concluded, would be to get one of the ones that walked alone. As he passed a group of three, he saw a loner about three hundred feet away, leaning on a light post. He accelerated toward her, hoping that when he got to where she was that he would not be disappointed.

As the car neared her, he could tell that he was in luck. The woman had distinguishing characteristics that he learned to look for that hinted that she was actually a man. Large hands and foot sizes were generally indicative of males. They were the first things that he looked for. He also looked to see if she had hairy arms, overly muscular legs, a chiseled face, or if he just had a gut feeling.

As he approached her, he slowed until he was parallel to where she stood. She pushed herself away from the pole as he rolled the passenger window down. McAlister thought that she looked quite alluring in her attire, which was all black. She had on a leather miniskirt and black satin blouse with a low neckline that made it look as though she had succulent breasts. "How much to party with you?" McAlister asked.

"Fifty dollars," she said, leaning through the window of his car. Her voice was raspy, also indicating that she was male.

"Get in!" McAlister said authoritatively. She looked around in both directions, making sure that she wasn't being watched the police. It was a habit she had learned early in her profession, McAlister assumed.

"You sure are a good looking hunk," the woman said.

McAlister knew that she probably told all of her customers that or paid them some type of compliment that made them feel special. Of course, some men ate it up while others could read into it as bullshit. It registered as just that with him. "You're quite the prize, yourself," McAlister lied.

The whole scene was repulsive to him, but he felt he had to endure it to get things to go smoothly. Too much time in silence, he thought, allowed too much time for doubt. The hotel he took her to was the location he chose since it was the first one that he came to without having to drive all over town. Before checking in, he told his passenger to stay in the car. He found the inside of the lobby of the hotel to be rather tranquil. There was only the attendant behind the check counter. It was unusually quiet, he thought, almost eerie.

After he had filled out the necessary paperwork, he gave the attendant forty-three dollars cash for a night's stay, and then went back to the car where the woman he had picked up was waiting patiently. He motioned for her to roll her window down so that he could talk to her. She complied. "Look, I'm low on cash," he said. "I had only enough for the room and what I'm going to give you for your services. I don't want the attendant seeing us walk in the lobby together, so give me five minutes before you get out of the car. I'll be in room 363. Just rap on the door a couple of times when you get up there."

When he walked into the room, he found that it had two beds. He wondered if a single room would have been any cheaper. It was only a matter of a few minutes that he had been in the room that he heard the knock on the door. The would be woman slipped her heels off as she entered the room, complaining that she should have bought a half size larger because the one she had on were hurting her feet. "Why don't you turn the lights off," McAlister said. "I don't like a whole lot of light in a room. Get undressed and into bed after you have turned the lights out. I've got to use the bathroom first."

Before going into the bathroom, he watched her as she started to undress. She turned her back to him. He went into the bathroom before she had undressed completely. In the bathroom, he could feel the anticipation begin to build. The inner feeling he had on the highway returned and was growing strong. He could feel himself tremble. McAlister removed the knife from inside his pocket and wrapped toilet paper around the handle so if anything unexpected was to happen, and he ended up losing the knife, his fingerprints would not be on it. Deciding that it would be a wise move, he removed every stitch of clothing he had on and folded everything neatly. After he had folded them, he placed them in a pile on top of the toilet lid.

The inner sensation had begun to cause him to sweat, but he paid little attention to it. He reached for the knife that he had placed on top of the toilet tank before removing and folding his clothes. "Here I come, baby doll, ready or not!" he said as he was exiting the bathroom. He held the knife concealed in the palm of his hand wanting to be sure she did not see it before he wanted her to.

If she had gotten her night vision before he wanted her to, there was a chance that it could happen. She laid waiting for him to fill the empty spot on the bed that she occupied. He crept into the room at a slow, methodical pace trying to capture her silhouette lying on the bed. As he neared her with each step, he clenched the knife tighter. His victim lay beneath the sheets, writhing in anticipation. Her eyes were glued to his body standing before her.

McAlister crawled on top of the bed and straddled her sheet enclosed body. She looked up at him through eyes that were not yet aware of what was about to happen to her. Clenching the knife even harder, McAlister broke the spell of silence. "Are you ready for me to give it to you?"

"Yes, give it to me now," she said. The knife was before her without warning. Her eyes immediately grew to the size of quarters as she tried to thrust him from the top of her, but the attempt was futile. McAlister plunged the knife through the center of her neck. It went easily into the soft spot just below her Adams apple. Blood squirted from the victim's neck as though it had been pushed through with a pump. It hit McAlister on his chest and splattered back onto the bed.

His victim was making gurgling sounds from her throat. She wrapped her hands around her own neck, trying to stop the blood flow from where McAlister had made entry with his knife. Blood seeped between her fingers. McAlister stabbed into the side of her neck, just missing the place where her hands were cupped across the front of it. Forcefully, he pulled the knife toward her hands, ripping a gash in her neck.

Her hands dropped as blood really began to pour. It was as though a faucet of blood had been turned on. Her body buckled a couple of times as she braced herself. McAlister could tell that she had very little life left. He pulled the sheet back just enough to reveal what he had known all along. She had the genitals of a man.

Looking into her eyes, he could see that she was barely hanging on. He knew that what he was about to do would bring out any life that was left in her. He grabbed the genitals in his hands. The transgendered man's hands went into motion toward McAlister's wrist, but there wasn't enough strength to ward off the power McAlister was wielding. "You won't be needing these again, since you really don't know what to use them for," McAlister said, pulling hard on the genitals. Her hands went lifeless and her eyes rolled back into her head. McAlister made the separation with the knife. More blood squirted on him, but again he paid little attention to it. He shoved the separated member into the victim's mouth.

His breathing that had been heavy during the activity suddenly subsided. He was sweating profusely. Still on the bed, he took his index finger and stuck it down in the puncture wound in the transgender's neck. With the same finger, he began writing on the wall, just above the headboard of the bed. When he was finished, it read, "Fooled no more." He made sure that all of his strokes were smooth so that there would not be a possibility of the police being able to detect any prints.

McAlister returned to the bathroom and found a towel hanging on the towel bar. With it, he wrapped around the knobs of the shower controls and turned the water on. He ran it as hot as he could stand it. When he was sure that he could bear the temperature of the water by testing it with his hands, he stepped into it and began cleansing the blood from his body.

The blood washed away rather easily since it had not had much of a chance to dry. McAlister was careful to pay attention to every detail of his body. With a washcloth, he rubbed at any area in which he saw blood. He grimaced as he rubbed some of the spots on his body that was still tender from where he had rubbed himself raw earlier. As much as he tried to ignore the pain, it was unavoidable, but he managed to get through the shower. After he had toweled himself dry with a fresh towel he put only his underwear back on. With the towel he had used earlier, he carefully began wiping down any objects that he felt he could possibly have touched.

He returned to the bedroom where his victim lay lifeless. Meticulously, he inspected the room to make sure that he would not leave anything behind. When he was sure that he had not forgotten anything, he began cleaning and wiping just as he had done in the bathroom.

Confident that he had tidied the place up well enough to remove any evidence that he was the perpetrator of the slaying of his victim, he returned to the bathroom where the rest of his clothes were. He dressed himself, being cautious not to touch anything. When he was done dressing himself, he washed the towel he had been using until he was satisfied that it was free of blood. He used the towel to turn the water on and off.

As he left the room, he used the towel on the door knob to open it. He slowly opened the door, peeking down the hallway as he did so. Seeing no one in the hallway, he slipped out of the room, closing the door with the towel. While walking briskly down the hallway, he balled the towel up as tight as he possibly could. Instead of the elevator, he chose the stairway. As he started down the stairs, he suddenly decided to reverse his direction.

McAlister ran up the stairs, not knowing how many floors were in the building. When he got to the top floor, he dropped the towel on the top step and began his journey back down. His hopes were that if the towel was found by the authorities and they would assume that it came from the room where the dead body was, that it must have been dropped by someone residing in the building.

McAlister noticed during his drive back to the apartment that the inner irritating feeling had been replaced by a gratified sensation of relief. It felt euphoric. He checked his watch as he parked his car in the same spot he had vacated from the apartment complex. It was 11:30 p.m. At least he did not have to shower, he thought to himself.

Even with the feeling of elation that he was experiencing, he just wanted to sleep. When he entered the apartment, the lights were turned off. A lit candle rested on top of the coffee table with a note beside it. Jeanette's handwriting read, "Please hurry, darling, I'm waiting for you." She had drawn a picture of a smiling face at the end of the notation.

"Damn!" McAlister said verbally. He wanted only to get some sleep. Now more was expected of him, in the form of energy. The energy he was feeling, he did not want to use, he wanted to gloat in it.

Chapter 23

Dash had figured it was going to be a boring night since The Weasel had settled in already. He was alarmed when he saw the car backing out of the garage, thinking that it may be The Weasel. He relaxed when he saw that it was just The Weasel's wife. The Weasel must have been just exhausted as he was, Dash thought. He could imagine how good sleep would feel that night for The Weasel and envied him at that moment.

When The Weasel's wife was a good distance from the house, she let him know that it was safe for him to get up from lying on the floor behind her seat. He instructed her to drive fast because if McAlister was going to make a move, he would be doing it soon.

They got to the apartment complex just in time. McAlister was getting into his car. The Weasel instructed his wife to stay with McAlister, but not to be spotted by him, like he had spotted the Blazer following him earlier during the day. The Weasel's heart pumped even harder when he saw McAlister pick up the transgender. He could not believe that is was so easy to catch McAlister the way he was. He used a 35 mm camera with a zoom lens mounted on a special miniature tripod to get pictures of the transgendered man before she got into McAlister's car.

As they were driving behind McAlister, The Weasel took a picture of McAlister's car including his license plate. He realized that in order to make the pictures stick in court, he would have to show a progression from McAlister picking up the transgendered prostitute, to him murdering her. As he took pictures, he jotted down times in a notepad that he had brought along out of habit.

The Weasel did not understand why the prostitute didn't get out of the car when McAlister came outside from the hotel to check in. After McAlister started walking back to the hotel, The Weasel became suddenly aware of what was happening. He immediately snapped as many pictures of McAlister walking into the hotel as possible. Then, he waited to see if the prostitute would soon get out of the car.

Five minutes passed before the female impersonator got out of the car. As soon as she did, The Weasel began snapping pictures fast enough that one might have been inclined to think that he was a professional photographer shooting a model. When he saw her enter the lobby, he jumped out of the car. He raced up to the door he had seen her enter. Cautiously he peeked around the edge of the door where it was glass and saw her standing in the lobby, waiting on the elevator.

As soon as she got on the elevator, The Weasel slipped into the lobby. He watched the elevator stop at the third floor, figuring he could catch her going into a room if he hurried. He located the stairway and made a mad dash for the entrance. When he got to the top step of the third floor, he collected himself. He slowly pushed the door open and looked down the hall to his right, he did not see anyone. Quickly, he shifted his attention to the left end of the hallway and saw the transgendered go into a room about seven doors down from where he was standing. The room was on the opposite side of the hall.

He knew that he would look suspicious just standing in the hallway, as well as the stairway. The lobby was the best place for him to wait. He noticed that there was a television in the lobby which served as a good front until McAlister would come down. Periodically, he checked his watch due to his impatience. He wondered what could have been taking place in the room that he had seen the transgendered prostitute go into. If his hunch was right, then he was sure of what he would find after McAlister was gone: a mutilated transgender.

The Weasel's heartbeat sped up as he saw McAlister exit the stairway. He noticed that McAlister looked calm. He did not make eye contact with anyone as he left the building. 'A smart move,' he thought. He made a beeline to the stairway. When he reached the third floor, he counted seven doors down from the entry to the room that was number 363.

Before removing his lock picking kit from his inner coat pocket, he checked to make sure that there was no one watching him. He knocked on the door several times to ensure that he was not breaking into the wrong room. When he did not get a response, he inserted the device, and then wiggled it around until the lock sprung free. He replaced the lock picking kit inside his coat pocket before opening the door and removed his revolver from the holster.

Cautiously, he entered the quiet room. The body was lying on the bed, drenched in blood. The Weasel knew it was hopeless to check for a pulse. He located the telephone on the nightstand beside the bed. As he looked around the room, he pulled a white handkerchief from his pocket. He wrapped it around the receiver of the telephone as he picked it up from the base. He dialed the police headquarters out of habit.

It was not long after he called that a large group of people found the room. Photographers were snapping pictures. Reporters were standing around, trying to get a story out of anyone that would talk to them. The Weasel was trying to explain to a small band of cops and detectives his own version of what had taken place. They all listened to him attentively.

Before the mob of people had gotten there, The Weasel had taken the time to inspect the place thoroughly. He found that it was very clean, all except where the victim lay in a bed of blood. He speculated that McAlister had taken the time to shower and clean the bathroom. It was very unlikely that he had left any prints. He also had used the time to document the events that he had witnessed. Now he was cognizant that his documentation was clear and concise. Looking at his watch, he approximated the times that each turn of events had occurred.

As the mob of people grew tiresome, The Weasel nudged his way through the room. A report had to be filed. He wanted to instruct a uniformed policeman to secure the scene as soon as possible before leaving to go prepare the report.

CHAPTER 24

Jeanette was alluring in her black satin negligee. A candle flickering on top of the nightstand illuminated her curvaceous figure as she lay on her stomach with her legs folded up toward her back side. She kicked her legs back and forth as though she were swimming. With her index finger, she motioned for McAlister to come to her. As he did so, he began removing his clothes dropping each item on the floor as he removed them. "That's right," Jeanette moaned, "Come to me, big daddy."

McAlister felt a stir in his loins at her suggestive voice. He liked it when a woman was assertive and knew what she wanted in her sexuality. He also liked the look of lust that shone from her eyes. She positioned herself on all fours. Her curvaceous hips began to wiggle slowly and methodically in a sexual dance. She looked at McAlister as she continued her gyrations. The look in her eyes became even more convincing to McAlister as he could feel a state of fury building in the form of sexual desire for Jeanette. Her every movement became even more excitedly pronounced. His clothes were off a lot quicker than he thought they would prior to entering the room.

Jeanette positioned herself on her knees for support, placing her right hand on the headboard. The other hand, she held out in front of her, slowly bringing it to her face. She put her index finger inside her mouth and slowly, sensuously, brought it out while looking at McAlister. He approved and his excitement grew to an enormous height. Slowly, he climbed on the bed behind her. When he was within reach of her, he began removing her negligee.

Jeanette slung her head back toward him as he kissed her along her exposed neck. She let out a short moan of approval, further exciting McAlister as a result. He worked smoothly at removing her negligee, kissing her about her neck and shoulders all the while. She positioned herself so that he could slide the negligee off her body, but it did not take much before he had it off. "You like?" Jeanette asked wanting him, as she spread herself flat on her back.

"Very much!" McAlister said with a smile.

He slid slowly over her body until he was even with her. Tightly, he began kissing her with his tongue darting back and forth. When he was sure that she was getting primed, he began kissing her elsewhere. Her sighs and moans sent the message that she was enjoying it. He was taking pleasure in making her happy.

Soon, they were each kissing the other's body indiscriminately. The prelude to entry worked their excitement to a fever pitch. Both being so worked up, it was only moments after entry that they achieved a united outburst. Jeanette's mostly induced by the strength of his own. "You're the best lover I've ever had," Jeanette complimented. "Where did you learn to make love like that?"

Her smile said that she felt thoroughly satisfied. "Hey, I'm a natural," McAlister answered.

Jeanette let her body sink into the cushioned mattress. Sleep was right around the corner. She did not feel like talking in the relaxed state that she felt. It took energy to talk because it sometime required thinking. Without continuously doing so, she drifted into sleep.

The energy that McAlister had just expended left his body with a glowing, relaxed feeling. He thought about the events of the evening as he listened to Jeanette begin a light snore. He felt good about what had happened. He eased out of bed so that he could get his cigarettes out of his coat pocket. He lit one, enjoying the taste and the way it seemed to have a relaxing effect on him. There was no ashtray on the nightstand, but there was one in the living room, he remembered.

When he returned to the bedroom, he slipped carefully back into bed so that he would not wake Jeanette. She had such a peaceful look on her face. As he smoked, he flicked ashes into the ashtray that he had placed conveniently on the night stand. Many thoughts began entering his mind. The first of his thoughts was that tomorrow would be a good day for Leroy. He was still intent upon having Leroy as well as Jeanette thinking that there was still a trial to attend. He thought about how devious he had been in getting Thomas Dash to pay two people to act as witnesses.

The plan could have even backfired if the store attendant had stood up in court and pronounced his guilt. But, things had worked out and Leroy's problem would soon be forgotten. His problems were paramount in comparison to the one that Leroy once had. There was Gene to deal with, better known as "The Weasel".

The first mistake made that he was sure The Weasel had picked up on was getting the time periods confused with Jeanette's on him moving in with her. Though it was minor, but still it bothered him. He knew that good detectives looked for inconsistencies in stories. Even more so than the time contradiction was the fact that The Weasel was focusing all of his effort on him instead of some other suspect. That meant that The Weasel had a pretty good hunch that he was barking up the right tree by investigating him.

McAlister had done the right thing by assigning Dash to keep tabs on The Weasel. That way, he would know when The Weasel was following him, or observing him during his night activities. It was pretty smart of The Weasel to send the transgendered man to his office. Actually, he had planned on making a trip to Barbara's residence. Thanks to Dash, he didn't make that mistake.

The thoughts slowed as drowsiness became a stronger part of McAlister's mentality. His eyelids became heavier as he took the last drag from his cigarette. He had become so sleepy, that it took great effort just to extinguish it. As sleep came easy, so did the dream that followed.

The first scene was of being at home with Kelly and Dane. It was during the evening hours, before the sun set. He had just finished playing a basketball game with Dane and they both were still sweating profusely from the rigor of the game. The patio door was open and McAlister could hear Kelly singing from the kitchen. Both he and Dane sat on the diving board, trying to catch their breath. Faintly, McAlister could hear the doorbell ring. "I wonder who that could be?" he asked, not really expecting an answer from Dane.

"I don't know and I don't care," answered Dane. "It's probably somebody for you or Mom."

"I'm not expecting anyone and your mom hadn't mentioned that she was expecting any of her friends to come by.

"Maybe someone just wanted to pay a surprise visit," Dane responded.

McAlister didn't bother to get up from his comfortable seat on the diving board. He reasoned that if whoever the person was had come to see him, that Kelly would escort him or her out to the patio. As he looked down at the water in the pool, his gaze was broken by Kelly appearing in the open patio doorway with a man whom he recognized immediately. It was The Weasel, holding a paper bag in his right hand.

McAlister could feel contempt beginning to mount just from the presence of the man. He cursed silently to himself. The Weasel walked toward him holding the paper bag securely in his hand. McAlister figured that whatever the purpose of The Weasel's visit was had something to do with what was inside that bag he was holding. He did not extend his hand for The Weasel to shake, only nodded. He could feel that Dane was just as curious as he was by the puzzled look on his face.

The first thing that came out of The Weasel's mouth caused him to raise his eyebrow. "You are one strange man," The Weasel said.

Still puzzled, McAlister frowned. "What the hell does that mean?" he asked.

As The Weasel reached for the item in the bag, he asked, "What kind of man does this to a person?"

When The Weasel's hand was all the way out of the bag, he saw that he held a mason jar that had fluid inside. Floating in the fluid was a severed penis. Dane sprung up hurriedly from his seated position on the diving board. He released a loud scream that reverberated in McAlister's ears. His eyes had grown wide with fear as he fled into the house.

McAlister kicked and jerked himself to consciousness. He sat upright in the bed, suddenly aware that he was not in his backyard, but had been having another nightmare. Jeanette stirred a bit from her sleeping position, but did not wake. McAlister looked at her, realizing how lucky she was to have such an innocent life.

Most people he had ever known well enough to find out had some skeletons in their closet, but he doubted very seriously that Jeanette did. He peeped at the clock on the nightstand. It showed that he had only been sleeping for an hour. With the intensity of the dream, it seemed as if he had been sleeping a whole lot longer. Another hour passed before he was able to fall asleep again.

****

Down at the police headquarters, The Weasel was busy preparing a report for his own personal use of the events that he had witnessed during that evening. He felt tired and irritable due to the lack of sleep, which his body desperately needed, yet he felt a sense of relief that he had not been concentrating all of his efforts in vain by focusing his investigation on McAlister.

He first became suspicious of McAlister when he questioned the employees of The Phoenix night club. He found out through questioning that McAlister's first victim, Natalie, was known by her neighbors to frequent the club. Upon further investigation, through questioning the employees of the club, he found out that Robert Sullivan, the doorman, had seen the slain Natalie leave with McAlister the last night that she was seen alive. He recognized McAlister from watching the news, where on several occasions, reporters would zero in on him leaving the court house with a client he was defending.

The Weasel felt that if he had been assigned to the case at the beginning, he would probably have been able to prevent some of the murders. He reasoned that McAlister had not started out intentionally killing transgendered men, but after his mishap with Natalie, he had developed a deep seeded hatred for them. It explained why he severed the sexual organs from his victims.

Instead of arresting McAlister right away, The Weasel decided that he wanted to wait until he had the case sealed up airtight. If he had been accompanied by another detective during his observation of McAlister, he would have gone immediately to McAlister to make an arrest. Realizing that a good lawyer would try to discredit his testimony as a lone witness, he knew that if he followed McAlister long enough, in the company of another detective, he would strike again and this time he would have someone who could corroborate his testimony. He did not want to let McAlister get off the hook.

After about an hour, he was finished with his personal report. Even though he was not responsible for writing the report because he had a uniform officer assigned to that duty, he liked doing it for his own records. That way, when something came up in court that he could not remember, he could always refer back to his notes. He was ready for the long overdue sleep that he needed.

On the way to the station, his wife asked to be dropped off at the house, but he refused to do it, remembering that McAlister had a man sitting out in front of his house who had seen his wife leave the house alone. It would not look good if she returned with him in the car, especially since he was still presumed to be inside his house, sleeping.

The Blazer was still in front of his house when he and his wife returned. His wife parked the car in the empty spot in the garage that they had abandoned earlier. The Weasel got up from the back seat once they were safe from Dash's view. Not much time had passed before they were inside their house and fast asleep.

****

The following morning, McAlister woke with an invigorated feeling. He felt good about the night he had spent and looked forward to facing the day. There was the business of surprising Leroy and Jeanette about there not being a trial. He shook Jeanette until her eyes opened. She stretched her arms as she yawned. Reluctantly, she tossed the cover away from her body. She joined McAlister, who was already getting dressed.

"After the night we just had, we ought to be able to remain in bed the rest of the day," Jeanette said.

Her voice gave hint that it was early morning. McAlister did not respond to her comment because he was busy thinking about what he had done before coming home. Realizing that she had said something, he snapped out of his momentary trance. He was standing in front of the mirrors, adjusting the knot in his neck tie. He fidgeted with it as he spoke. "I'm sorry Jen, what is it that you said?"

"I'm not going to get mad about repeating myself. It's a bad habit you have, getting lost in space, that is. What I said was that after the night that we just had, we ought to be able to remain in bed for the rest of the day."

"I have to agree with you. It really would be a pleasure to remain in bed for the remainder of the day, but we work for a living. Besides, I don't think Leroy would appreciate it if we don't show up today."

"That's right! How could I have forgotten today? It's Leroy's big day in court. Poor fellow, I'll bet he's pretty nervous right now."

"He'll be alright. This will all be over before you can know it," McAlister said, smiling.

"You sure sound confident," Jeanette said. She had her clothes on, but had just begun putting on her make-up. To McAlister, that part always seemed as though it took longer than the dressing did.

Checking himself for approval in the mirror, he was pleased with his appearance. "I think I'll have my morning beverage of choice," he said as he started out of the room.

"I knew that you were going to do that anyhow," Jeanette said in response to his statement.

McAlister was halfway to the kitchen, but he still heard her. He laughed to himself about what she had said. It was an age old habit that he was not about to break at this point in his life. He found the products he needed in the usual place to make his Highball. After tasting it, he was satisfied with its consistency and went into the living room and turned the television on and plopped down on the couch.

The news was just coming on. *'Perfect timing,'* he thought to himself. Surely it was too soon for the body of his latest victim to have been discovered, he was thinking, but his thought was virtually interrupted when he heard the newscaster say, "Another body was found early this morning at a hotel in downtown Greenville in what authorities say is the doing of a very sick man."

"Who the hell are they calling sick?" McAlister exclaimed, slamming his Highball down hard on the end table beside him.

Jeanette was just entering the room. She caught the tail end of his reaction. "What are you getting so worked up about?" she asked changing her chipper tone.

McAlister showed his surprise of her presence by suddenly jerking his head toward her. "It's nothing," he answered. "I was just remembering that I forgot to do something personal," he lied.

"Very well, are you ready to go?" She asked. "We have another big day ahead of us. You know, I'll bet you that Leroy didn't get much sleep last night."

"I don't care to take you up on that bet," McAlister replied as he downed his Highball. He grabbed his coat from where it rested on the back of the couch. The drive to the office was pretty routine, neither of them had much to say. Mornings were the times that both cherished not having to spend energy talking. The elevator ride up to the office wasn't different than the ride in the car. If someone had been on the elevator with them, he might have assumed that McAlister and Jeanette were strangers to one another.

As they entered the office, Jeanette headed straight to the coffee pot. She turned it on so that it could start percolating. She realized that she had forgotten to get something – the newspaper. She snapped her fingers when the thought came to her. "I didn't think about it on the way up, either," McAlister said as he hung his coat up on the coat rack that was in the corner of the room. He smiled at Jeanette, knowing that he had read her mind. "I'll do my own coffee while you go downstairs," he told her.

"Be back shortly," she replied, exiting the room. McAlister took a seat in his high back chair. When he was settled in, his mind went into gear. His first thought concerned the events of the working day before. Barbara popped into his mind. Suddenly, he felt excited. He knew that Barbara was a plant of The Weasel's. The cleverness of how The Weasel operated tickled him. He knew that he was now involved in a game of cat and mouse.

McAlister reasoned that if something fatal were to happen to Barbara, it would give The Weasel a hell of a guilt trip. He picked up the receiver of his desktop telephone and plugged seven digits into it. It rang two times before Dash picked up his cellular phone. "Yeah!" Dash spoke gruffly into the receiver.

"Dash, good morning!" McAlister greeted him. "How are you feeling?"

"Like shit," Dash answered. "I'm ready to get the hell out of this truck. I've never been so cooped up in my life." He sighed briefly. "So, what's brewing so early in the morning?" he asked.

"Do you remember that man, I mean woman that you saw The Weasel give money to? Chances are that she hangs around that same area that you saw The Weasel approach her. Drop your tail on our boy for a while. Try to locate our impersonator. Once you do, I would like for you to give her a message for me."

"What's the message?" Dash asked.

"Tell her that it is very urgent that you get her to understand that I want her to call me just as soon as she's done talking to you."

"I'm hopping on it right now." Dash responded.

McAlister could hear him start the engine to the Blazer. "I'll talk to you tonight," Dash said, just before hanging up the telephone.

Shortly after McAlister hung the telephone up Jeanette returned to the office with a morning paper. She walked into the office as a rushed pace. After dropping the paper onto McAlister's desk, she stopped at the coffee pot and poured herself a cup. McAlister didn't say anything he just sat at his desk and watched her move about the office. Finally, after the silence and observation, he spoke up. "So, do you think Leroy is up by now?"

He had propped his feet up on his desk. Smoke lingered in the air from the cigarette he had lit up. "Do I think he's up yet? What kind of sick and crazy question is that? Do you think that he actually slept at all last night? I feel so sorry for that poor kid. I know he's innocent. I just know it. Don't ask me how I know, I just know, that's all."

McAlister took his feet off of his desk. He looked at Jeanette with serious eyes. "If I did not know any better, I would think that from the way you are acting, you are more nervous than he probably is right now." He got out of his seat so that he could stand closer to her. She turned her back to him as she drank her coffee.

McAlister realized that she needed to be comforted. He leaned forward, extending his upper body so that he could see what her condition was in regards to her nerves. He saw that her hands trembled as she held the coffee cup and her eyes showed a hint of fear. "Come over here and gather yourself," McAlister said to her.

He put both hands on her shoulders to move her to the seat that he had vacated. She seated herself so slow that it was almost like she had aged forty years and had an arthritis condition. McAlister pushed the remaining part of his cigarette into the ashtray. A thought ran through his mind to go ahead and tell Jeanette the truth about Leroy's situation since she was so worked up about the whole thing. That would even make his surprise more effective as he passed on the idea of telling her.

He walked around the corner of his desk until he was directly behind the seat in which she was sitting. With both of his hands, he began gently massaging her shoulders. After a few minutes of doing so, she began to loosen up. "Oh, that felt so wonderful," she said, after much of her tension subsided. "You sure know what buttons to push, don't you?"

"Aren't you glad that I do?" McAlister asked.

"Yes, I am!" Jeanette answered. "I must have been quite hysterical," she added.

"No, you weren't, but you were getting there," McAlister told her.

After he terminated his administering Jeanette rose, triumphantly from her seat. She felt as though her attitude was right for working, thanks to McAlister. "You know we really don't have much to do today besides going to court. I've got a few things that need to be typed, so I need to get busy. Lucky for you, there's nothing that is presently demanding of your time. Better take advantage of it," Jeanette said. "Have you prepared well for Leroy's case?" she asked. She waited for his answer. He hesitated for a while before speaking.

The hesitation, he knew, would make Jeanette nervous. That was what he wanted, to make her nervous. "Well," he started out slowly, "I have been so damned busy doing other things that I really haven't had much time to work on Leroy's case."

McAlister tried to look as if he held guilty as he told her. She believed him. "Mac, this is Leroy's life we are talking about here!"

Jeanette had become upset again. Her hands were clasped solidly to her hips as she spoke. McAlister could tell that she was serious. He wanted to laugh at how well his plan was working. It had been quite some time since he had this much fun playing a joke on anyone. Glancing at the clock, he saw that it was getting close to 9:00 a.m. Pretty soon, the joke would come to a climax. "Look, calm down," he said, trying to look serious as he spoke.

It was hard because he could feel himself wanting to laugh hysterically. "We will not have any problems in court. I'm pretty confident that things will go well, even if I haven't prepared for the case," he mumbled.

McAlister watched for her reaction. "I've been asking you all along if you were prepared to defend Leroy properly. Now you tell me that you haven't. What the hell have you been doing?"

McAlister walked away from her. When he had his back to her, he bit down on his lower lip to keep from laughing. He had never seen Jeanette so upset since he had known her. He gathered himself as quickly as he could. When he was positive that he would not have an outburst, he posted a serious look on his face and turned to face her. Looking at her sternly, hoping that she would not see any hint of humor in his eyes. "I've been very preoccupied," he told her.

"You've been doing more damned partying than you have work!" She screamed out. "If I had known that you did not have your act together, I would have been on your ass every day, making sure that you did. Now, a poor, innocent kid may end up suffering at the hands of your neglect."

Jeanette hurried the remainder of the contents of her coffee cup down her throat, then slammed the cup down hard on the desktop and walked away from McAlister's desk. She was almost stomping as she left the room and went into her own work station. McAlister wished that he had not played the joke on her because he felt that she was getting overly emotional about the whole thing. He was not sure that she would get more upset once she knew the truth. Reasoning assured him that since she was a woman, that her mood would inevitably be unpredictable.

He took his seat that Jeanette had vacated. As he reared back in his chair, he propped his feet on top of his desk. When he became settled, he realized that he did not have anything to do. The morning newspaper that Jeanette had dropped on his desk was close to the edge furthest away from him. He found it hard to reach it due to the position he had put himself in.

Not wanting to remove his feet from his desk, he extended his right arm until he was able to reach the paper and read over the headlines of the upper section of the front page. There was nothing mentioned in the upper half, but he found that down in the lower left corner of the paper, a section was dedicated to the finding of the body at the hotel. The article only mentioned what the television had reported earlier that morning. There was even the same reference that the television anchor man had reported police as saying that the person responsible for the murders was very sick.

Again, the notion of being called sick infuriated McAlister. He gritted his teeth as he simultaneously clenched his right hand into a fist. He slammed the fist down hard on his desktop. There was a loud noise made resulting from the impact causing the objects on his desk to momentarily go airborne. Two wooden figurines that had been resting on the edge of the desk fell to the floor.

Jeanette, who just prior to the reaction, had managed to settle herself enough to take her seat at her typewriter, jumped from her seat because of the sudden shock that McAlister had caused. She put her hand over her heart as though she had just experienced cardiac problems. She turned from her seat frantically. "What in the hell was that noise?" She asked.

McAlister did not answer her. He did not hear her, although she spoke loud enough. He was slamming his clenched fist down hard repeatedly on his desktop. Each time he did the objects that were on top of it bounced around. To Jeanette, McAlister looked ridiculous acting the way he was. He looked like an overgrown child having a temper tantrum. She had no idea why he was so disturbed.

McAlister had no idea that Jeanette had gotten up from her seat and was standing in the doorway looking at him. He had begun to feel the involuntary visceral reaction that he had felt just before he had gone out and slain his last victim. His entire body began to tremble. Jeanette became afraid. He looked as though he were a caged animal. His eyes were wide and unblinking. They exhibited an intense look of hatred. His jaw was clenched tightly. Jeanette could tell from looking at his expression that he must have been biting down hard on his teeth.

Jeanette felt a cold chill go through her body. She had never seen anyone in such a state before. He had been looking in her direction, but he had not even noticed her standing and watching him. It was as if he was looking right through her. Now both of his fists were clenched as he held them rigidly out in front of him in a gesture that looked as though he had a certain person in mind to beat up.

Jeanette soon realized that he was in a trance. She swallowed hard as she decided to approach him. Cautiously, she walked toward him, expecting something to happen. McAlister's expression did not change. He was still unaware of Jeanette's presence. Instead of approaching him directly, she chose to do so from his side. If he was going to react to her trying to snap him out of the trance, she didn't want to be the victim of any wild blows. She stopped and took a deep breath when she was about a foot away from him.

Rationalizing that if she grabbed him and started shaking him, it would give him an opportunity to hit her, she opted against it. The safest thing she could think to do was give him a strong push that would possibly cause him to fall to the floor and break his trance. With all of the physical strength that she could muster, she shoved him with both hands against his left shoulder. The force behind the push sent him stumbling off balance and his body crashed into the wall. He then toppled over to the floor.

Jeanette raised her hands up to her mouth and covered it as though she had said something bad, but wanted to ensure that nothing else came out. She was glad that she had hurt him. As she saw him trying to collect himself from the floor, she ran to help him up. He shook his head from side to side vigorously. He felt disoriented and drained as to what had happened. The look on his face showed the truth. He knew that something strange had happened, but he did not know what.

McAlister raised his right hand to his forehead and grimaced. He felt faint enough to pass out, but he maintained his composure long enough to find his desk chair. He let his body fall into it like a sack of potatoes. Jeanette had not left the room. She stood close to his desk, not saying anything, but was very observant. As he began slowly regaining his state of awareness, he noticed that she was staring at him. "What are you staring at?" he asked.

"I'm not sure yet," she answered. She still looked baffled. The sudden ringing of McAlister's desktop telephone interrupted the air between them. Both of them averted their eyes to the telephone. McAlister picked it up on the third ring. Jeanette left the room.

"Hello?" McAlister said into the receiver of the phone. He still felt slightly disoriented from the attack. His body felt wrenched. "Hi, Mr. Johnson, do you remember me?" the voice on the other end said.

It sounded of a mixture of male and female persuasion, but more convincing of male than female. McAlister recognized that the voice belonged to Barbara. "Yes, this is Barbara, right?" McAlister answered.

"Yes, it is," she said. "How have you been doing?"

"Fine," he answered. "Well, there is something urgent that I need to talk to you about," he took over without letting her give her reason for calling. "I'll be too busy to talk to you at the office, but I'd like to get your address so that I can drop by this evening, that is if it's alright with you."

There was a brief silence on the other end before she spoke up. McAlister thought that she must have been thinking about what plans she must have made for the evening and whether she had time to slide him in on her agenda. She had no plans for the evening. What she was actually contemplating was whether she should allow him to come to her house. She had gotten a funny feeling about him when she met with him at his office. There was no way that she was going to trust him. "Let me see, what do I have to do this evening?" She said into the telephone. "I think I can spring free at about 9:00 p.m.," she said, sounding quite convincing.

"That's good!" McAlister said sounding pleased. "I'll see you tonight then."

"Mr. Johnson, don't you want to know how to get here?" She asked sarcastically.

She wanted to laugh at his eagerness, but she held it within herself. "Yeah, I guess I need that," he said grabbing a pen from his desktop and jotted down the address that she had given him on a memo pad. "That's 101 Gordon St. It's the green house with yellow shutters."

"Yes, I know that area. I'll find it. Thank you. See you at nine." McAlister sighed after hanging up the telephone. He was determined that he would give Detective Foley something to think about. He was sure that The Weasel would feel responsible for what he was going to do to her.

Barbara had a bad feeling that McAlister had some mischievous intentions. She rummaged through her pocketbook until she found the card that The Weasel had given her with his home and work telephone numbers on it. Since she assumed that he was at work, she decided to give his office number a try first. The Weasel picked up the receiver after it rang several times. "Hello?" he said after placing the receiver to his ear.

"Detective Foley?" she said, sounding unsure of whether she dialed the right number.

"Yes it is," The Weasel said. "What can I do for you, sir?"

Barbara pulled the receiver away from her ear and frowned at it as if she could see The Weasel through it. "It's not sir it's ma'am," she said with a tone that let him know that he had offended her.

"I'm sorry, ma'am, what can I do for you?" Barbara felt offended that first he recognized her voice as that of a man, and secondly, he did not distinguish her voice as that of someone he had spoken with before. He had even relied on her to complete a task for him. Of course, she had been rewarded monetarily for her good deed. She dismissed the slight as a small injustice. If given the opportunity, she would deal with it later, but for now, she had a hero's deed ahead of herself to worry about. "It's me – Barbara Davis," she said into the transmitter.

She waited for a few seconds in silence for Detective Foley to recognize her. "Oh, yeah!" snapped The Weasel, suddenly cognizant of who he was speaking with. He was in a fog as to why she would call him. Then he thought about McAlister. "What's going on?" he asked. "Something come up with Mr. Johnson?"

"Yeah, he wants to see me at my place tonight at 9:00 p.m. I don't feel comfortable about it so I decided to call you. I just have a bad feeling about this guy."

"I do, too," The Weasel said to himself. He would not say it verbally to Barbara for fear that he would alarm her even more than she actually was. "That's great!" he said excitedly. "This will probably provide us with the opportunity that we need. I'll make sure that you have plenty of protection when the time comes."

Barbara realized that her meeting with McAlister could turn out disastrously if things did not go right with the so called protection that The Weasel promised. "We will need for you to wear a wire so that we can monitor the activity. Do you have any problem with that?" he asked.

"No problem," she answered.

"What are you doing this afternoon?" he asked.

"Besides having lunch, you mean?"

"Right – besides having lunch."

"Absolutely nothing!" she answered.

"It really didn't matter what you were doing anyway, because if we plan to do this thing, you need to come by my office so that I can brief you on how we are going to handle this thing. A situation like this you just don't go into blind, you know?"

"What time do you want me to come by?" She asked.

She could hear The Weasel figuring out loud, but to himself. "Oh, let's see… Hmm… lunch at 12:30 p.m., paperwork afterward… Can you make it here by 2:00 p.m.?" he asked.

"Sure, I'll see you at that time."

"Do you know how to get here?" he asked before she could hang up.

"You're at the Law Enforcement Center on McBee St. Let's see, don't tell me – I enter through the front double doors, take a right in front of the big reception area, go down the corridor, make a left, and go straight back. Your office is at the end of the hall. How did I do?"

"How did you know that?" he asked, sounding surprised.

"I just know these things," she said with a smile that she wished he could see. "I'll see you at 2:00 p.m." Before he could say anything in response, she hung up the telephone.

Chapter 25

While Jeanette was busy typing at her desk, McAlister was kicked back, doing absolutely nothing at his desk when Leroy entered the office. He was dressed nicely in his double breasted suit. It was conservatively gray and fit him as if it had been tailored specifically for his wear.

Jeanette leaped from her typewriter as if she had been spring loaded. With outstretched arms, she ran to Leroy before he could get to her and wrapped herself tightly around him. The response elicited a smile from his face. "You act like you're glad to see me or something," he joked. It was good enough for a laugh from Jeanette. He made her realize that she had been very responsive.

McAlister witnessed the episode from his desk. He could see through the glass how jubilant Jeanette was about seeing Leroy. Of course, that was not surprising to him after the commotion she had caused with him about the fact that he was unprepared. "Hello, Leroy," McAlister said, standing in the doorway.

"Hi, Mr. Johnson," Leroy responded. "How you been doing?"

McAlister flashed his toothy grin. "I've been doing pretty good Leroy, how about you?"

"Other than being scared, I've been okay," Leroy answered. I can't wait till this is all over." He looked into McAlister's eyes as he spoke. Jeanette had broken her grip on Leroy and stood close to him while he talked to McAlister. She had locked her hand in his. "Don't worry about anything, Leroy," McAlister said boastfully. "This one is in the bag."

McAlister looked at Jeanette to see if she would respond to what he had said. Of course, Jeanette did not want to alarm Leroy with McAlister's lack of preparation. She only gave McAlister a malicious look, hoping that he would understand the message. McAlister avoided laughing for fear that Leroy would become inquisitive. "Make yourself comfortable," he said as he walked away from the doorway and toward where Leroy and Jeanette were standing.

Leroy saw that he had extended his arm and responded by shaking his hand. As they released grips, McAlister checked his Rolex to see what time it was. It was getting close to 10:00 a.m. More precisely, it was 9:35 a.m. Leroy's trial was due to start in another hour and a half. "Are you guys about ready to get over to the courthouse?" he asked.

Jeanette checked her own watch. "What's the big rush, Mac? We've got an hour and a half before court starts and we're only five minutes from the courthouse. I don't want to get over there just to have to sit around for a long period of time. Let's leave here at 10:30 a.m."

"Sounds good to me," Leroy said taking a seat on the couch.

"Jeanette, have you got all of the paperwork together that we need?" asked a smiling McAlister. He knew that she was still angry with him, but she had too much class to pitch a fit in front of Leroy. "I'm getting on it now." She went immediately to work, gathering all of the things that they needed to have available in court. "So, did you sleep well last night?" Jeanette asked as she gathered the items.

McAlister lit up another cigarette and began walking around the room aimlessly. Leroy didn't hear the question because he had tuned in on McAlister's actions. Realizing that Jeanette had said something to him, Leroy turned his attention away from McAlister. "I'm sorry, I didn't hear ya!" he exclaimed.

"All I asked was if you got much sleep last night."

Still somewhat perplexed by McAlister's constant motion, Leroy hesitated before answering. "Ah, no I didn't. I was too worried to sleep, ya know what I mean?"

"I think I can understand that." Jeanette laid all of the things that she had gathered in the middle of her desk. After doing so, she went over and took a seat beside Leroy. McAlister was still pacing the floor. She put her hand on top of Leroy's nearest thigh. It did not affect him much because he was still checking out McAlister while he paced aimlessly. Both Jeanette and Leroy looked at each other quizzically. "I think he's even more nervous than I am," Leroy said, breaking the silence.

They both burst out in laughter. McAlister was oblivious to it. He then caught their amused eyes and figured that they must have found a point of interest in his actions. "I'm just doing some heavy thinking," he said.

"I was thinking about a little problem we have with the trial," he lied. "Oh, it's nothing to be alarmed about, Leroy. Just forget I said anything." McAlister had really been thinking about The Weasel and Barbara. Revenge was going to be sweet. He sat Jeanette's facial expression change understanding why she did not want Leroy to be alarmed by his lack of preparation.

Leroy thought about how easy it was for him today, but he kept it to himself. He would rather believe that McAlister was competent so he dismissed the doubt from his mind. "I'm sure you'll handle it," he said. "I've got confidence in you."

Jeanette could feel her blood begin to boil. She tried to think of something that would keep her from dwelling on McAlister's incompetence. "Would you care for a cup of coffee?" she asked Leroy.

"Sure, I could go for a cup," he answered as he stood up. He followed Jeanette into McAlister's office where the coffee was kept. McAlister remained standing. He was still thinking about Barbara. Jeanette and Leroy returned to the room, chatting away as though they were oblivious to McAlister's presence. He left the room as they came in for coffee.

From his desk, he retrieved the briefcase that he kept his important paperwork in. Of course, it did not really matter what was in the briefcase because there was not really a trial. He put his jacket on and checked his appearance in the mirror. It was satisfying enough to elicit a smile from his face. "Let's be off to do battle," he told Jeanette and Leroy, who were waiting for him.

They stood and proceeded behind him, looking only half eager. It was a short walk to the court house. Jeanette and Leroy could feel themselves becoming nervous as they entered the building. Leroy realized that his whole life could be changed depending upon whether the people deciding his fate believed him or not.

As they entered the court room, Leroy noticed that it was full of people already involved in some trial that looked pretty serious. Three of them took a seat on an empty bench on the left side of the court room. The defendant on trial was a young man who looked to be in his early twenties. He was a handsome man with strong masculine facial feature and a square chin. He had the look of a ladies' man.

As a few minutes passed, the details of why he was on trial came out. A zookeeper had been caught trying to have sex with one of the sheep. A girl who looked to be in her late teens was testifying to the details of how she had caught the young man with his pants down, snuggled up behind the sheep. She looked embarrassed as she spoke. Other people in the court room seemed to be quite amused. Even the judge appeared somewhat flustered as the young girl described what she had witnessed.

Leroy seemed surprised that the young man was being tried in the General Sessions Court. Something like that, he thought, would have been a misdemeanor. McAlister explained to him that South Carolina took bestiality very seriously and generally punished the offenders to the fullest extent of the law.

As time passed, so did the number of cases. Some of them lasting a lot longer than others. Leroy's eleven o'clock appointed time came and went swiftly. Out of the corner of his eye, McAlister saw Jeanette frantically checking her watch. Leroy broke out in a cold sweat sitting between McAlister and Jeanette. She bent forward with a puzzled look plastered on her face. She spoke harshly, but quietly as she could. "What the hell is going on, Mac? Leroy's trial should have been underway long before now."

"What trial are you talking about?" McAlister asked, trying to look untouched. Jeanette's puzzled look became more pronounced.

"What do you mean what trial? You know damned well what trial!"

Still looking calm and unmoved, McAlister repeated himself, "What trial?" Then, a look came over his face that told Jeanette the he was trying to hold back his laughter. Leroy was just as perplexed as Jeanette was. His face was tight with misunderstanding. He pulled a handkerchief from his coat pocket and wiped the sweat from his face. Jeanette looked at Leroy, seeing that he was as nervous as he could be. It angered her that she did not have a clue what was going on.

What made matters worse was that McAlister was acting like such an idiot. "Excuse me, Leroy," Jeanette said, stretching around him to get close to McAlister. "Can we step outside for a minute?" She asked rising from her seat.

"We can all step outside," McAlister said. "There is no need for us to stay here. Our presence isn't required."

"How do you figure that?" Leroy asked, even though he had wiped his face clean of the sweat from earlier, beads of moisture had returned on his forehead.

Jeanette had sat back down, but on the edge of her seat. She had no clue as to what McAlister meant by saying that they had no need to stay there. It was Friday and surely the day that Leroy was set to be in court. "Well, you see, Leroy," McAlister started with a sneaky smile on his face, "I've managed to get you off the books already.

A few days ago, I got curious and I went to see the store attendant who said that you robbed the place. After questioning him for a while, he finally broke down and told the truth. He was the one that actually took the money. I called the cops who came down and arrested the guy. After that, I went through all the necessary channels to ensure that you did not have to go to court. So you see I saw this whole episode as an opportunity to have a little fun with the two of you."

McAlister pressed his lips together and tilted his head with a look that said, there you have it. Leroy was astonished. He could not believe that after all the months of worrying, it was all over, just like that. He started to pinch himself as a smile washed over his face. A state of euphoria consumed him.

Jeanette's mouth was wide open. She could not believe what she had just heard. She felt compelled to leap from her seat to express the joy she felt, but realized that it would not go over well in the court room. She placed her hand on Leroy's thigh and squeezed. He smiled at her approvingly.

Once they were out of the courtroom, Jeanette let out a loud yell, with her fist clenched high over her head. She embraced Leroy tightly for a moment. Then, she did the same to McAlister. As she broke her embrace from him, she balled her right hand into a fist and punched him squarely in his chest. "You asshole! Why didn't you tell me?" she asked.

If I had told you, then it wouldn't have been a practical joke as effective as it has turned out now would it?" McAlister said. He began to laugh. Then, he laughed even harder as he thought about how well the joke had gone over. The laughing became contagious with Leroy, but not with Jeanette.

Soon, McAlister and Leroy were laughing uncontrollably. They were rolling on the walls just down the hall from the courtroom. When the elevator door finally opened, Jeanette grabbed them both by the arm and pulled them into it.

Feeling festive, McAlister suggested that they go back to the office only long enough to put a "Closed for the Day" sign on the door and retreat somewhere for a celebration. The trio ended up at a quaint little bar and grille located on Main Street. The smiles that their faces bore acknowledged that there must be some type of celebration going on.

There were only two other patrons in the establishment, with the exception of the bartender. The other two were engaged in conversation, paying no attention to McAlister, Jeanette, and Leroy. The absence of other people signified that it was still early in the day.

Behind the bar was a big burly man with a rugged face. Some of the small scars on his face revealed that he had seen a rough life. His hair was a wisp of salt and pepper. His eyes, which were almost black, were tight at the outer corners, but were soft and intelligent. Jeanette was taken aback by him. She found it hard to take her eyes off of him. McAlister picked up on it during the course of their conversation, but he paid little attention to it. He was talking about the case and knew he had gotten a strong hunch about what had really happened.

McAlister was seated facing the door that they had entered through. As he talked, he paid little attention to the furnishings and surroundings of the atmosphere. At least in the beginning, that was the case. Jeanette and Leroy listened tentatively as he spilled his piece about the store attendant. As the conversation turned to other topics, McAlister began to fade out of it. During the conversation he checked out the surroundings of The Network while Jeanette and Leroy talked.

At the back wall was where a baby grand piano rested without anyone playing it. McAlister surmised that at night, someone would be behind it and play for a contented crowd. He did not understand how he could have overlooked the ceramic vase containing orchids that sat on the right corner of the piano. Since they had to him become symbolic of a negative icon, they did not hold the beauty that they did for other people. Instead, the sight of them sent a chill throughout his body.

McAlister's first thought was of his marriage gone astray. He remembered buying enough orchids to fill his bedroom, by suggestion from Dane, in order to please Kelly. The notion had worked in that he and

Kelly had made up, only to find that it backfired the next day. He recalled how he had felt when he saw them on the lawn.

Jeanette and Leroy were still engaged in conversation, almost forgetting McAlister's presence. They were not aware that he was going through somewhat of a trauma. He had a very tight grip on the glass that contained his drink. That grip became even tighter, but that was not voluntary. Still fixated on the orchids his grip became stronger and stronger. He had begun to tremble due to the strength he was using on the glass. The drink inside began to spill out. Before all of the liquid could spill out of the glass, the pressure that he was applying to it became too overbearing and came apart in pieces all over the table, startling both Jeanette and Leroy.

The liquid that had been in the glass splattered on top of the table at which they had been sitting. Fortunately, none of the spilled drink got on either Jeanette or Leroy. They both sat with their mouths gaping open. Blood was oozing from the hand of McAlister which had broken the glass. His body began to tremble enough so that Jeanette and Leroy could see it. "My God," Jeanette said, "Something's awfully wrong with Mac."

Panic stricken, but not wanting Jeanette to notice, Leroy grabbed her by her arm so that he could summon control of her. McAlister was staring blankly as he still trembled. Leroy leaned close enough to him so that he was able to extend enough to shake him violently by his shoulders. "Mac, Mac, snap out of it," Leroy said forcefully.

Suddenly, the blank expression left his face and was replaced by a puzzled one. His raised eyebrows were a testament to it. McAlister, still perplexed, turned his head rapidly from side to side, gathering his surroundings. Seeing the orchids had triggered in him a sense of why he had just experienced what he thought of as an odd physical episode. Not wanting it to happen again made him feel uncomfortable about remaining at the bar. He felt fidgety.

Jeanette and Leroy momentarily turned their attention away from McAlister and looked at each other as though they were speaking a silent message that they both understood. Leroy was the first to stand. Jeanette immediately followed suit. "Well, I think we had better get going so that I can let you guys get back to work," Leroy suggested.

"We put a sign on the door that we were out for the day," said McAlister. "Remember? So we don't have to rush because I just had that anxiety attack. Now sit down so we can enjoy ourselves. The party is just getting started." He shifted in his seat so that his body's position made it uncomfortable to turn his head toward the Orchids and placed the napkin in his hand to stop the bleeding from the small cut he had just received.

Chapter 26

The Weasel's office clock displayed that it was 2:00 p.m., the time that Barbara had agree to show up. She entered the office as he was looking at a scattered pile of papers atop his desk. "Please, make yourself comfortable," he said as he motioned toward a plush armchair which was caddy corner to his desk.

There was a twin chair at the desk's other corner. Barbara was somewhat shocked at the homelike atmosphere of Detective Foley's office. There was a wall unit on one wall that had figurines of model cars and ships. Plants hung from the ceiling as well as those that were on top of his desk. Also on his desk were photos of people who Barbara figured were significant to him.

Noticing that Barbara was observant of his office, The Weasel spoke up. "I like feeling at home when I'm at my office. I don't want to feel like I'm stuck behind four walls all day.

"It gives the place a nice effect," Barbara said, as she let her rear end drop down into the comfortable armchair. "Those orchids in that black vase are beautiful. Where did you get them?"

"I went on a trip to South America last year. They were everywhere down there. You normally find them in tropical places like that, but they can be found worldwide. What I like about them is that they have unusual shapes and colors. There's almost something mystical about them to me."

Detective Foley stood up from behind his desk slipping both of his hands into his pockets and began slowly walking to and fro in the office without speaking. Barbara watched him, waiting for him to speak. "I'm pretty convinced that this lawyer, McAlister Johnson, is the man who has been killing transgenders in our city," he said, finally breaking the silence. He stopped pacing as he stood only a foot away from her. His eyes locked onto hers as he proceeded to speak. "You can be instrumental in helping to bring these killings to a stop."

Barbara suddenly started feeling sort of nervous. She had a notion that The Weasel was going to ask her to put herself in a position of danger. Her confidence in the police department had never been very strong. "I'm not going to ask you to put yourself in any position of real danger," he said, almost as if he had read her mind. We have people in our department who are trained to do that.

"What I would like to do is plant one of our people in your house when Mr. Johnson shows up tonight to meet you. Not anyone that will be hiding in the closet or anything, but someone visible that he can meet."

The Weasel began pacing the floor again as he continued to talk. Barbara listened to him attentively. "You see, I think our lawyer friend is drawn to murdering transgendered men who sexually assert themselves verbally toward other men. You haven't done that yet. Our man will!"

Feeling a bit relieved, Barbara sank even further into the comfort of the armchair listening attentively to what Detective Foley had to say.

****

Jeanette and Leroy had already become uncomfortable with McAlister's behavior so they were not reluctant to leave the establishment. Each of them hastily pushed away from the table. McAlister reached into his pocket, searching for money. When he felt what he thought was money, he retrieved it. He saw that it was a five dollar bill and tossed it on the table.

The sun was shining brightly when they got outside. They all squinted from the intensity of the rays being beamed at them. As they walked to the car, each of them contemplated what he would end up doing with the rest of the day. McAlister decided that he was going to go back to the apartment. His body felt exhausted after the episode. Getting some sleep was the foremost thing invading his thoughts. He would deal with Barbara at the time that they had discussed. He felt that he needed a fix.

Leroy came to the conclusion that he would go play some pickup basketball games, now that the trial was over, he could resume his life, and possibly enjoy himself. McAlister and Jeanette dropped Leroy off at his car. Jeanette hugged him and advised him to be careful in life. Leroy promised Jeanette that he would drop by the office occasionally to visit her.

As they rode toward the apartment in silence, Jeanette searched for words to start a conversation. She didn't want to come across as though she were making small talk so she just decided to ride the rest of the trip without saying anything at all. It was all that McAlister could do to stay awake as he drove. It was unusual for him to get sleepy during such an early part of the day. "You look pretty tired," Jeanette said as they walked to the apartment from the car. "Maybe you should get some sleep."

"That's exactly what I intend to do," McAlister said as he opened the door to the apartment. He practically ran to the bedroom. Jeanette took her car keys from the hook that hung from the side of the refrigerator and left immediately. McAlister had his clothes off in no time. He set the alarm to wake him up at 7:30 p.m. That would give him just enough time to get up, take a shower, shave, and get dressed before meeting Barbara at 9:00 p.m. McAlister had an astounding thought as he got into bed. He was not going to kill Barbara for the same reason he had done the others. His interest was to kill her just to piss off The Weasel.

When the alarm went off at 7:30 p.m., it startled him. He didn't realize when he set it that he turned to volume louder than he would have liked it. He shot up from the bed. "Damn," he said as he hurriedly turned off the alarm.

Taking a few deep breaths he tried to collect himself. His feet hitting the floor helped him start. He looked in the chest of drawers and pulled out a pair of fresh underwear and quickly discarded what clothing was still on his body. The shower felt refreshing. As he cleaned his body he felt as if he were cleansing himself of all the wrong he had done. He found himself applying a lot of pressure with his washcloth as he bathed. Before he went too far into the shower, he remembered what had happened the last time. Hurriedly, he turned off the shower and stepped out.

In front of the mirror, he inspected himself closely. He looked tired and aging. There were bags underneath his eyes that had begun to darken. He cursed the fact that had taken the toll on him. He thought about it as he applied shaving cream to his face. He cursed Kelly for bringing the dark side out of him. If it wasn't for her bringing Carolyn to the house that day, none of this would be happening.

Carolyn had been one of his clients. She had sought his services for the matter of settling a family will and testament on a multi-million dollar estate. She found McAlister appealing the moment that she laid eyes on him and made countless approaches, hinting to McAlister that she wanted to sleep with him. He wasn't naïve to what Carolyn wanted, but was insistent upon maintaining his cool. He knew that Kelly had never trusted him.

After nine years of marriage, he had managed to remain faithful. He was proud of it, yet at the same time, he was somewhat frustrated, because he had never gained Kelly's trust throughout the entire time. After those nine years, he gave up on trying to convince her he was trust-worthy, and decided that as long as he was enduring the punishment, he would actually get to have the fun of committing the crime. For the last two years, he did commit adultery, but never got caught in the act. He loved his wife, but he had given up on that love because what is love without trust?

What they had left was tossed out the window one day when Jeanette had gone out to lunch and Carolyn still happened to be in the office with McAlister. When she sat atop McAlister's desk, facing him with her legs open, revealing that she had no panties on, McAlister was taken by surprise. Although it was shocking, it was also arousing to him at the same time.

Carolyn picked up on his excitement and took the bull by the horns. As he plunged toward her depths, he felt guilt and sweet release at the same time. Before leaving, Carolyn wrote her telephone number on a piece of paper and pushed it into his pants pocket. He forgot about it.

The unexpected finding of Carolyn's telephone number by Kelly changed the flow of McAlister's marriage. Before he had only been assumed to have had affairs with other women, but there was no proof. The telephone number alone made him look guilty of all of the accusations, not just one. As mad as Kelly had been when she stormed out of the house, she returned like the calm after the storm, much to McAlister's surprise. Following Dane's suggestion, there was a bedroom full of Orchids when they made love that night.

As McAlister stroked his face carefully with his razor, he gazed into the medicine cabinet mirror. It was not his face that he saw. Far off in his mind was the sight of the orchids on his lawn that next day when he returned home from work.

Instantly, he remembered the feeling that went along with seeing the flowers on the lawn, a deep feeling of despair. He thought about how that moment had changed the course of his life. Haphazardly, he ventured from his home due to the surprise of the situation with Carolyn's presence. His next move was even worse, because it led to the murder of Natalie, his first.

All of McAlister's recollections of his sightings of orchids had led to negative occurrences in some form or another. Before all of this had happened, he did not ever feel influenced one way or another about orchids. Now, all of his gut reactions were adverse toward them. "Orchids are Deadly!" he said loudly as he wiped the remaining shaving cream from his face.

When he returned to the bedroom, he checked his watch. Time was not sitting still. Already, it was after 8:00 p.m. Not rushing, he dressed and checked his appearance in the mirror. Once he was satisfied, he put on a splash of cologne. Figuring that it would take about twenty minutes to get to Barbara's house, McAlister opted to concoct himself a Highball. He sat on the couch in front of the television as he sipped it. When his glass was empty, he checked his watch again. There was just enough time to get to Barbara's if he left right away.

Visual images flashed in his head of different incidences that had taken place since he had left Kelly. The murders that he had committed dominated his thoughts. He felt justification for all of the murders he had committed. The people he had terminated needed to be gotten rid of. They were nuisances, he thought to himself. "I'm doing this because it makes me feel good," he said openly. He could feel his adrenaline rev through his blood.

The Highball he had earlier had gotten him slightly buzzed. It was a warm feeling as he felt his senses becoming numb. He thought about how sly The Weasel had been. It was a good thing that he had sent Dash, who had done a great job, to play I spy on him. He made a mental note to give him a bonus.

Gordon Street was located between White Field Rd. and Rose Ave. It was a little stretch of street only about fifty yards long. Barbara's house was the third on the left. McAlister saw that it was not actually just a single house, it was a duplex. Not seeing a driveway, McAlister surmised that he would have to park on the edge of the road next to a Honda Accord that was parked in front of the house. He carefully pulled his car up close to the Honda's rear bumper.

As he walked to the front door of Barbara's residence, he patted his pocket to make sure his knife was still there. Since he had turned onto the street, he noticed that it was particularly busy. Feeling arrogant, McAlister whisked right up to the front door. Instead of using the doorbell, he knocked hard three times and dropped his head after doing so.

Immediately, he saw a row of orchids planted in a flower bed on each side of the cement on which he was standing. He felt his legs go weak and his stomach felt empty and his heart became heavy. Perspiration came from nowhere. Breathing became difficult. He reached for the knot of his necktie, loosening it to get some air. Luckily, no one had answered the door yet. He turned to hurry to his car, but as soon as he did, the door opened. "Mr. Johnson, it's good to see you," Barbara lied.

She felt nervous, but was doing all she could not to show any signs of it. She saw McAlister's perspiration, which she thought was strange, but the look on his face was even stranger. Like Barbara, McAlister was trying to suppress what was going on within him. If anything was out of the ordinary it may give him away, it had to be the look in his eyes. The fear was still present. '*Calm down, calm down,*' he kept saying to himself as he stepped into Barbara's half of the duplex. His heart rate actually began to slow down, but it picked up again when he saw that Barbara had company. Instantly, he noticed that it was another transgendered man. "Man, you look yummy," the stranger said to McAlister.

Barbara's aggressive behavior slightly overwhelmed him. She was just the type that he hated – aggressive. Suddenly, his focus was not on Barbara. "So, who's your friend?" he asked.

McAlister took a seat on the couch that Barbara's friend was lounging on. Checking her out, but cleverly so, McAlister felt slightly impressed with the job she had done making herself look like a legitimate woman. If he had not noticed that the stranger was a phony by his own awareness, her voice would have given her away. When she spoke, there was too much masculinity reverberating through her vocal cords. "I'm Carlile Sugar, what's your name?" the husky voice asked.

A couple of seconds passed before he answered. Already, he could tell that he did not like her. She was exactly the type that he sought out as victims for slaughter. "McAlister is my name," he said as he crossed his legs, "McAlister Johnson."

"Oh, you're the attorney that I've heard so much about," she said enthusiastically. You're really something," Carlile said. She eyed him admiringly, not trying to conceal that she was doing so.

McAlister noticed it. *'How disgusting she is,'* he said to himself. To her, he asked, "So, what have you heard about me?"

As though she were a school girl, Carlile blushed. "I heard that you were married, but it didn't matter because you had made yourself available by leaving your wife. They say that because your wife is a judge and you're just a lawyer, you couldn't handle it. Are you a male chauvinist? I also heard that you were better looking in person than you are on television. It's true," she said smiling.

'You should be a male chauvinist, yourself,' McAlister said in his head. *'As a matter of fact, you should just be a male,'* he added. "No, I'm not chauvinistic," he told her. He was being truthful. "I believe in total equality. I would not be in the business that I'm in if I didn't."

Barbara was sitting across from McAlister, patiently listening to the exchange of dialogue between them. She could feel the wire taped to her chest brushing against her skin as she moved. Hopefully, it was working.

About a block and a half away, The Weasel was sitting in the back of the Sheriff's police surveillance van. A pair of headphones was draped over his head. Along with him were two deputies in uniform, monitoring the recordings. So far, nothing interesting was happening. One of the deputies was complaining that they were wasting their time. Detective Foley ignored him.

At first, The Weasel was going to have only Detective Carl Banks wear a wire, assuming that McAlister would lose interest in Barbara because she was too subtle. Barbara did not feel as sure as the detectives did that McAlister would go for Detective Banks instead of herself. She insisted that she would not go along with the plan unless she could wear a wire as well. After getting tired of arguing with Barbara that she had nothing to worry about, The Weasel threw his hands in the air and consented to it.

It became apparent to Barbara that McAlister was quickly losing his interest in her because of his focus on Carlile. She became just a bit more comfortable when she saw what was happening. What amazed her was how well Carlile was playing her role.

McAlister felt uneasy that he had not apologized to Barbara for ignoring her presence as the hostess. "That's ok, you two go ahead and get acquainted," Barbara said, feeling relieved that McAlister was not concerned with her.

McAlister had forgotten about the purpose of his visit. He had already made up his mind that Carlile would be his next victim. Carlile could see that McAlister was expressing a lot of interest in her. She beefed up her performance.

It was on Gordon St. that The Weasel had set up a house, wired well enough to hear a pin drop. It was the location the Detective Banks was instructed to lure McAlister to. Waiting patiently near the perimeter of the house were a half a dozen detectives who had been chosen carefully by Detective Foley. Each of them carried a walkie-talkie on his hip, and a 9 millimeter Beretta tucked close to his abdomen. They had been instructed by The Weasel to keep sight of McAlister at all visible moments of his presence. Also, they were told not to shoot him unless he threatened to kill one of them.

Detective Banks had played the role of the drag queen on previous occasions. He had been very convincing on his performances. The men on the job thought that he was an ordinary cop who had an extraordinary talent for passing himself off as a woman once he was all dressed down.

Banks, himself, was glad that none of his comrades knew the closet life that he led at home. If they knew that he frequently enjoyed dressing in women's clothing each day after work, it was likely that they would disassociate themselves from him as well as ostracize him. Playing the role of a woman on his job was the ultimate for him. He could bring his profound joy of cross dressing into public view and not feel guilty about it. He sure was a lucky man, he thought.

Something about McAlister deeply disturbed Barbara. She had a visceral feeling that he was the person responsible for the transgender murders that had been taking place over the previous few weeks. As she sat on the couch and watched McAlister and Carlile, she felt better inside about calling McAlister to set up the meeting.

The Weasel felt impatient because things weren't moving fast enough with McAlister and Carlile. He tapped his fingers methodically against the surveillance audio equipment in front of him. It was annoying to the two deputies with him in the van. They didn't say anything to him about it because they all felt he was somewhat of a lunatic. "Come on, come on, come on. Let's go!" The Weasel shouted.

The other deputies jumped from surprise at The Weasel's abrupt speech. The Weasel had flung his hands into the air out of disgust for how slow Detective Carlile was working. The deputies looked at each other without saying anything, but they each had the same thought pattern concerning The Weasel.

Detective Banks, who had been sitting, stood up, stretched his hands and arms high above his head. He yawned as though he were ready to call it a night. "I think I'm ready for a nightcap." He looked at McAlister, who was watching him very closely. "Do you care to join me?" he asked. "I just live a couple of houses away. Come with me, I'll make you feel real cozy."

McAlister rose from his seat. He looked at Barbara who appeared to feel complacent and apologized that he had not made much conversation with her. She assured him that it was no big matter and that she was glad that he had come by. He apologized again as he and Carlile were leaving. As she closed the door behind them, she felt relieved that they were gone.

Carlile grabbed McAlister's hand in his as they walked toward the set-up house. Knowing that Carlile was actually a man, he was tempted to unclench their entwined hands, but he didn't want to alarm her. The thought of another man's hand entwined in his sickened him, but he had to bear with it. They would soon reach their destination and then his hand would be released.

Detective Banks enjoyed the feel of McAlister's hand. It felt strong and sure to him. He was really enjoying his work and couldn't wait to get to the house. Being there would be sheer excitement for him. The house that they entered was small, just as all of the houses on that street were. Before entering it, McAlister glanced at the area of the dimly lit street. It did not appear as though any of the neighbors were observing them.

High up on Detective Banks' thigh, he could feel his nine millimeter resting securely in the holster he had rigged for it. If the need to use it were to suddenly arise, all he would have to do is lift the bottom of the dress he had on. He had practiced it many times before and was comfortable with the speed with which he could retrieve it. The danger excited him.

Nothing seemed unusual about the house that Detective Banks and McAlister were in. As a matter of fact, it was rather quaint and warmly decorated. Most of the furnishings were oak antiques. The room that they were in was brightly lit by the color of the wall. They had been painted white. Numerous oriental rugs with colors matching the furniture and walls blended well with the room.

The Weasel clapped his hands together when he heard Detective Banks and McAlister enter the room. Again, he startled the deputies that were with him. The dullness of the activity had caused them to go to sleep. They both sprung to their feet, nearly hitting their heads on the ceiling of the van. "Pay attention, it's about to go down!" he snapped at them.

Neither of them resumed their seated positions, but instead they each checked their weapons for surety. They listened intently to the dialogue taking place between McAlister and their planted man. "Can I pour you a drink?" Carlile asked. She kicked her shoes off and waited for McAlister's reply.

"Sure, Highball," McAlister responded. He watched as Carlile waltzed off to the kitchen. *'Who the hell does he think he is fooling with those big ass feet of his?'* he said to himself. *'These damn trannies are crazy.'* It wasn't long before Carlile was back from the kitchen with two drinks in her hands. She gave the Highball to McAlister, who had already seated himself on the couch. After handing him the drink she took a seat beside him.

Inside his gut, McAlister could feel a stirring. His anxiety slowly crept upon him. It was uncomfortable having a man sit so close to him. They were always so aggressive. Carlile was going to have fun with McAlister. The gun on her inner thigh assured her that she would be safe. Being a

Detective, his fourteen years of experience had taught him much about the streets and the criminals that ran them. He could tell nine times out of ten when someone was packing heat. He knew that McAlister did not have a gun and suspected, though, that if this was the right man, he would have a knife on him.

Carlile stirred her Bloody Mary with her finger. Her legs were tucked underneath her on the couch making sure that both knees touched McAlister's thigh. The remote control for the entertainment system was resting on the empty spot beside her. She hit the power button, which brought the sound of jazz to their ears. After taking a sip from her drink, Carlile began playing with McAlister's closest ear to her. She rubbed it gently between her thumb and forefinger.

If it had been a genuine woman playing with his ear, McAlister probably would have found it arousing, but Carlile wasn't a woman and he found it repulsive. It was all he could do to refrain from hitting her. He knew however, that if he acted angrily, he would blow his cover before he was ready. "You're a rugged one, aren't you?" Carlile said coyly, rubbing his face. "I like rugged men. They turn me on so much, you know."

In the van, the two deputies were laughing. "Boy, he sure is pouring it on thick," the heavier one said.

"Yeah, he's too damn convincing. I'm getting a hard on," the other one replied.

They began laughing hysterically until The Weasel stopped them. "Alright, that's enough!" he shouted. He was loud enough to capture their attention. Each of them suddenly brought his laughter to a halt. They did not want to push The Weasel too far. The look on his face exuded alertness. He was anxious to capture McAlister – the mad killer. The thought of catching the transgender murderer had been eating at him to avenge the death of Natalie, the first one that McAlister had murdered.

Natalie had been The Weasel's secret lover and was shattered when he learned of her death. His wife noticed a sudden change in him, but she attributed it to stress from not wanting to take the assignment, but that was quite contrary to his real feelings. His wife had been only an average lover to him, at least compared to Natalie who pleased The Weasel in every way he could imagine. If it were not for the image he felt that he had to maintain as a law enforcement officer, he would have left his wife and moved in with Natalie. "Yeah, I guess you could say I'm pretty rugged at times," McAlister told Carlile.

The two of them laughed at the comment. Carlile pressed her lips to his neck while she breathed softly. "Hunks like you make me swoon with desire. What are you going to do about that, Mr. Johnson?"

"What do you want me to do about it you sleazy bitch?" McAlister said surprisingly. He had begun to get an erection from Carlile's administering and the fact of it had pissed him off.

"I like it when you talk dirty to me." She was surprised by McAlister's sudden change in attitude, but she regrouped before she allowed herself to become offended by McAlister's snide remark. She made a skull note to be prepared for any unexpected moves that McAlister might try in order to overpower her. She could see that he had become suddenly edgy.

McAlister stood up without warning. The movement slightly startled Carlile, but she remained calm. She stood up so that she could remain close to him. "I'm going to go in the bathroom to freshen up while you get undressed," McAlister said.

Just as he was about to walk away, Carlile turned to sit down. As she did so, her blouse became slightly crumpled between two of its buttons. It was just enough for McAlister to see her false breasts. That was not all he saw. He caught a glimpse of the wire that was taped to her chest. Suddenly, he became aware that he was about to make a big mistake. Logic assured him that The Weasel was somewhere close by. McAlister's mind went to work. It was useless to try making his move on Carlile now. He wondered how many men The Weasel had assigned to watch him.

In the van, the tension was mounting steadily. Actually, The Weasel was unsure exactly what it would be that McAlister would do to initiate his slaying. He knew that he would just have to play it by ear and hope that their timing was right once they burst in on McAlister's attempt. He knew that the moment had risen when McAlister said he was going to freshen up. That would be the moment that he would have a chance to get his stuff together. All of them took a last feel of their weapons. They were about to exit the van when The Weasel instructed them to wait. "My, it sure is a lot later than I thought. Hell, I almost forgot that I've got something terribly important to do. I'm sorry, but I must run," McAlister apologized.

Suddenly, Carlile realized that something wasn't right. If this was the right man, then he was certain to make an attack on her. It angered her that McAlister had decided to leave and not go through with his ritual. Detective Banks, Carlile, had begun to revel in the excitement that had mounted. The moment that he had waited for was going to pass him by. "Hold on!" The Weasel instructed the eager deputies. "Something's gone wrong." He wondered what could have triggered McAlister to decide to leave.

'What could have spooked him?' he asked himself. He listened intently to the dialogue that was being exchanged. They heard the screech of the walkie-talkie. One of the detectives that had been stationed on the perimeter had reported that McAlister was leaving the premises. "What do you want me to do," he asked, "follow him?"

"No!" The Weasel answered. "He's not going to do anything tonight," he added confidently. "You boys can go on home," he instructed one of the deputies to drive them back to the station.

Detective Banks felt dejected. His fun had been ruined. He had felt himself reaching an ultimate peak in his performance with McAlister, until McAlister destroyed it. Banks would not allow himself to feel down for long. He was going to go home and dress himself in all of his feminine lingerie. A smile broadened on his face.

CHAPTER 27

McAlister drove for a block in order to give the black van he had seen sitting at the end of the street time to leave. Just across from the end of Gordon St. was a church parking lot that was ideal for McAlister to park where he could see the van leave. Not only did he see the black van leave, there were a couple of detectives who got into a dark colored sedan further down the street. "Clever son-of-a-bitch!" McAlister said as if there were someone in the car with him to respond to his comment watching attentively as the sedan drove out of sight.

Detective Banks was unaware that he was being watched as he left the house. Had he known that McAlister was watching him, he would have been aroused. Danger excited him. All he could think of as he drove toward the east side of town was how his whole night had been blown. He wanted revenge on McAlister for not carrying through his intentions. If the opportunity would ever present itself again, he would see to it that McAlister paid for the agony he had caused him.

McAlister made sure that he kept a safe distance behind Detective Banks. As he drove, he thought about Kelly and Dane. He really missed Dane and wondered how he was doing in school. As far as Kelly was concerned, he wondered if she was seeing anyone. It did not matter. His thoughts were interrupted by the continual flashing of headlights behind him. At first, he thought it was the police. Then, he realized that the vehicle was too big to be a police car. It appeared to be a Blazer. "Damn!" McAlister protested. He turned his car into the parking lot of a shopping center and waited for Dash to follow suit.

McAlister rolled his window down, expecting that Dash would do the same. "Mac, what the hell is going on?" Dash looked puzzled as he waited for a response from McAlister. "Look, there is something you need to know, because sooner or later you're going to find out anyhow. Right now, I just don't have enough time to explain everything to you, but I promise I will."

Dash blew out the air that had filled his lungs as he had held his breath in anticipation. He realized that McAlister was in very serious trouble and he had suspected so since the beginning of his surveillance of Detective Foley. "Were you tailing Banks?" Dash asked.

"Yes," McAlister answered.

"I guess I blew your tail by stopping you, didn't I?"

"Yep!" McAlister was hitting the palm of his right hand against the steering wheel.

"Don't fret, my good friend, I can direct you to where that weird bastard lives." McAlister perked up. There would be a better time to talk to Dash he hoped, but for now, he just wanted to get to Detective Banks. "The address is one fifty six Houston Rd."

McAlister made a skull note of the address. "Hey, listen, Dash buddy, there's no longer any need for you to keep your tail on our man, Foley. Come by the office in the morning and I'll have your money."

"You bet," Dash answered. "Check you soon, and be careful." There was a look of concern in Dash's eyes.

They each sped off in different directions. As Dash drove toward Kelly's house, he thought about her in the many negligees she had modeled for him. He had bought several of them, himself. The others, she had accumulated over the course of her marriage to McAlister. It did not matter which ones she wore; she looked good in all of them. Dash thought back to when he first saw Kelly and how ravishing she had looked at the dinner party he had been invited to by McAlister. She had worn a black dress that clung to her body. He knew that McAlister and her were not that stable in their marriage because McAlister had often complained to him about Kelly. The night of the dinner party McAlister had been in and out of the room where everyone else was as his phone rang off and on. Kelly obviously noticed Dash's sneaking stares at her and returned them with warm smiles. Upon talking to him she could not help but feel the electricity between them and welcomed it, mostly because she felt her husband had been unfaithful to her. From that night onward Dash would make small advances to Kelly but she did not bite until he told her that he had followed McAlister once and saw him with another woman. Dash assured her that he was a good shoulder to lean on so she let her fury for McAlister turn into passion in hotel beds with Dash. He wanted her to always wear a well fitting dress when they met for their blissful escapades.

Each time Dash saw her in one, he felt fortunate to have her. Now that McAlister was out of the picture, he felt somewhat relieved. It always scared him to be in McAlister's house, not knowing what time he would come home. He didn't like the idea but Kelly liked living on the edge. It was a side of her that McAlister had never known about. As he thought about Kelly, he drove faster hoping that Dane would be asleep when he got there.

Houston Rd. was an area that had high dollar homes. Mostly doctors, lawyers, and executives made up the communities. McAlister could not figure a policeman living in that area. Even if Detective Banks was moon-lighting, it seemed unlikely that he could afford Houston Rd. unless he was into something illegal.

He checked his rearview mirror as he drove slowly, looking for one fifty-six. Bingo, there it was. It was an incredible brick house with tall column posts on the front side. It must have been at least four thousand square feet. The lawn was neatly manicured, all of the shrubbery squarely cut. From the outside, the place looked immaculate.

There were a few lights still on in the house. McAlister had no idea how many people were inside. He should have found out from Dash whether or not Detective Banks was married. He had a strong hunch that Banks was not married and had no kids. It would be very risky trying to enter the house.

The first thing that he had to do was find an inconspicuous place to park the car. He drove past Banks' house, slowly maneuvering the car and carefully looking for a place to park. He did not want to park too far away; the closer the better. Banks' house became further and further away as he continued to look.

A light flickered in his rearview mirror. A car was approaching him. He did not want to arouse any suspicions. As the car got closer, almost to the point of having to slow down, he saw a church just ahead on the right. The church parking lot would be a decent place to park. After killing the engine to his car, McAlister started mentally preparing himself for his mission. From inside his glove compartment, he retrieved a pair of latex gloves and shoved them into his inner coat pocket.

Underneath the box of gloves was a black velvet pouch. Inside of it were all the tools he needed in order to break into Banks' house. He shoved it into his other inner coat pocket. Of course, he knew that he had his knife. He had checked to make sure that he had it before he left the apartment. He never left home without it since he had gotten used to car-rying it.

Since his prison days when he carried a shank, he had learned to always have some protection with him. Feeling confident that he hadn't forgotten anything, he set out toward Banks' house. He felt a bit over-dressed for a man walking through a residential area at night. If a car were to come toward him, he would turn his head in the opposite direction. No one could get a good look at him that way. He walked with urgency and it did not take as long as he had thought that it would. He was not going to be bold enough to hang around the front of the house. Someone would be sure to see him and get suspicious.

Around the back side of the house, he found that there were a swim-ming pool, a tennis court, and a basketball court. It kind of reminded him of how he hand landscaped his own back yard. There was an above ground deck that ran almost the entire length of the house. Underneath it was a sliding glass patio door. McAlister chose it for his entrance. He was careful not to make any noise. He worked his lock picking tool with speed and accuracy. Bingo, he was in.

The room that he entered was dimly lit, but he could see from the light that illuminated the room that Detective Banks had exquisite taste for furnishings. Expensive paintings clung to the walls. All of the coffee tables, end tables, and book shelves were made of a deeply textured mahogany. Brightly colored oriental rugs added life to the vast array of the dwellings furnishings. There were numerous wood and glass cases of rifles and handguns. Some of the handguns looked to be from the days of the old west.

He listened intently for any sound that would give him a clue to what part of the house the occupants were in. It was eerie knowing that someone was in the house but there was not a sound to be heard. It was like the occupants knew that he was there. He waited patiently for a thump, a thud, the sound of running water, a television, a stereo, or any other sound of life, but none came. Anxiety was building within him. His pores opened and released beads of perspiration. He could hear his heart beat like a steady drum.

The excitement was mounting so much that he found he had established an erection. A new sense of confidence prevailed within him. It showed with burning intensity in his eyes. He stalked on further, like a lion after his prey.

****

Dash blew out the smoke from his cigar. He always enjoyed one after he had finished a major job or after a good sexual episode. This one, he was really enjoying. He had just satisfied both in one night. The assignment for McAlister was complete. He had also completely satisfied Kelly. He untied her wrists and ankles. Now, she was snuggled up next to him, her face buried in his chest.

Kelly had always marveled at how cool and reserved Dash was. She figured that most men who had just slept with another man's wife in his own bed would be itching to get away from the scene after he had his fun. Not Dash, he did not seem the least bit eager to get up and go. It was dangerous, but it excited her for him to be that way. To her, it made him even sexier. "When you finish your cigar, take me for another trip around the world?" Kelly purred.

After exhaling a cloud of smoke, Dash turned to her and said, "Yeah, Baby, we're going for a trip. We're going to visit some of the most beautiful places on this earth." He extinguished his cigar in an ashtray on the nightstand and rolled over to her and gingerly positioned himself on top of her so that he could see that look in her eyes that turned him on so much. Slowly, they started a new journey.

Dane found it difficult to sleep due to the creaking sound his mother's bed was making. He lay in his own bed with his fingers stuck in his ears. A frown was molded on his face. Mad at his mother for having Detective Dash as her boyfriend. He was mad at Dash for befriending his dad and sleeping with his wife. Most of all, he was mad at his dad. He had been mad at him and now that anger had turned to hatred.

Dane cursed his father each time he heard the bed in his mother's room creak and then bang against the wall. He vowed to himself that he would never get married. He also wished that his father would die.

****

The silence of the house was beginning to pluck at McAlister's nerves. He was tempted to purposefully make some noise, himself. That would send Banks to investigate. He could overcome him when he entered the room. The problem though, was that he was sure the Detective Banks would come armed as well as alert. Also, he did not know if there were others in the house. It was best that he proceed on, silently stalking, until he found his prey.

His hand was clenched tightly around the ivory handle of the switchblade. The long shiny blade glistened as glimpses of light hit it. His mind flashed a picture of his victims. They had deserved what they had gotten, especially Nathan, his first victim. When he got to the door leading out of the room, he stopped and pressed his ear to it. He could hear nothing but the constant beat of his heart.

Adrenaline coursed itself rapidly through his veins. His eyes were wide and alert and his whole body felt tight. He turned the doorknob slowly until it stopped. With about the same amount of pressure, he pushed the door forward until he had enough space to slide his body between it and the door frame. He found himself in a hallway. It had expensive looking paintings hanging on the walls. There were also various showcases displaying objects made of pewter, ceramic, marble, brass, glass, ivory, gold, and silver, all of which were charming in some way.

Just across the hall was another door. McAlister handled it just as he had done the other. He let himself into the room only to find that it was a game room. It had a billiard table, pinball machines, table tennis, and a host of video games. Nothing was going on in this room. He could see from the doorway that at the other end of the hall was a staircase. It would probably lead him to Detective Banks. He approached it with caution, just as he had thus far.

As he climbed the stairs leading to the next level, he did so staying to the outside of the stairway. If anyone was coming down the stairs, it would give him a better chance of seeing them first. When he reached the top of the stairway, he could see that he was on the main level of the house. He speculated that he was in the living room. It was very spacious and was decorated to suit the style that he had seen thus far.

There was another hallway to his left. He could see that there were two doors on the right side of the hallway that led to the other rooms. To the right of where he stood, but not too far away, he could see another hallway. He headed for it. As he turned the corner, he came upon the kitchen. It had a large bay window that made it look airy.

No one was there, so he kept on walking. He checked the laundry room, which was just past the kitchen. As he had suspected, there was no one there, but he approached it with caution just as he had done the rest of the rooms. The house was still just as quiet as it had been when he entered it. His heart felt and sounded as though it were beating faster and louder.

There was another door just ahead of him. It was closed. McAlister gripped the doorknob and turned it slowly. Once he felt it would not turn any further, he counted to three in his head. He rushed the door open. Once inside the room, he found that he was the only person there. He went back to where he had seen the two doors in the hallway to the left of the living room. Fortunately, the first door was open. The lights were off. There was enough light illuminating from the window to see that he had entered the study.

A multitude of books lined the walls. A huge mahogany desk sat off to one side of the room. The desk was positioned so that a person sitting at it could easily look out the window over his right shoulder and see the big pond that was about a hundred yards from the back of Detective Banks' house.

There was one more room on the floor that McAlister had to check out. If Banks was not in that room, he was sure to be in the room upstairs. He knew that there was just one room upstairs because when he was approaching the house, he could see the upper level of the house did not extend half the distance that the lower level did. As a matter of face, McAlister thought that the house was kind of odd in that respect.

Not until he had gone around to the back side of the house did he realize that the house actually had three levels. Unlike before, the door to the room beside the study was not open. Of course, McAlister's heart rate picked up its intensity each time that this was the case. He clenched his grip more tightly around his knife. He almost felt like an idiot, though. Here he was, about to kill someone, and he had only brought a knife.

There was not a cop that he knew of that did not own a gun. Why should Banks be any different? Well, at least he had the element of surprise aiding him. He pressed his ear to the door, listening for any sound of life. He could hear nothing. Slowly, he turned the door knob and pushed it open when he felt the latch give way. The lights were off. He couldn't make anything out, so he stood still until he got his night vision.

Slowly, the obstacles in the room came into view. Still, there was no human presence in the room. Just as he was about to depart the room, he heard the sound of the floor creaking overhead. His heart raced wildly as he headed for the room upstairs.

McAlister had not relinquished his grip on the knife. If anything, his grip had become tighter. His body felt tense and his movements were robotic. His anxiety began to increase as he felt the inner tremble that had overwhelmed him before. This time, the sensation was different. He no longer felt that he had no control over it. Instead, confidence invaded his mind. He felt like a Bengal Tiger, stalking its chanceless victim.

The beat of his heart set the stage as he approached each step. His eyes were keen and alert. As he reached the top of the stairway, he saw that he had another closed door in front of him. Behind the door, he knew that he would find what he had come to the house for. When he looked at the bottom of the door, he could see that light emitted from underneath it. His heart now beat to a fever pitch. It had never beaten so hard in his life. It pushed the adrenaline through his veins like bullets out of a gun.

McAlister took a step back from the door. He collected his mental energy and delivered it with the force of his right foot on the door. The door flew open, revealing Detective Banks standing in the center of a king size bed with a black negligee on. He was posing in front of mirrors that were on the wall behind the head board. He also had a leather whip in his right hand. McAlister expected him to react with surprise. Detective Banks showed no fear or surprise.

When he was fully turned to McAlister, a big smile spread across his face. "Come over here and give me a big kiss, big boy. I've been expecting you!" He cracked the whip down toward the floor, creating a loud smacking sound.

"I'll give you a kiss, alright," McAlister said, his face showing determination. He went at Detective Banks with the knife extended in his hand. Banks tried flogging him with the whip. His first two tries were unsuccessful. The third swing found its mark on McAlister's left arm. McAlister was so charged up that, he was oblivious to the pain that the whip had caused.

McAlister persisted toward Banks with the knife. He held out the lashed left arm as a sacrifice for the whip, which landed two more times before he was able to cut one of Detective Banks' lower legs. Banks laughed as he felt the warmth and searing burn of where the knife slicing a deep gash into his leg.

McAlister landed two more strokes before he heard a loud thud and saw The Weasel come racing from the closet in which he had been hiding. He looked like a mad man. His hair was standing wildly on his head. He was sweating profusely and his eyes were as wide as fifty cent pieces.

McAlister had turned his back to Detective Banks so the he could watch The Weasel. The whip caught him across the back and shoulders.

Out of the corner of his eye, he could see a vase of Orchids on the dresser. He felt despair set in. The whip kept coming and the blood kept oozing.

The Weasel was standing in front of him looking like a mad dog. He was gritting his teeth. His right hand was in his pants pocket. McAlister kept feeling the punishing lashes of the whip, but he would not move away from its reach. Immediately, everything seemed as if it were happening in slow motion to McAlister. He saw The Weasel's lips moving. He said something about this being for Natalie.

Suddenly, the hand that had been in The Weasel's pocket was before him. In it, he clenched a knife identical to the one that McAlister had, except that the tip of it was not broken. Realizing what was happening, McAlister made a plunge at The Weasel with his own knife. Unfortunately, The Weasel had the same thing in mind.

Each knife found its entry at belly button level. They both found that the pain was piercing through their bodies. It showed outwardly with the horror written on each of their faces. Their energy had begun to subside. The whip had taken a toll on McAlister. His mind told him to pull upward toward The Weasel's heart with the knife still plunged into him, but his body would not respond to the demand.

The Weasel's strength was dissipating quickly. With what strength he could muster, he pulled upward with the knife, ripping at McAlister's insides. Blood suddenly poured out of McAlister's mouth. His eyes grew faint as his body pulsated violently, and then stopped. Finally, there was no more light.

THE END